What people are sayi

Night Waves

A vivid and engaging hyper-sleazy wet horror novel, evoking those early 1980's seaside monster films we all grew up on. A blaring siren of a novel so long missing in horror literature.
Josh Hadley, 1201beyond.com

Refreshing, raw, British humour, *Night Waves* confronts a more eerie side to the human psyche and offers up a range of delicious dark horror.
Emily Caroline, vampiresquid.co.uk

Paints the story vividly in my mind, wonderfully enticing, you get to the end of a chapter and hearing your brain demand you carry on reading, brilliant.
Stuart Bannerman, FromPage2Screen.com

Enthrals from the first page, pulling readers into a seductive and glamourous abyss. A siren song of sexy scares!
Kelly Dunn, Mutation Nation

An intriguing modern chiller which sees an ancient exile become an ungodly disaster. *Night Waves* is instantly enticing. A novel that evokes sea beasts like the Kraken and Godzilla-like mythology, but places them bravely up against contemporary fictional classics like *Cloverfield* and *A Quiet Place*.
Andrew Bullock, MailOnLine

Night Waves

Night Waves

David Irons

Winchester, UK
Washington, USA

JOHN HUNT PUBLISHING

First published by Cosmic Egg Books, 2019
Cosmic Egg Books is an imprint of John Hunt Publishing Ltd., 3 East St., Alresford, Hampshire SO24 9EE, UK
office@jhpbooks.com
www.johnhuntpublishing.com

For distributor details and how to order please visit the 'Ordering' section on our website.

ISBN: 978 1 78904 026 5
978 1 78904 027 2 (ebook)
Library of Congress Control Number: 2018936232

A CIP catalogue record for this book is available from the British Library.

Design: Stuart Davies

UK: Printed and bound by CPI Group (UK) Ltd, Croydon, CR0 4YY
US: Printed and bound by Thomson Shore, 7300 West Joy Road, Dexter, MI 48130

Prologue

As the sunset dulled on the British south coast, Barry Slater threw his eighth and last empty can of cheap lager into the soft ripple of the sea. His drunken, blurred vision lied to him as he stared at it floating on the dark green surface. He tried to concentrate as it seemingly separated into two cans: a ghostly double of the original, mimicking the slow sway of the ocean.

He wondered for a second if there actually were two cans, perhaps he had already dumped another 'dead soldier' in the 'drink' and only recalled one? It wouldn't be the first time his addled brain had malfunctioned in this way, nor, he knew, would it be the last. He rubbed his tired eyes. Seeing straight, as if by magic, the two bobbing cans returned to one.

See, he thought, *I ain't that pissed,* and a dirty, delirious, black-toothed smile spread over his face.

Seeing double had been a problem for Barry lately, it was a problem on top of a stack of others his life was filled with. This was a more sinister and menacing problem though, darker than any he had ever had to deal with.

He pushed his rough hand through his greasy hair and drew it into a fist, his fingers sticking to one another inside his palm. Opening his fist, he looked down. His entire hand was red with blood. Blood that wasn't his own. His face turned sheet white. The thing he had tried to forget crept to the forefront of his mind again.

Barry rubbed his hands madly down his filthy, yellow, high-vis jacket. A piece of clothing that was more of a shell than a suit, thick with dirt, grease and oil, the added smears of blood made the supposed 'high visibility' a shade more akin to a dulled mud-covered pumpkin.

Seawater lapped up and into the hungry mouth of his old beer can, weighing it down to the ocean floor. A hollow shiver penetrated the numbing drunkenness that he had spent the last of his change to enjoy. His mouth relaxed into a slack jawed drool and his cold eyes glazed over as he remembered his last job out at sea.

This memory seemed to have a life of its own, forever returning, like a vicious, barbed boomerang into his brain, leaving deep lacerations which could never heal.

The job, he remembered, was one, that for once, he hadn't got fired from, but had himself – almost stone cold sober – walked away from.

His friend, Dirty Derek – a man with as much personal hygiene as himself, with a putrefying aroma so pungent the army could bottle it as a new form of chemical warfare – had told him that there was, 'Some real good Spon-doolies if ya fancy it.'

'Fancy what?' he'd asked, chugging back the dregs of a bottle of vodka that he may or may not have at some point topped with a cheaper bottle of mouthwash.

'Old Bob said they need some drilling out on a jackup rig. They're putting up a load of them wind turbines out at sea. Ya know, that re-usable energy shit. Massive bastards they are. Want blokes with experience and a bit of muscle they do.'

Barry, sucking his gut in as far as possible and as a result belching fumes into Derek's face, slurred, 'Yeah, I'm ya man for that.'

'Need ta be sober though, Bazza, need ya down the dock in Lancing at nine tamorra. Do ya fink ya can make it?'

'Course I can,' Barry said swaying. Of course he would be there for nine. Put out that a man as he might be doubted in such a way. It was easy, all he had to do was find a dry place to sleep under the docks at Lancing, then slither up at nine like a giant slug, good to go. Easy.

And so he did. He found himself standing on the dock, surprised that he'd remembered the job offer and that there actually was a job to be offered. Dirty Derek hadn't let him down. At nine a.m. sharp, the boss of the crew, with no questions asked, had enrolled him for 'cash in hand' work that day and before he knew it he was standing on the rig's steel platform, staring across the waves back to land.

In a romantic recess of his mind, he would think of himself as a nomad, a man of the world with a case of wanderlust. The passing world that would stare at him asleep under a bridge in a pool of piss would call him otherwise – a hobo, a filthy layabout, a tramp.

His life's priorities lay in the good times of a bottle and the cloud of his own filth. Living near the sea helped feed into his careless attitudes. He had worked on the docks all his life. Nothing ever too formal, just a hired hand, a rented grunt to do things no one else wanted to: Trawling fish, general maintenance, working the oil rigs, getting his hands dirty. It was all well-paid work at a casual pace, a pace he could more than live up to. He liked it out at sea, away from society, from the people who looked at him with disgusted eyes. They seemed a million miles away from him, stuck on the island. He had liked that thought; liked being away from them, and gobbed a huge green membrane of phlegm in their direction with a sneer.

The people on the rig left him alone, too, partially due to his foul attitude, partially due to his foul aroma.

In their own individual ways, the people there were nomads like him, too.

There was a woman out there, dressed for action in safety clothes, but beautiful and blonde. He had never really seen too many 'lookers' out on the rigs. She seemed intelligent but could have been one of those stunners from Page Three that he used to 'shoot his load' to. He'd tried to talk to her, tried to make her laugh. A Polish worker nearby talked in his native tongue to two others. Barry had turned his nose up at them, looked at the blonde, and then flicked his head in their direction.

'Listen to em,' he'd cackled. 'I bet the fuckers couldn't even laugh in English!'

She'd raised her eyebrows, and then walked off. 'Up tight bitch,' he'd spat out, stripping her with his eyes as she went. For the rest of the day all he did was look at her. She'd seen his lascivious glances, the way he licked drool from his lips like a starving man looking at a plate of steaming chicken, and ignored it like she always did.

Day disappeared. Night pulled in like death's ragged robe and shrouded the entire sky in darkness. Barry had stood on deck, staring above as speckles of rain began to hit his face, striping his filthy visage with clean streaks. The cold, steel rig was lit by high-powered spotlights now, their beams reaching through the gridded platforms, making cross-sectioned shadows like spider webs on the rolling waves.

It reminded him of an old haunted house film he had seen at the pictures years before. He couldn't think of the film's name but remembered how it felt: somber, claustrophobic, a deep sense of dread that seemed to emit from the screen in cold, chilling waves. The moon peered from behind thick banks of grey cloud, staring at him like a huge glowing eye.

Dodging as much work as he could, he couldn't believe his luck when the rig's huge industrial drill had locked up boring one of the wind turbine's foundations. The huge yellow drill had hit an unplanned patch of thick seabed. A loud grinding of stone ended the chewing of the diamond-encrusted drill bit. The pained cry of twisted metal and chugged black smoke rose into the night. It was instant panic stations all around, suits and clipboards going into meltdown mode. 'Gutted, ya cunts,' Barry had sneered, finding a nearby lifeboat to hide in. It was the perfect makeshift shelter to roll some fags and smoke the hours away. 'Stay broke,' he'd smirked. 'I need some overtime.'

After four hours of picking through the other men's lunches while their hands were dirty with work, the free ride eventually came to an end. With cheers and claps, the crew managed to throw the drill into reverse, making its big engines groan back to life and Barry groan at the thought of actually having to do something again.

But below the chatter of the crew and the steel rig they stood upon, deep in the ocean, something had been disturbed by the enormous drill. No one noticed the loud reverberating tectonic cracks from the breached stone, something that, had they known about it, would have garnered a lot of interest; a thing that would have been considered to be of great archaeological interest if discovered.

Sunk down into the seabed, deep in the fresh, watery, dust clouds, was a time worn stone monument, its covering slab destroyed by the drill's ravaging bit. Beneath was a sealed off, oversized tomb, a place that was never supposed to be opened again, now broken into. Its contents flickered to life as if a switch had been flipped. Something had been awakened, something that had waited a long time to escape. Finally, its time was now. Its way to freedom was here. Inside the living darkness, a bioluminescence blinked with a malevolent intelligence. Things that were never supposed to rise again seeped up through the drilled hole like thick oil. Beings condensed to hydrophobic molecules that refused to mix with the ocean as they rushed out and pulped together into living protoplasm that tingled with a conscious cold desire. A hunger pulsated in it, aroused and stimulated by all the warm flesh it knew was above.

Men peered down from the steel walkways as high-powered lights lit up the massive drill shaft, the giant bit slowly retracted from the seabed, bubbling to the water's surface. It's over worked engine juddered a rumbling groan before seizing up again with a steaming hiss. Before the hard-hatted workmen were able to do anything, before any sigh or grunt was able to leave their cold, chapped lips, another sound was heard. An animalistic scream emanated from the watery depths – a long, desperate cry. The sound of the things unleashed. A scream that silenced everything.

Barry had heard wild stories of things dwelling in the ocean as a child, from men as drunk and rotten as he was now. But that's what they were: stories. He hated those stories. He liked things with substance, things grounded in an understandable reality, but his idea of reality was about to change.

The thick, cancerous blackness bubbled to the sea's surface, polluting the water around it in big, gagging, glugs. 'We've hit oil!' Barry cried, pound signs rolling in his eyes like the reels of a fruit machine.

Ignoring him, like they had been all day long, a few of the crew noticed something that made no sense. The black tar leaped from the sea, wound itself up the drill's bit, wrapping itself around its shaft with fast swipes, like dark, reaching tentacles. It was a grotesque living thing that morphed into what looked like hundreds of elongated arms, winding around each other with a desperate clawing.

Stringy, flailing arms whose ends became sharpened daggers, thick pointed cat-like talons that curled to perfect pin sharp ends.

Everyone watched in horror as within only a few seconds of reaching the rig's cold, steel deck, the liquid arms separated, spread out into pools of darkness at the shadowed corners of the deck. Another banshee scream thundered out, not pinpointed to the foamy water below, but around the crew, next to them, on the very platform where they stood. A scream that sounded like it came from a hundred rabid mouths that now circled them. One of the workmen frantically shone his torch around, his trembling hands making the beam quiver.

They rushed to turn the high-powered lights back from the drill to the platform. But something else illuminated. Sets of primal, yellow eyes opened all around them, evil burning bright in the black night.

Barry, suddenly the soberest he had been in his working life, turned his head frantically from side to side, watched as swiping claws appeared from nowhere, exploded from the shadows, slashing the protective clothing from the workmen, tearing into their flesh – cries and blood all around him. The soft, cold spray of sea on his face quickly turned to a warm coating of crimson as shrieking creatures, clawing in the night, grabbed their victims and dragged them over the rig's edge, plunging, screaming, down into the icy sea below.

Barry backed away, somehow unseen and left alone as madness erupted around him. The beautiful, blonde girl exploded from the darkness, running towards him. She grabbed him by his shoulders; her wide, blue eyes brimmed with fear as she screamed for him to help her. He didn't understand her words; she may as well have been talking a foreign language now as each syllable was muted by sheer terror. One of the creatures advanced towards him, its eyes blazing, lighting up the rows of razor sharp teeth that were grinning hungrily in its gaping mouth. Barry grabbed the girl back, his first physical embrace with a woman – a woman he hadn't paid for – in his entire life. He flashed her a regretful, rotten smile. 'Sorry love,' he said as he lifted and swung her around, turning her into a beautiful, blonde shield as a creature's razor sharp talons slashed towards him.

The sound of tearing filled the air, a mask of pure agony dropped across her face. The beautiful face he'd fantasized about touching turned a sickening white, blood drained from her flailing body as she was wrenched from his grasp, pulled down into the black sea.

He stared at a bubbling patch on the water. For a second, on top of the waves, he could see the blonde, her face doubled; he rubbed his eyes, double, but not a reflection, not the same. One was naked, one wasn't. One had glowing yellow eyes, like the black, oily creatures: the other, a wide-open mouth and endlessly staring dead eyes.

The yellow-eyed blonde held the other dead blonde – the one

he had used as a human shield – arms wrapped around her as she floated on the waves. She sneered at him, then sank below, bubbles rising from her lips, dragging the girl's corpse with it as it folded backwards. And somehow, as it went, with the ripple of the waves, or by an unknown force, their features merged, fused into one as they disappeared into the abyss.

Barry felt a warm stream shoot down the leg of his trousers; the strong smell of his own piss filled his nostrils. Frantically backing away, he remembered the lifeboat behind him. Jumping in, he lowered himself down. After several attempts, the motor started, his wide eyes frenziedly searching the night as he navigated back to land, not even stopping to be sick over the side into the watery graveyard of his former colleagues.

Somehow he had managed to get the small boat back to the secluded bay in a Shoreham industrial area. That was a day ago now. No one had known that he was out on the rig, cash in hand work; the contract wasn't worth the paper it was printed on. Officially, he hadn't been there to see any of what happened, unofficially, he knew every detail. Eventually, staggering back onto land, shell shocked, he went to a twenty-four hour off-license and spent the last of his money on eight cheap, shit beers and a bottle of cheap, shit whiskey.

The whiskey went quick, the beers paced out. Falling asleep, the booze did its trick, temporarily erasing the images of the creatures' nightmarish eyes from his brain. The shock of death on the blonde girl's face. The shower of blood in the air as they tore and swiped flesh. But as that final beer can sank down into the sea, it all came back. He remembered everything again. Still feeling the tackiness of the dead girl's blood on his hands, he emptied his stomach's contents over the edge of a guardrail, hearing it splatter into the sea.

That's when Barry Slater turned his back on his idea of being a nomad, of being a man of the sea, happily accepting a mundane, prosaic way of life. All he wanted to do now was drink more than he ever had before, to escape, to erase that memory of what he did. He finally saw himself as the rest of the world did, as filthy Barry the tramp. A loser in life. He was a coward, a fat, stinking coward. Wiping puke from his chin he went to find something that resembled shelter to call home. To find something in a bottle that would clear his head of those images again.

It never crossed his mind to tell anyone of what had happened, of what was still out there. It never occurred to him that it wasn't over. That the death he had experienced was only the beginning.

CHAPTER 1

Charley Reynolds wrapped one of the curls of her dyed, red hair around her finger over and over. This was a thing she found herself doing more and more these days, fixating on the slightly fraying ends, noticing the changes in color from countless dye jobs. It was an easy distraction, driving out here in the Sussex countryside with the man next to her – her boyfriend, Darren, wearing his usual grease-stained T-shirt. He pulled down the gear stick of the old, orange, Mark 3 Escort Mexico, a car he considered to be his pride and joy. A mechanical mass of fought back rust that she knew meant more to him any day of the week than she did.

She pulled the strand of hair in her fingers straight, transforming its tight curl into a long, wiry, dyed fuse, she let it go and it immediately sprang back into its original form.

'Pull the car up,' she said.

'Wha..?'

'Pull up.'

'What, you need a piss or something?'

'I want to get out,' she said with a stronger tone.

'Oh, here we go. Not this shit again. You been reading them women's mags ain't ya? Filling your brain with shit about how I treat ya?'

A flare of revulsion coursed through her like a warhead, infusing her with an overwhelming feeling of wanting to escape.

Without hesitation or care of the consequences, she reached out and grabbed the steering wheel, yanking it towards the side of the road. Loose stones, the smell of burning rubber all combined with the objecting tyres dragged in a direction they weren't prepared for. Darren hit the brakes hard, the car screeched to a halt, his refurbished rims barely missing the protruding six-inch concrete curb.

'You dumb bitch! What the fuck are you doing?' Darren yelled.

Quickly grabbing her handbag, Charley jumped out. Slamming the door behind her, walking away from the car, the dust caused by the sudden stop still hanging in the air like a mist.

'Get back in 'ere!' he screamed, a shower of spittle spraying from his mouth.

She thought about those melodramatic, grey TV shows, soap operas set in boring pubs, with down beaten people backstroking in depression and misery. Thought about screaming back, about telling him the old clichés. 'It's over.' 'I never want to see you again.' Or the council estate classic: 'You're doing my head in.' But she didn't.

Realizing where she actually was, walking on a random road, with nothing around apart from long stretches of tarmac and sundried green fields. She turned back to him, raging in his orange car, wearing his black-stained, yellow T-shirt, looking like a wasp maniacally trying to escape the insides of a particularly sticky piece of fruit.

The sound of his ranting, calling her all the 'bitches' and 'whores' he could muster, becoming distant as she stared forward and carried on. She narrowed her vision down to a thin tunnel, ignoring him, the outside border becoming a black blur, like darkness was consuming her.

After a few minutes of determined walking, a slick orange bullet flew past her, pulling as close to her as its furious driver would dare. She ignored it, throwing her handbag further over her shoulder. Silence suddenly seeped into the soundtrack, making her decision to be alone and away from him more real. The heat from the afternoon sun beat down on her, glad now that she had chosen to wear a cropped, white vest, tiny shorts and low top Converse.

She wondered where he would go, if he would come back,

what she should do to keep him away. She remembered the family party when she introduced him as he swayed drunkenly in the doorway. 'You're late, Darren!' she moaned. 'You've been drinking again!'

'I'd rather be pissed and late than early and fucking bored with you lot,' he slurred.

Charley had back pedaled, tried to make his first impression more pleasant.

'This is Darren, he's a mechanic,' Charley said with pseudo enthusiasm in her voice.

'Fuck off, am I! I work on the bins, innit fella? Driving the dust cart.' He smirked as he patted her father on the back.

She had known her father hated him from day one. He had never said this outright to her, just to her mother. She'd always defended Darren, but now she wanted him out of the flat. Daddy's flat that he had bought his little girl. She knew how to play her father when she had to, and she knew he would make it his personal project to get Darren out.

She checked her bag for her phone. '*Shit,*' she whispered closing her eyes, remembering she had left it in the Escort's center console, knowing his grubby fingers would be working at the password, trying to unlock it; trying to find the messages from the other men he had constantly accused her of seeing.

A breeze caught her hair, the curls rising and falling, propelled by soft gusts as she wondered if anything else could possibly go wrong today.

She continued to walk, making it from the main road, wandering by instinct to the south, going back to the seafront. She found her way to Eastbourne's promenade and headed west, back towards Hove. It was a long walk, the afternoon fading to the long shadows of evening.

The walk gave her time to think; to contemplate the decision of living with Darren, libido and petulant youth had overcome good sense when selecting a live-in life partner.

Maybe she should get a job, live like the regular people of the world and not live from Daddy's wallet. She never understood how they did it; she would often go shopping during the day, watching people work, managers, assistants and cashiers. Bored after ten minutes of viewing them run the rat race, she wasn't able to fathom spending eight hours there. It would send her mad, consumer retail incarceration, locked behind a till pressing buttons like a chimp trying to type Shakespeare.

Deep in her shallow thoughts, she looked up ahead at the nearing Brighton pier. It looked mystical in the setting sun, like a mirage that bridged the gap between the sea and the pebbly beach she walked on. She couldn't believe she was here already, her head so far away it distorted time.

Long, thin strands of rotting seaweed were caught on the structure's underside, hanging down and gently swaying in the wind like ghostly shredded curtains through an open window.

Above, on the promenade, a group of young men – boys in actuality, all drinking from cans of larger – shouted down to her. She looked up at them. Here was an entire gang of dick head Darrens, five of them in total. Dopey, Brainless, Gormless, Toothless and Fuck Wit – a small seaside tribe of lowbrows. They all had the same vocabulary as him, using their pub charms in her direction. 'Oi babe', 'Oi bitch'. 'Come suck on this,' one yelled, grabbing his genitals.

She thought about giving them the finger, using that old daytime TV dialogue she had mastered. Telling them all to piss off without the censoring bleep of a producer to stop her. But she didn't. She just looked forward and continued to walk, putting distance between her and their leering voices. Moving quicker, the wind picked up, its hollow timbre coldly whispering past her ears.

A few minutes passed, the sharp smell of the sea drifted to her senses, distracted her, immediately making her forget the bench full of morons. She looked up at the promenade again, and then stopped. Another figure was looking down towards her. There, as if in mourning, a dark-haired woman stood, wearing funeral black.

The woman raised the dark veil from her hat, looked down at Charley with eyes blackened by tear-stained makeup. She was middle-aged, beautiful, her expression gaunt and vague, masked by sadness. The woman's black, tar-like pupils defied the twenty feet between them, her mesmerizing gaze rushing through Charley like a pair of dark spears. Sharing a moment in time together, the lady in black sharply turned then walked away, disappearing from view.

Charley raised her hand to her hair, pushed it from her face as a breeze took hold of it again. The image of the woman in black turned in her head as she moved to the underside of the pier. She had never known anyone who had died, had never been to a funeral before. She wondered what it felt like to lose someone. The only feeling she knew of in life was the slow bubbling of wanting rid of another, not the grief or sadness of their unexpected departure.

Beneath the pier's metal structure, decay and rot clung in abundance. Hanging seaweed tendrils reached towards her like hundreds of miniature tentacles. She could see the sun in the distance pushing out its final orange glow, dipping on the horizon like a ball of fire slowly being extinguished by the sea. A refreshing coolness caressed her skin.

Taking this moment for herself, she suddenly felt anguished and worn out from the fight earlier, from the common foul abuse thrown at her by Darren. Reaching in her bag, she passed a cigarette in between her lips and lit it.

As the pier's acoustics reverberated, completely immersed her, the soothing sound of the wind mixed with the hypnotic roll of the waves and created a tranquility in her soul. She had never allowed herself these quiet moments before, she found a rock and sat down, her legs crossed in a meditative position, eyes shut. There was always a drama, a party, or a trip to the pub with Darren, manmade noisy nonsense, people creating their own pointless dramas all for the purpose of having something to talk about. She pulled three more drags on the cigarette, tasting its rough pleasures that her mind longed for and her lungs repelled.

The sea rolled in, a breeze touched her face.

The cigarette fell from her fingers as she dropped from consciousness. Slipping into a light but far away sleep, she thought of that deep look in the eyes of the woman in black. Her hypnotizing eyes. She had real problems. She didn't know how she knew this, but she felt it with an intuition she didn't really understand, a heightened instinct that she had drawn from her gaze.

A shattering shriek, an almost animalistic cry pierced the bubble she had put herself in. Her eyelids flew open. Panic surged in her blood. She swung her head around trying to find the origin of the sound that made her tingle in terror, her skin rippled as cold as the waves before her.

Then, as soon as the shriek had come, an alluring, ethereal song, not too many octaves away from the slight whistle on the wind, distinctive enough to be its own eerie thing, replaced it; a soft, female voice, romantic but empty, cold but warming. There was no understandable dialogue, just long drawn, sensual sounds. A soft sexuality entwined within a child's lullaby twisted into its tone.

Charley gasped at the air with parted lips, slowly calming herself, her rough fear smoothed as the strange song entered her mind, caressed her body and overcame her.

Her head lolled, her eyes closed with a slow, soft joining of her lashes, like the closing mouth of a Venus fly trap, ensnaring her in the darkness of her own mind. A tranquility as vivid as REM sleep washed over her. The song became more intense, closer and more personal, firing pangs of sexual excitement between her legs.

Suddenly, the song stopped. Immediately the foggy, intense desire in her mind dissipated. She opened her eyes and looked around, trying to discover the song's source. There was nothing, just the dying sun's final touch on her face.

The tide pulled out, the wind's icy bite now noticeable. Between the pebble beach and the sea there was something she hadn't noticed before. A collection of curved, black rocks, two feet high and four feet wide, all spread out in front of her under the advancing waves, each of them a similar shape and size, as they dotted out away under the shadowed length of the pier. As the tide rolled out again, momentarily, the song wafted up from the sea's creased blanket of waves, the desire filled drowsiness bubbled in her brain again.

She stood, transfixed by the pattern of black rocks, transfixed by the song.

That was where the song was coming from, the rocks.

A heightened intuition tingled through her, fueled her curiosity. Everything seemed like a dream, the song pulled her forward.

The tide drew in, lapping up at her feet before being sucked back out again. Her grin broadened, she felt drunk, filled with something that made her feel far away. *The song... the song.*

Something whispered in its soft tones. A word – her name –

'Charleeyyyyyy.'

It was calling her, drawing her to it.

Without thinking, she moved forward dreamily, almost floated forward. The nearest black rock was only a few feet away now. With each step closer, the rock becoming bigger, the rock... wasn't a rock. Its thick surface seemed to pulsate with a webbing of veins, like it was somehow... breathing? With each rhythmic pulse the veins conducted a small glow of energy through them. A neon surge, like the bioluminescence of deep-sea fish, shone deeply below its surface. Each pulse matched the dreamy rhythm of the song. Yes, she understood, somehow, this… thing was generating the song. She wanted to run, but it held her in place, became stronger, whispering her name over and over.

'Charleeyyyyyy, Charleeyyyyyy, Charleeyyyyyy.'

Re-adjusting her dreamy eyes, she began to notice recognizable contours. Thin limbs wrapped around folded legs. A smooth, black head bent to thin black knees. A long, thin spine rose in its middle, separating two halves of a human-looking back. Charley gasped, the fog in her mind thinning, settling, understanding, no, this was no rock. No, it wasn't a rock at all. It was a curled up humanoid form, a living, breathing, vein covered shadow.

The tide crashed in and pulled back out. A thin, spindly arm moved from the curled creature towards the wet sand, its fingers tipped with sharp talons that stretched into a vicious tarantula-like paw.

She wanted to turn away, wanted to run, but somehow the song held her in place, tears building in her eyes. Fear and intuition said, *Run! Run! Run!* The silky, slithering song said, *Stay! Stay! Stay!* The creature slowly unfolded, stood up, restructured into a sheet of darkness that blocked her view. Tears fell from her face, a jolt of panic broke the songs spell, she fell backwards, toppled down, landing violently on to the pebbly beach with a winding blow. The thing loomed forward, Charley's mouth curled to scream as two, fiery, night-time eyes drew down.

There was no scream, only the song filling her again, muting her from the inside.

It slashed her with its taloned hand, five, sharp, meaty holes gouged into her front, splitting the fabric of her white T-shirt, tearing down in her soft flesh, dragging across her breasts, pushing deeper, nicking at her ribcage with claw-like blades. Agony overwhelmed her and the next flush of tide was a deep crimson, polluted with her warm blood. It grabbed her, dragged her backwards. Her open mouth filled with water as she was pulled deep below the waves into a stagnant, silent place.

Hollow, cold, isolated, where her terrified, bubbling screams would never be heard. She looked up to the surface of the sea, watched as it rapidly disappeared into the distance. Blood plumed around her, like a contrail of red haze from a plane. Wide-eyed, petrified, her lungs filled with gory, freezing, water, twisting and turning in panic, she was dragged straight down into the murky gulf. Straight down to her death.

CHAPTER 2

In a trendy, overpriced but rundown part of Hackney, down a graffiti covered back alley, up a rusted fire escape and though an old, red brick warehouse door. A pair of deep-brown eyes stared mannequin-like, not blinking, as intense flashes hit their retina, licking them with light.

'OK turn to your left again... drop your arm... come on!' the photographer barked as he unloaded a rapid fire of camera clicks.

Modelling was Kirsten Costello's job; this was her way to pay the bills. She had been a fortunate girl at birth, blessed with all the right attributes in the facial department to be classed as beautiful. She had the cheekbones, the jaw line. Her nose was perky, her eyes held the correct distance between them to be cat-like and alluring. Others in her immediate family held just a few of these physical characteristics. Nice eyes, full lips, perfect cheekbones. Whether through good genes or the stars cosmic alignment, she naturally had the attractiveness many others searched for in surgery.

At 18, living in the tacky surroundings of South End, she felt London calling. A place that, in her mind's eye, promised to be a creative catalyst, a fuel pump for ideas she could feed directly to her brain. A place where she could revel in culture, rather than doss in run down arcades and chip shops. Originally, she had not relied on just looks for her future, but used her artistic talent instead. Skills and talent that were based behind the camera, not just standing in front of it, skills that had now become largely redundant. Applying for a photographer's position at a fashionable magazine, they quickly became less interested in her portfolio, and more so in taking her picture.

Sometimes in life, things just fall into your lap, even when you may not have wanted them. She had a face people wanted to look at, a face that had been chosen for others to see. There was only one other person she knew who had the good sense to leave their hometown. Her cousin, Simone, the one no one spoke about at family dos, and if they did, it was with a condescending tone and a disdainful flash of the eyes.

More flashes burst in her own eyes. Her pose tilted to match the line of the expensive, German-designed dress that she wore. She was starting to feel hot, sweat running down her back, her thick brown hair wasn't helping. She was positioned only a few inches from the hot red bars that the studio was dressed with. Not neon bars, no that was too easy. The stylist wanted authenticity, wanted those 'volcanic oranges and reds'. Behind her was a heated metal grid, basically a giant grill – a health and safety nightmare. All for that 'look' they wanted. Someone trying to be 'artistic' with their decisions, someone who should spend an hour in front of it to see how it feels.

She listened to the man in front of her again. A guy doing a job she should be doing, and her doing a job he could never do.

'Turn to your left a little, that's it... chin up, a little more... a little less... No, no, no... can you just be more seductive?'

She did what she was told. That was her job. Looking good and shutting up. What could she do? She needed the money. Before her was a man with a reputation of being the 'best' at fashion photography, a man who was highly respected in his field, an original. You would never have guessed this from his look and ensemble: the beard, the skinny jeans, the branded cup of 'designer' coffee. Originality had taken a holiday in the arts and pop culture as of late, the mediocre admired, the awful graciously given a pass if their 'face fit'.

Just like the man who took the pictures now, the tinpot Karl Lagerfeld, a man who had seen Antonioni's Blow Up one too many times at art school. But that's how the world worked, wasn't it? You act like the thing you want to be and then you become the thing you act like.

'Show me something. Make me want to buy this outfit! Come on, do what you're supposed to do!'

She turned, striking another pose that showed off her body in the well-cut outfit.

In a way, modelling was like being trapped behind her own eyes, caged in her own head, her old self a slave to the movements her body made. It was easy money. You stand and you stare. No brain, no pain. But her caged side, the creative side, the side that was actually her, had grown tired of its prison and now it wanted out.

A flash popped off; it took her by surprise, making her flinch and almost touch the hot wire grill behind her.

'When do you think we'll wrap?' she asked, surprised the words passed her lips.

The photographer looked up at her, his face filled with theatrical dismay, over exaggerating his expression for effect. The old wiring had been reconnected in her head, and she wondered what exactly was she doing here? For a second, it was like an out of body experience, she saw herself. The aspirations of her life inverted and reversed, not using her brain, but using her face, not using her talent, but using a forced ineptitude and dullness molded to what other people wanted to see.

More flashes from the camera. A bead of sweat trickled down her brow; luckily, the photographer didn't notice it. Unluckily, his sour-faced assistant did. She turned to him, whispering in his ear. Non-emotional eyes stuck on Kirsten, a mix of resentment and boredom.

The photographer dropped the camera down and snorted. 'Getting hot in there?

'A little,' she replied.

'Not much longer now,' he said in a drawn out breath.

'When do you think we'll wrap?' she asked again, the words just falling from her mouth, anchored with a deep honesty.

He dropped the lens he was about mount on the camera's

body onto a small metal table, making a loud, dull clang ring out.

'Busy are we?' he replied with a well-oiled passive-aggressive tone. Her mouth started to speak, saying words she felt, but knew she shouldn't say.

'I have some work I need to do today, that's all'.

'This is work,' he said with cold eyes. 'What's more important?'

She looked at the assistant as a sneer brushed over her face.

'I'm a photographer, too. I do what you do,' she said.

Her outer shell, the model part of her almost dropped its jaw in shock. She was doing something she hadn't in a long time. Saying what she thought.

Something caught his attention, there was honesty in her words, something he found deeply challenging. He turned to her.

'Right, that's adorable. If you want to get out of here quicker, how about you not keep your jaw moving up and down so much, and we get some decent pictures?'

She filled with rage. Reattaching a lens, he began snapping in her direction, more aggressively now, as if the camera was some kind of weapon in his hand.

'Are you too good to be just a model then? It's not enough you think you have good cheekbones but you think you have a brain as well?'

She tensed, her hands gripping tight for a second. Everything reconnected inside, port to port connection with common sense, with having a backbone, having an opinion. Consciousness rose in the waif like model she pretended to be, with it her old self emerged. 'Photography has always been number one… not this.'

'Not this?' he scoffed 'I can tell. HEAD LEFT!'

Kirsten slowly moved her head left.

'So, this pays the bills while you dream of being an artist does it?' He threw a look at his assistant, who smirked back at him.

'It's not dreaming if you are actually doing it.'

'So, are you actually doing it then, Princess?'

She knew she wasn't and hated the fact he was right. She had to change that, she had to change everything.

She thought of her photography. Of her equipment and work, sitting, gathering dust. Her own portfolio was now just a place where plates of toast, crumbs and dead cups of coffee sat. Her neglected work had ended up second best, not even second, third, fourth. It had become nothing, caught in the social whirl of Dalston and Brick Lane. A place she had unconsciously started to call Prick Lane in her head.

With the flash of the photographer's camera, something erupted inside her, brought her to life like a bolt of lightning to Frankenstein's monster. Suddenly, she wanted to leave, wanted out, any pleasantries of pretending to be something she wasn't had burned up and evaporated like a spilled glass of water on a burning hot pavement.

She wasn't a model; she wasn't put here for others to stare at. She was a photographer.

'Yeah, I'm doing it' she said. 'I'm good at it, too. And I know for a damn fact that I don't have to act like an arsehole, like you, living in this little bullshit made up world of yours, with all of your arse-kissing little friends around,' she pointed a finger at the assistant, 'to try and get a fucking decent picture.'

He threw the Canon Mk 3 camera to the floor, the sound of its broken sensor tinkled in the air. It was the same camera she had bought back in Essex, an expensive one that she spent a year working in a café to buy. To the over privileged idiot before her, it was just another toy thrown in a temper tantrum.

'Did you just answer me back? Did you just answer me back? he bellowed, foaming slightly at the side of his mouth. 'You are here to look good for the camera. I don't want your life story. You get paid to keep your eyes dull and your face pretty. Trust me, thinking is not a strong point for a pretty face!'

A smile broke on her face seeing his ridiculousness, the

ridiculousness of the entire situation. It enraged him even more, 'I think I'm using the wrong thing to shoot you with,' he snarled 'I need something with bullets! In fact, I'd blow your bloody brains out if I thought you had any!'

He walked towards Kirsten, his eyes ablaze, his ego fueling them like two flame throwers that shot from his eye sockets. A similar rage started to burn in her eyes; she curled her hand into a fist. As he got closer, as he got in spitting distance between them, she threw a punch, aimed straight for the face, and nailed him perfectly in his bearded mouth.

He reeled back, staring in astonishment, lost his footing and landed straight on his backside. Kirsten quickly removed her oversized earrings, throwing them in the direction of the stunned assistant.

'Fuck this!' she screamed, storming out, letting the heavy, metal door slam satisfyingly behind her.

Outside, three vacuous looking models all chewed gum in unison. They stared at Kirsten, blank and lifeless, a look she herself had perfected in an attempt to be one of them – to fit in. Their gaze followed her as she grabbed her jacket and rushed out the door, a trio of glass-eyed, ceramic dolls.

London was done. She had no idea where she was going to go, no idea how to pay the stack of bills on her desk, no idea how she was going to pay the rent. But she knew she would never model again, and that was a promise she intended to keep forever.

CHAPTER 3

Kirsten threw open the paint-flaked door to her small, rented room in Dalston and looked towards the old, oak desk in the corner that held her photography equipment. Afternoon sun filtered through the dirty window, highlighting her collection of lenses. Her life's creative work neglected and discarded.

Dropping her bag to the floor and walking over to the desk, she drew in a deep breath and blew a layer of dust from a printed glossy of an actress named Alexis: middle-aged, beautiful face and blue eyes like a deep oasis.

'Need to get more of these going, get back into the headshots,' she thought, angry with the boozy nights she had let get the better of her. Spending money she should have used investing in keeping her gear up to date, now all pissed away with trendies with their pockets filled with their parents' cash. They were people who valued status and vapidity over any real talent in themselves or anyone around them. She had fallen into that old trap, becoming a bi-product of her surroundings. Being immersed in the persuasion of others and losing any individuality in the process.

Her artistic output had become nothing more than a bragging right when challenged in conversation, her having the edge of not being 'just a model' when it would be a convenience. Much like today, when the guy taking her picture asked what her real job was, she spouted out the answer in a second. A photographer. Yes, she was that, her past could corroborate it. But to be this in the present she had to do one thing: take photographs.

She hated people who never finished things, had met a lot of people like this but never considered herself one of them. She knew that the sparkling, yellow brick road to good intentions was paved with unfinished creative work. And here she was, just one of those people, 'a dreamer', someone who was all mouth and no trousers, a person who used their own talent as a shorthand to better herself in casual banter.

Signing with her modeling agent, thinking about the money, she had immediately fit right into the East London scene. Just like all the others in her position, the hand of capitalism had reached around and gagged her with money, while from behind, her knickers were quickly yanked down so the industry could have its way with her.

The life of a model was an emotionless one; having an opinion and being your own person was a social stake through the heart.

It was a superficial thing, bright with color on the outside, drab and cold on the inside. Hitchcock said actors were cattle, in her eyes, models were just cardboard cutouts. Two-dimensional beings, existing only to be looked at. Displaying all the things you personally lacked in real life on the pseudo world of social media. On Instagram, if you described yourself as a feminist, you were in the club. On Facebook, if you described yourself as a vegan you were in the club. Being seen as a good person was more important than actually being one. Besides, you could keep all the selfish self-indulged parts of your personality hidden, like a surprise for anyone who believed everything they read on the Internet.

Go out, get fucked, get treated like a bitch, then eat a kebab on the way home in the morning. If it didn't happen on social media, did it happen at all?

If you refused a job though, if you let those morals get in the way, if you didn't want to lie wearing only a smile on a real fur coat, if you refused a big paying job that would get your face out there… that was different, that was 'el stupido'. All those old social media morals would have had to disappear straight out the window when exposure and a check came into play.

At one shoot, she remembered how a dull looking girl said 'honesty? What is that anyway? It's like a secret, right?' without a splash of irony in her voice.

She was done with all that shit. Done and dusted.

She looked around at her room. It was a bare space, white walls that had been refreshed with a splash of cheap, white emulsion for each new, paying tenant. Her double bed always unmade, with stale smelling sheets. Her clothes strewn around the room in various states of cleanliness.

She lifted her portfolio up; a square section of mirror lay covered in smears of cocaine beneath it. Instinctively, before she even knew she was doing it, her credit card had racked the white remnants into a line. Nothing special, just a quick toot. It was always just a quick toot. Even when she was buying it three times a week it was 'just a quick toot'.

Another explosion, like the photographers camera, went off in her mind. A cold surge struck her body: defiance against taking the fiver from her purse and sticking it up her nose. Acting on a momentary impulse, she threw the mirror against the opposite wall and watched it explode in a cloud of powder and shards of glass.

It had to end, everything had to end.

Everything had turned out a way she hadn't expected, and now it was time to move on again, to do something else.

She tried to think clearly, tried to think... think.

The rent was cash in hand at the end of the week, it was Thursday today and the money would be gone by Friday. So why not spend it on her escape from this? On a new start away from all this crap.

Grabbing her phone, she scrolled down the long list of contacts, looking for one name that she had been meaning to call for a long time. Simone. Kirsten had walked away from Essex with a gracious bow, ending an era that she could always be welcomed back to. Her cousin, Simone, hadn't just burnt the bridges to her past; she had blown them to smithereens with a rage filled nuclear strike.

Kirsten touched the screen where it said her name, and, after three rings, Simone picked up, and in that instant both knew that despite the years of not talking, nothing had changed.

'Oi! Alright ya fucker? Long time no speak!' Simone exclaimed.

Kirsten smiled, their connection over time and space instantly bridged with her cousin's crude but warm, colloquial tones.

Kirsten told her she'd had enough of London and Simone, with no hesitation, asked her to live with her in Brighton. The call lasted less than five minutes, but in that time, all the worry and frustration that had been growing in Kirsten was gone.

'Babes, fuck that place. Do one. Just come down here!' said Simone.

'Are you sure? I mean, I don't want to be a burden I…'

'Get the train down this arvo. Meet me at work! I'll text you the address!'

'Are you sure?'

'Wouldn't say it if I didn't mean it.'

Kirsten looked around at her room; it was an image she already felt slipping into the past, away from the now and into the back of her memory. 'I guess I'll see you tonight then,' she said.

'That's my girl! See ya soon!' Simone blew a huge kiss down the phone. A loud smack that made the small speaker on Kirsten's phone crackle.

Without hesitation, Kirsten grabbed her suitcase, loaded it with the clothes she needed then carefully packed the important stuff on top: her camera, her portfolio – the real work. Slamming the door behind her, she walked past a few of the housemates downstairs. Foreign students studying in the UK, some legit, some here to just earn the British pound.

'Oi!' she said in a tone that seemed to mimic Simone's, 'give these to the landlord.' She threw the keys on the dining table with a crash.

The timid Indian girl jumped, the Polish art student, who always came home in cement and brick dust, sipped his tea. The blonde Dutch girl called after her as she neared the door, 'So, you are going?'

'Yeah...' Kirsten said with pride, 'and I'm never coming back.'

Now in control of her life again, without a backwards glance, She left London for good, for a new life by the sea.

CHAPTER 4

Leaving for Victoria on one of London underground's confined sweatboxes, Kirsten looked around at the grey city workers, the tone of their skin mirroring the dullness of their suits. Each one rigidly sitting, with a stony expression that defied human interaction. The etiquette of the underground baffled her. She never understood the unified ignorance of the others around her, the judging look of disdain if you attempted to communicate with another.

Once, she saw a woman, quite obviously not drunk, homeless or an addict, fall to the floor vomiting. Maybe she was pregnant; maybe it was some kind of food poisoning, who knows? She was one of them though, she wore the same markings; the same uniformed shade of grey, fitting in perfectly with the banality of the other corporate types around her. And as she retched on the floor, down on her hands and knees, projecting something orange up from her insides, all of her own kind, the grey people, lowered their newspapers, stared, then raised them again, shielding themselves from the undignified woman who was letting the side down.

Kirsten stood in front of the information board and tried to make sense of the rows of flashing times, as usual, trains were cancelled. She had heard about how bad Southern Railway was by word of mouth, but now, here she was, experiencing it first-hand. She shuffled along with the rest of them, as a bored looking guard ushered them towards a replacement coach. Managing to bag a window seat, resting her warm forehead against the cold glass, she watched as London's colorless buildings and roads rolled by, becoming a blur of concrete and glass. Soon her view was replaced by the greens and browns of the countryside and as the bus travelled along the motorway, she felt a wave of relief that she was moving away from the confined urban maze behind her.

Drifting in and out of sleep, she awoke properly to see rows of old Victorian houses painted in either subtle pastels or vibrant graffiti. Posters advertising bands, parties and events, were plastered over any free space on empty buildings. She looked at the people wandering the streets, each one different in their attire. The flamboyant, the trendy, the retro, everyone here thought they were somebody, an individual, all-conforming to their own sub-sect of style.

The bus finally pulled up next to the sea. She sat back letting everyone off first, tourists, exchange students, two boozy old idiots who had watched Quadraphenia too many times. Taking in the sea air and slowly exhaling, she felt the rust and decay of London's pollution leaving her body. She looked out to sea, the red sun pushing out its' last rays of the day, casting long shadows around her.

Kirsten surveyed her new surroundings, she caught sight of the famous Brighton Pier. It was a structure covered in people having fun, like they were all aboard a giant climbing frame in the water. But below, in the pier's darkness and shadow, the smash and crash of waves of the natural world waited to drown and wash them all away. She smiled at this; this was the old way of thinking. She took her camera out, framed the pier in the viewfinder and clicking the shutter, took her first picture on the right side of the lens. The picture turned into a dichotomy; an equinox of day and night, the light above and the darkness below. It wasn't the best, but it was something.

Finding her phone, she checked the text message Simone had sent her, copied the address to the map app, and followed the blue arrow as it pointed to her destination.

Soon, Kirsten was outside the place. 'SIMONE'S D'SIGNS' glowed in tropical neon on the shop front. In the window, an array of neon signs moved in their basic two-step animation. Cocktail glasses chinked, coffee steamed and giant hands pointed with their index finger. Perfectly crafted, colorful and sleek, she knew these came from the creative hands of her cousin. Next to the front door a little plastic container held a file of Simone's business cards, she took one and popped it in her jacket pocket, a memento if all else failed in this new chapter of her life.

Her bag of possessions suddenly felt heavier in her hands and looking down she saw her fingers had taken on a purple hue. Opening her stiff fingers, she felt the blood rushing back to the tips as she pumped her fists, enjoying the sensation, making her way to the workshop around the back.

There, a pair of old, wooden, sliding doors were wide-open, Kirsten peered around them. An old metal-framed table was filled with toolboxes, heaps of fast food wrappers and an old boom box playing '80s synth music. Something caught her eye, an orange flash from further around the door, pushing forward, not trying to intrude any more than she felt she already was, Kirsten stopped at the sight in front of her.

There, wearing huge goggles that shielded her face, dyed hair side combed and sprayed into place like a giant blue and blonde arch, was Simone. Moving to the music in a pair of oversized clown-like overalls, away in her own world, caught in the moment, bending glass over a flame, sculpting thin tubing into curled handwritten letters.

Simone noticed something from the corner of her eye, a figure in the doorway. She looked up, letting her work fall away from the exposed flame. Pulling up her goggles, two clean circles now on her face. 'You came!' she happily exclaimed, carelessly putting down the glass tubing with a fizzle on an old wet work rag.

'I did,' Kirsten replied, beaming.

They moved towards one another, smiles plastered on their faces. Simone quickly and playfully punched Kirsten on the arm, Kirsten quickly and playfully punched Simone back, then they fell into a hug. In that moment, the feeling from the phone call was solidified, their old childhood bond rekindled. There are not many things in life as simple as this; most reconnections through time were awkward and forced. But the difference between this moment and others was the genuine sentiment behind it, one that hadn't changed since the days of their youth. Simone loved Kirsten, and Kirsten loved Simone.

Shutting up shop, Simone was full of exhilaration, talking at the speed of light, her mouth a literal vomit comet of stories as she dragged Kirsten down towards the pier. The pair ran through the streets like two children escaping school early, buying two portions of chips and stuffing them in their mouths between the non-stop conversation.

Standing on the pier, they leaned on its old, iron guardrail looking out to sea as the sun set in a sky of two perfectly contrasting colors, hot pink and baby blue. Kirsten soaked up the wide-open space around them. Space for her had been overwhelmed and concealed by tall, confining buildings. Now space was postcard-perfect, a wide, panoramic view. She resisted the urge to pull her camera out again, just enjoying the moment for what it was, with a person she regretted not staying in touch with.

On the evening air, the sound of a saxophone intruded over the sound of the sea. To their right, a cropped haired, middle-aged woman was attempting to play the instrument. Ninety percent of her playing hit the notes as intended, the other ten finding that special auditory place that puts your teeth on edge.

Simone rammed chips into her mouth like a ravenous animal. 'Mmm... my... God... these are the best chips in the world.'

'Hungry?' Kirsten asked, doing the same.

'Ain't been out the workshop all day. I'm a real arse for not eating at times. The only good thing about it is at least I'm not gonna fill out those work pants.'

'I don't think you could ever fill those.'

'If I ate what I wanted, I could give it a bloody good try.' She shoveled in another fistful of chips, turning and smiling at Kirsten with fried potato pieces popping out her mouth like a bunch of yellowed piano keys.

'Beautiful,' Kirsten said, raising her eyebrows.

'Ha! Alright Miss Model. Miss super-size zero. Just because your mates lose the calories with the flick of two fingers on the old tonsils.'

'They ain't my mates any more, I'm done with that. I shouldn't have done it in the first place.'

'Well it earned you some wonga didn't it?'

Kirsten sighed, 'Yeah, but... I just need to get on with what I'm supposed to do now. I need to start over again. I think I've lost it a bit... with everything you know...'

Simone stared at her, not understanding.

Kirsten raised a finger to her nostril and snorted in.

Simone clicked, 'Oh, that.'

'It's become... it was a bit of a problem.'

Simone thought about this, 'It's okay. I get it.' She threw another long fat chip in her mouth and began to talk trying to break the somber tone.

'You know what they say, you gotta do what you gotta do. And you can do photography, Kirst, you got that eye. You know it, too.'

Kirsten smiled. 'Look at you, you're doing it, too. Do you know how cool your shop is? Seriously?'

Simone didn't like compliments, never had and never would. 'Yeah, yeah,' she said flippantly, picking a chip from the pile in her hand and throwing it out to sea, watching a flock of seagulls hit the water making short work of it.

'Do any of the family know about the sh—

Blocking her off before she could finish her sentence, Simone butted back in. 'No they don't. And as far as I'm concerned, they never will.'

Awkwardness filled the air. Kirsten felt like she had out stayed her welcome already.

'Do you still speak to them?' Simone asked, her hyperactivity gone and a deep seriousness replacing it.

'Now and then. They seemed more impressed when they saw my picture advertising perfume in a trash mag than when I had some stuff in an exhibition.'

'Oh, I bet they did,' she snapped back. 'Getting paid to pose with a bottle of stink, that's success to that lot, is it?'

Simone thought about this for a second, she dwelled on those old attitudes from the past. The simple five-word sentence from her mother's mouth, 'Why can't she be normal?' was almost the lyrics to her life. Her family was content with five days of work, a Friday night in a pub. A Saturday afternoon in a shopping center, a Saturday night in front of a TV, then the Sunday thinking about doing it all again.

Simone wanted more, she wanted every day to be a Saturday night. Hot color, hot clothes, sizzling neon, heavy metal rock and roll or the thump of a synthetic drum machine, she wanted all of this at a hundred miles an hour, with her hair on fire. Art, clothes, self-expression. Etiquette was a thing for good girls in lace gloves. She wanted chipped nails and dirty fingers. Ink stained, paint stained, smeared lipstick by hyperactive sweat or hard, heavy sex.

Simone knew from an early age she was gay, knew when watching schmaltzy romantic comedies she always wanted the two leading ladies to ride off into the sunset, leaving the leading man with his dick swinging in the dust.

It was just one of those things, Simone was confident; she knew who she was and what she liked. The teenage questions of 'Who am I?' and 'What do I want to do?' were mere chicken feed in the bigger scheme of things. There was too much to do and too much to see. The only problem in Essex was fitting in.

After a while, 'Why can't she be normal?' didn't cut the mustard when her family described Simone anymore, a meaner, more hard-spirited statement was heard. 'She's a fuck up,' became the go-to phrase. Her choice of career, her outrageous choice of clothes, her choice of sexuality, everything was met with, 'she's not like us,' and a roll of their eyes.

Hitting twenty, she knew what she had to do. Packing her things, slamming the door behind her, she never looked back. She emancipated herself from everyone. Simone wanted to head butt banality right on its fucking nose, breaking it in three places, leaving it concussed. She wanted everything she could get and she wanted it in stereo and style. And on the south coast she found it.

'Just stay as long as you want, Kirst. Everything's different here, people are more open-minded… less arse-hole-ish than London. Urgh, London's a rat hole! Fuck that place. Down here by the sea, you can be anyone you want to, babes.'

'I appreciate you putting me up, I know it's been a while since we spoke.'

'Shhh,' she hissed. 'Don't worry about that nonsense. Let's set you up in your new home.'

They began to walk, Kirsten thinking she should have kept her mouth shut about back at home, about the past, a place she could tell still haunted Simone. But then walking past the saxophonist, Simone sprang to life, hyperactivity coursing through her veins again, stuffing her empty chip wrapper in the end of the saxophonist's horn. Surprised, the saxophonist let off a high-pitched blast that should have had every dog in ear shot standing to attention.

'What the fuck are you doing?' the saxophonist yelled.

Simone swung round, putting a pair of red-framed sunglasses on. 'You a favour, love, you couldn't carry a tune if it had handles!'

Relieved, Kirsten laughed out loud with Simone. Any worries of putting her foot in her mouth had vanished as Simone's hedonistic humor returned. Breaking into a run and wailing like harpies, they moved through the bustling streets again like the children they once were.

CHAPTER 5

Simone and Kirsten slowed from running to walking arm in arm, gassing over fun times. The times they had spent together, the times when they were apart. They cut through a dark subway underpass, their eyes adjusting to its gloom. The old green tiles had been set into the walls back in the sixties and had hardly ever reflected any light from the world above.

Ahead, was a pile of old cardboard boxes making a dark, shapeless form – taking up a third of their path – both unconsciously stepped to one side to pass it.

Simone squeezed her cousin's arm in excitement, 'Kirst, you should have been down here years ago, big time! You need to meet some of my mates, they're ace!'

From the shadows of the boxes, a rough, filthy hand shot out and grabbed Kirsten's ankle.

She screamed, staggering backwards, almost falling as the grimy grip tightened on her. Grasping for the wall behind her, yelling in shrill surprise, her fingernails scrabbled against its tiles, as Simone began to swing her handbag repeatedly down onto the unknown assailant.

'Let go of her, you fucking arsehole!' she screamed.

'Get off!' Kirsten shouted, twisting and struggling to loosen the vice like grip.

From the floor, rising through the layers of boxes, a middle-aged, fat man in a florescent work jacket pulled himself into the light. Foul smelling, dirty, looking like he'd been sleeping rough for quite some time, Barry the Tramp squeezed the girl's ankle harder, a flourish of excitement passing through his groin as he did.

These days he tried to suppress those kinds of urges, he tried to be an upstanding member of society now, and he had made a personal promise never to sail the seas again. He had been trying to forget the memory of his last day out there, and the homemade cocktail of white lightning cider mixed with special brew helped, but a magic bottle of mind wipe it wasn't.

He let go of the girl's slim ankle, feeling his rough hand pulp into a fist, then reached for his bottle. Simone gave him one more giant whack for luck then backed up against the wall with Kirsten.

'Watch it will ya!' Barry coughed.

'You alright, Kirst?'

Kirsten, shaken, gasped at the air trying to find words, heart pounding so loudly it felt like it was going to explode from her chest.

'Sorry, love,' the creature from the boxes mumbled. 'Don't s'pose you got any spare change for an old man, eh girls?' he slurred at them.

'We're not paying for your beer you stinking old cunt! Go get a job!' Simone yelled, getting as close as she felt comfortable to the foul-smelling wretch in front of her.

Barry laughed, slithering from side to side like a giant slug as he attempted to sit up. 'Job? I 'ad one love.' All of a sudden, his eyes darkened and he became agitated. 'I'm not going back out there again, do you hear? I'm not going back! I'd rather be under here in me boxes.'

'Out where?' Kirsten asked in scared confusion.

'Out there on the seas, old Barry was doing a bit of cash in hand, working on the rigs, been doing it all my life but... I give it up about a month ago. Not again. Not after what I've seen out there. You think you've seen everything in life at times, love. Truth is, we haven't seen anything at all. There's always something out there trying to get you. Trust me, girls, trust me.'

'Oh, piss off!' Simone yelled, grabbing Kirsten's wrist and dragging her away from the vile entity. They stomped away from Barry the Tramp and without looking back they broke into a run, hearing him laughing as they went.

Dribble began to form at the side of his mouth, turning into white goo that strung from his top to his bottom lip. His laughing stopped and he stared coldly into thin air, his ears ringing with the sound of the creatures, the unearthly screaming. His mind pitched to the sea again, to the blonde, to the Polish workers, all dead and gone and only him as a witness, cowardly Barry the Tramp. When thinking back to the blonde again he thought of the thing that sent the biggest sting of fear though his oversized frame: the twin. The blonde's underwater double, with the eyes. Another shiver drove through him, the 'mind wiping juice' that he was drinking was not doing its job. He downed the rest of the bottle. What he had left apparently hit the spot as he fell back into his collection of boxes. Barry the slug had now become Barry the snail, the boxes around him his sweat stinking shell. Squirming down in his own filth and stench he didn't dream of things with glowing eyes and other people's faces. He didn't dream at all, just the way he wanted it.

* * *

They didn't hurry back to Simone's flat, they walked, talking about the run-in with the horrible tramp, talked until the whole experience became funny to them. An hour passed before Kirsten found herself back at Simone's front door. Her friend had bought herself the top floor of an old Victorian house, spacious and roomy, wooden floors spreading throughout.

Simone's décor was pure '80s styling: VCRs, old stereos, a laserdisc player, woodchip wallpaper, black frames that boarded-in Patrick Nagel prints, images that celebrated the curved female form. The flat was a space filled with things from the past; it had become a four-walled time capsule that Simone – in her red converse, stone-washed jeans and oversized T-shirt – fit into perfectly.

She stood in the hallway with her arms outstretched, the grin on her face as big as a crescent moon. 'So, where d'you want, loft or sofa?' She jumped slightly on the spot reaching up high and grabbed a piece of rope attached to a loft hatch, partially pulled down the foldout ladder.

'Does the loft have windows?' Kirsten asked.

'No.'

'I'll go with the sofa then.'

Simone bowed her head with the graciousness of a maître d. 'A fine choice, a room with a view,' she said, taking Kirsten's bags through.

'This is a nice place.'

'I know, right?' Simone dropped the bags and lit a cigarette, moving over to the bay window. Kirsten joined her, automatically taking a cigarette from Simone's pack and lighting it.

Staring out into her thick, jungle-like garden below, they noticed an awkward looking teenage boy, who threw awkward teenage boy glances up to the pair of them.

'Who's that?'

'Mickey. He comes around every now and then to do some work on the garden.'

Simone tinkled a little wave down to him, followed by a wink. He was cute in a boyish way, shabby clothes with huge curls of dark hair. He looked up to the girls at the window, nodded in a way that might be charming or roguish later in life. But now, trapped in a hormonal body, he looked as if he wanted to slip free of his own skin and escape from their gaze.

'Silly boy has a thing for the girls. Not that he'd know what to do if he got one. All the better to walk all over him with. Geena, my girlfriend, is always talking to him, bleeding him dry for cigarettes.'

With that Simone flicked her ciggie out the window and called down to him, 'Oi! You missed a bit!' She shut the window down with such a crash that Kirsten thought it would break the glass in its frame. Then, leaning in, Simone placed her red lips on the glass, puckering up and smacking a huge kiss print on the smooth surface.

'He'd love a bit of that.' She laughed before ushering Kirsten on for the complete whirlwind tour.

In the bedroom, there was no bed frame, just a mattress on the floor. Simone let another smoldering cigarette dangle from her lip while she challenged Kirsten to a two-player game of Galaga on an old refurbed arcade machine in the corner. Engaged in shooting down the constantly spawning bad guys, Simone spoke in broken distracted words. 'Mi casa es su casa. You want peace and quiet to start your work up, you got it. Set your stuff up in the living room I'll keep out your…'

There was a knock at the door.

'Ah shit. Don't s'pose you've got a tenner I can borrow till later, Kirst?'

'No, not on me.'

Drawing herself away from the game, Simone held a finger up like an exclamation point, an idea coming to mind. She gave Kirsten a cheeky wink. Dropping her jeans to reveal short but well-shaped legs, she pulled her T-shirt over one shoulder, ruffling her already messy hair.

'Watch this.' She laughed.

Simone ran like a light-footed imp to the front door, spying through the small security hole to the gloomy corridor. There – rearranging his hair, dusting his clothes down and trying in his own way to make himself look pretty – was Mickey.

Slowly and seductively she answered the door, curling around it with a bare leg. Soft light from inside the doorway penetrated the hallway. Mickey, wide-eyed and speechless, stared at it, before looking up as Simone let smoke pour naturally from her barely parted lips, filtering across her lascivious snake eyes.

He squirmed. 'Erm… yeah, I… I came to, err, pick up my, err, money.'

Simone, the larger than life loud mouth, was now a slinking

seductress who oozed sex appeal.

'Hmmm, maybe you should come back later? Actually, give it two nights, I'm in then… alone…'

Mickey's eyes popped out like two over-inflated balloons. 'Alone?'

Simone gently nodded.

'Yeah but, you owe me for last week as well, so that's twenty…'

'Bye, Mickey, see you then.' Simone cutely smiled at him then slammed the door, sending him back into darkness.

Running back into the bedroom, she kissed her right index and middle finger and placed it on Kirsten's forehead, like the blessed touch of a priest, before shrieking with laughter as she jumped right back into the game.

'Sorry about that. So, just help yourself to anything you want. Oh, and the spare keys are on the hook near the door.'

Kirsten nodded but kept her eyes on the screen. 'What're your plans for tonight?'

'Dunno. I think Geena's coming over. It's just a quiet one. We'll leave you to get on with your work.'

'So, what are you going to do?'

'Oh, I don't know. Play a few games on this thing, I suppose,' she said flippantly.

And later that night that's just what Simone and Geena did. First Geena bent over the arcade machine, hands on the joysticks, arse pushed out, with Simone using her tongue to push her buttons. Then Simone climbed on to the machine's fascia and buried Geena's face between her legs.

Kirsten never even got introduced to Geena; she had heard the door go while she sent out some emails, trying to catch a few paid gigs, and had expected the pair to stick their heads in to say hello.

But within ten minutes of her coming over, the quiet soundtrack of the old house was gone as their moans travelled down the hallway to the living room. Kirsten stared at the screen, completely distracted by Simone's whimpering as it beat the same pulse as the cursor on the screen of her laptop. Her mind finally giving up and breaking away from her work due to her cousin and her girlfriend's passionate cries. Sounds that grew more and more intense.

'Jesus Christ!' She sighed and rolled her eyes, throwing her work and camera into a bag as she began to leave. She caught sight of Simone through the crack of the bedroom doorway, eyes closed, mouth open curling into a smile, a blonde buried deep, face first, into her from behind, *Oh so that's Geena,* she thought, meeting her in an image she really didn't need to see as she walked out of the front door and off into the night.

CHAPTER 6

Kirsten wandered alone around the hustle and bustle of the Brighton lanes, everybody reveling in the good times of a Thursday night. Loud music, burning colored lights, pushing, shoving, drinking, drugging, everything regurgitating in a blender of excess.

Even though this carnival of hedonism marched on around her, her mind was still tethered to the laptop in her bag. She could easily slip in with the crowd, going back to what she'd been doing in London – not much of anything, and waking up with a hangover the next day because of it. She needed to move forward, wanted to move forward. It was like a test of will, always easier to just say, 'I'll do it tomorrow,' a day that never actually came. But she wanted change. Christ, that's what she had come here for in the first place.

Taking a break from the constant deluge of pushing bodies, the merging of one face into another, Kirsten backed up against a flyer-covered wall, looking at the people who surrounded her. Brighton felt full of people who seemed to be their own thing. The gay community, the straight community, people who defined themselves by color and style rather than any conformity.

She tried to think of where to go, where to get a slice of quietness. Unconsciously, her fingers found the wall behind her, picking at old, peeling paper that rustled like leaves. Turning around, she came face to face with a plethora of posters, not for bands or parties – 'lost' and 'missing' posters, some old and crispy from exposure, some relatively new.

She stared, dumbstruck for a second. She had only ever seen these for lost pets, rarely for lost people. And there were so many? Why were there so many? They were like the layered rings of a tree, you could literally peel them back and watch the dates change on each of them – dates that were strangely all within the last month. The wall had become a time capsule to lost people, all young and attractive. But why so many in such a short amount of time? She looked at the newest poster on top of the rest.

'Charley Reynolds'

She silently mouthed the girls name as she read it, as if she expected the girl to climb out of the picture and introduce herself.

Another young and attractive face, a head of curls as big as a lion's mane. Her father's direct phone number at the bottom of the poster, the promise of a healthy reward for any information. Kirsten looked into the green eyes of the girl, wondering how someone so close to her own age could just go missing?

Uncomfortably, she looked to the floor, a copy of the local paper – The Argus – trod on in a murky puddle, its headline – 'DISAPPEARANCE AT SEA – CREW STILL MISSING FROM RIG'.

Her mind popped like a flash of the photographer's camera, the disgusting tramp that grabbed her, his words. 'Out there on the seas, old Barry was doing a bit of cash in hand, working on the rigs, been doing it all my life but... I give it up about a month ago. Not again. Not after what I've seen out there.'

Pulling herself away from these images and thoughts, she pushed her way back through the crowds, clinging to the thoughts of straightening out her photography business, trying not to lose them, trying to find a place to hole up. She came to a pub tucked away on a back street, The Heart and Hand. Peering through the windows she figured that it seemed quiet in comparison to any she had just walked past. She pushed open the door and went in, ordered a drink and sat down.

For three hours, and with three G and T's, she fell back into her work. After updating her website, she looked back through rolls of digital images, manipulating them into a symmetrical gallery to display online, photoshopping headshots and a fashion shoot that had lain dormant on her hard drive for almost eight months. This was the longest she had spent in some time with her own ideas, away from others and in her own world. She fell in love with it all over again, with the medium, with the mental isolation, with being able to plug into that consciousness, that wave where ideas for future shoots just washed up into your brain.

And after the three hour session, her head hurt, she became distracted, the thinking became harder and harder. Moving from the table, she went to the bar. Changing her scenery and giving her mind a break, she watched from the safety of her bar stool as the people in the outside world moved past, hearing their voices and watching as they all twisted around one another looking for the next thrill. She took out a sketchpad and began making a list, feeling invigorated. New lenses, new bounce boards, there was an excitement of starting again, a freshness to it all, that old enthusiasm from the past reignited once more. Soon there was another dead G and T in front of her, a fourth being sipped from, not gulped like the others.

The pub was empty apart from the barman, a couple who canoodled in the corner and near the back, in shadow, nursing a drink, a paperback and a cigarette, looking tired and lonesome, a brunette woman in black. It was the same woman in black who had looked down at Charley Reynolds from the pier. A woman who – unknowingly – had been the last to have seen her only a few minutes before she was lost forever.

There was something alluring about the woman. Kirsten somehow felt, by the striking image of her sitting alone, that she was a woman who marched to the beat of her own drum. For some reason, instinctively, she felt a strong connection to her. She reached for her camera, touching its cold metal casing, wanting to capture her image for posterity. She stopped herself, the social restrictions of just taking random pictures of random people in a pub.

'Psychic,' a booming male voice said. Kirsten turned to look at the barman, a short, fat man, sporting the same physique as Danny DeVito.

'What?' Kirsten replied, confusion on her face.

'Her in black, that's what she does for cash. Reading cards, crystal ball, all that seafront gimmick stuff.'

Kirsten turned back to the woman. 'You let her smoke in here?'

He shrugged. 'Not supposed to, but…' He paused, lowering his tone. 'Her husband did the real work – paid the bills. Poor sod died last week. Bet she didn't see that one coming.'

He took a sip from a pint of lager, laughed at his own joke.

'I'm not gonna tell her she can't have a fag, especially when it's so quiet in here, anyway.' He shrugged.

Kirsten ignored him and looked back down at her notepad, trying to drift back into the zone again, but was rudely interrupted.

'See, you gotta be diverse in life, gotta be able to do as much as you can. That way you don't end up drownin' going straight under, ya know?'

Kirsten stumbled in her own headspace, unable to concentrate as the man droned on. She placed her pencil to the side of her pad, and then raising her eyebrows, pulled her uninterested eyes open to give the man her full attention.

'People sell all kinds of stuff on the seafront. This one bloke, ten years I saw him trying to sell taxidermy birds. Roadkill he'd stuffed. He got older and his stuff just stayed the same. I ended up buying one out of pity in the end.'

He pointed up to a shelf where a badly formed stuffed seagull sat, a misshapen thing, an abomination to aerodynamics with oversized, cartoon googly eyes poked into its skull.

'I don't know who the idiot was: him for making that shit or me for buyin' it.'

Kirsten rolled her eyes down to her pad again, that tethered interest pulling her back towards it. Suddenly she felt her personal space being invaded as the barman leaned in closer, wanting to continue the conversation.

'What I mean is, the old man kept her. She ain't got nothin' now, some good looks that are starting to fade. How far can that get ya? It's a real shame. You have to be versatile, you have to keep changing, you don't want to end up lost in the shuffle.'

Moving in closer he leaned over, allowing him a better look at her note pad. He stared down at it for a second, then raised his eyebrows seemingly genuinely impressed.

'See, you get it, thinking forward, making lists, planning, you're not just another pretty face, are you love?'

Kirsten's face fell to an unimpressed position, knowing she wouldn't get any peace here. Her mind drew back to the place she'd left only just this morning – the photographer's studio – a place that seemed a million miles and a million years away now. A place where she was just a pretty face. Suddenly, a glass smashed and everyone in the bar turned around. Rising from her seat, the woman in black put on a pair of dark glasses. She swayed slightly, trying to hide her intoxicated state; her Dr. Marten boots crunching through the sparkling shards of her smashed glass without a care.

Whether her inelegant sway be alcohol induced, meds or straight up street drugs was unknown. What was known was that she was functioning enough to make it towards the door, breezing past everyone with a quick, sharp gust of air. The kissing couple pried apart for a moment, tongues untangling, watching as she went. Knowing all eyes were on her, she made a concerted effort to act normal, turning her buckling legs into long, gliding pins, her huge, brunette hair bouncing with every step.

'You gonna leave that for me to clean up then?' the barman called out. Ignoring him, she pushed the door open, letting in the cold from outside. She stepped out and disappeared as the door slammed back in its frame, making the barman's drink fall from the counter, hitting his oversized stomach and smashing at his feet.

'Bloody hell,' he muttered, half of his drink now poured down his mid-section, looking like he had pissed himself.

A smile drew over Kirsten's face as she packed her notepad quickly into her bag.

'Shame you're not psychic, maybe you could have seen that coming,' she said to the barman as he wiped himself down with a filthy bar rag.

'Yeah, piss off,' he grumbled, kicking glass to one side with a trickle of rage, he waved his hand at her dismissively and went to get a dustpan and brush. Knowing her welcome had been more than overstayed she got up to leave, then noticed the woman in black had dropped something by the table that she had been sitting at. A paperback was on the floor. Reaching down to pick it up, the title, 'Life after Death: a handbook for the bereaved', sent a small stream of sadness through her. Inside was a bookmark made from a business card.

'MADAM MELISSA CLARKE – TAROT – PALM – CARD READINGS'

Below this was her address in Kemptown. Kirsten put the card back in its place in the pages of the book, then slipped it into her bag, making a sharp exit. It was time to go back to her new home, the work done for the day, a satisfied feeling surrounded her.

Walking back to Simone's flat along cold, lonely streets, she thought about the woman in black. Melissa Clarke – psychic. No one in her immediate family had ever died; all of her relatives were still walking planet earth. Aunts, uncles, nans, grandads, people who flirted with the grave but never actually wanted to go both feet in. For some reason, death itself spared them the dignity, but not from the care homes and piles of pharmaceutical medication that ran through her elders' veins.

She thought about Simone, how she had discarded the family

life like Melissa had her glass, shattering it into pieces and walking over it, never looking back or caring.

Her life was here now, her family just strangers from the past, all of them as good as dead in her everyday existence.

Already mentally mapping the geography of the area, before she knew it, she was back at the flat.

Taking exactly seven steps up the blue-carpeted communal stairs, she paused, shocked that she was again listening to the sounds of Simone's rabid sex session still underway. Heard the unseen Geena yell, 'Keep rubbing it you dirty bitch!'

Kirsten rolled her eyes again, whispered 'Jesus Christ' and left exactly as she had come, taking seven steps back down the stairs again.

She checked her watch; surely they hadn't been in the throws of passion for three hours? Kirsten was impressed; impressed they were still going, impressed they hadn't rubbed themselves out of existence completely.

With a sigh, she headed back out into the dark once more.

CHAPTER 7

A colder, lonelier chill filled the air on her second trip out into Brighton. The night had calmed down, everyone saving their hedonistic energy for the weekend. Now, she heard only the echo of her feet on the pavement as they beat a rubber soled beat.

Kirsten headed back down to the seafront, the sky above now a wash of grey cloud that hid the glowing moon beneath it. The pebble beach was barely lit by the streetlights on the promenade, the small, twinkling lights of passing ships in the distance trickled softly back onto land.

The sea, almost invisible in the night, made its presence known by a loud crashing onto the shore. There was a solitude that Kirsten liked about being by the sea, the same feeling that made Simone originally fall in love with it here.

Walking down to the beach, a line of bleached white foam pulled towards her on the tide as the moon crept out from the clouds that shrouded it.

Slowly, her eyes adjusted to the night, the entire ocean revealed itself as a vast black sheet in front of her now, a rippling, moving tar that covered the unknown below. Behind her, on land, lay the beginning of the manmade world, a place she knew and resented only too well. It was the start of the buildings, of concrete, of made up rules from a made up society.

But here, in front of her and out to sea, lay a place to escape. A deep, endless place, a shimmering darkness that held mystery and wonder that, with all of his efforts, man had yet to completely kill with pollution.

She walked further and the sound of waves and night wind became more soothing and dreamy, making her drift off into her thoughts. She hadn't realized the distance she had walked. The beach became a void, a long tunnel of pebbles, tide as black as if she were wandering into nothingness.

Looking ahead, Kirsten noticed something emerging from the gloom, materializing piece by piece like an inverted mirage; the skeletal structure of Brighton pier began to appear. Being this close to it at night made a slight dread coil around her throat like a thick, choking snake. Long, dark shadows crisscrossed underneath into an abstract grid of rectangles and triangles, all reaching out from the shore and into the sea like a submerged cage.

She climbed under the pier into its darkness. Finding an iron beam at waist height, she perched herself on it like a bird, sitting in cut off solitude. This was the first time since she'd arrived that she was alone and away from people. It was, in fact, the first time in a long time she had been away from anyone. London was like a barrel of eels, everyone writhing around one another, living in each other's pockets, all looking out for number one.

The house she had shared, public transport, Oyster cards, taxis, nights out, nights in, congestion charges, Ubers, everything cost money, everything you did and everything you thought of doing cost money.

She was just another morsel for the meat machine of London. The place was a conveyor belt, one constantly running backwards into a pit of poverty, starvation and homelessness, and all you had to do to avoid it was keep running. Keep pointlessly treading water while trying to pull anyone around you backwards, keeping a smile on your face as you went. Conformity was the secret; you just did what the others around you did without question.

That's how society worked.

But she hadn't succeeded in reaching the end of the conveyor belt, you weren't supposed to, no one ever did, your moving just kept the machine moving, powered it. It used you and you used it. She had made the decision to jump off, only turning back to look at everyone else running. Glorified hamsters on a glorified wheel. And here she was, the bird who escaped in her steel cage under a pier by the sea.

Even though she had to ask Simone for help, she was apart from all of that now. Taking out her camera, she popped open the flash and aimed the lens out under the dark pier. As her finger hovered over the shutter button, something grabbed her attention. An eerie lullaby stole through the night towards her, gently touching her senses.

A word whispered on the wind, secret but sonorous. A name. Her name.

'Kirstennnn...'

A chill went to pass through her, then stopped, caught and snared as quickly as it came, a new feeling replacing it.

Her eyes started to feel strangely heavy, closing with a woozy dreaminess. Her head vague, a feeling of excitement passed through her, sexual excitement. Flashing in her mind was a vision of the first time she was kissed, a boy from her school, a boy she fancied, taking her into a stockroom cupboard, holding her chin slightly as he moved towards her lips with his own. The same tingling sensation ran through her again, an almost romantic feeling.

Abruptly, the song stopped and any amorous feelings died, turned off cold like a light switch. Her eyes losing the rose tinted filter. She looked around, on edge, panic rising, trying to trace where the sound had come from, the night too dark to distinguish anything.

There were only the waves now, the seas calm sway.

She waited, listened intently, tense, filled with fear. Clicking the camera's flash, three bright explosions went off giving garish nightmare detail to the rusting, monolithic structure. She looked down at the digital images on the camera's display, over exposed shots of the pebbled floor, the incoming waves, and the pier's thick, insect-like legs protruding from the ground.

She wanted to leave, a cold shiver rippled through her flesh.

Then she heard it again. Closer now, the mellifluous, ghostly song drifted up, her toes curling in her shoes, sensual thoughts of being touched rippling through her body. That beautiful voice, its alluring song, the hairs up on the back of her neck on end. Its words, her name repeated, slowly sensually.

'Kirstennn, Kirstennn, Kirstennn,'

The tide rolled in, the song stopped, her heart was thumping in her chest and a new sound slithered into the soundtrack, a sound that she had become accustomed to being her own on the beach: the sound of pebbled footsteps.

Swallowing hard and sliding down from the iron beam, she put both feet on the ground. A chill surged through her like an electric current as she saw, moving up from the crashing waves, two, yellow, glowing dots hovering in the air, coming towards her. Dots that were quickly cut off by dark, blinking lids, dots that became eyes that glowed like those of a nocturnal animal.

The mesmeric song started again, 'Kirstennn, Kirstennn.'

Somehow it belonged to this dark creature and for some reason, staring into its advancing eyes, she turned to a statue, hypnotized to the spot.

She rose the camera again, the eyes drew nearer, now only a few feet away. Almost on top of her.

'Kirstennnnnnnnnnn.'

With no time left, she desperately resisted the song that stiffened her bones. Fumbling, panicking, with her teeth gritted and sweat on her brow, Kirsten pressed the camera's button. Two lightning flashes burst out, highlighting in its white blasts a slick, oily skinned humanoid form in front of her, all sharp teeth and claws. Amorphous, but clearly feminine, bald, veined, and coal black skin. It was a shadow, hidden in the pier's darkness, come to life and it came for the intruder that wandered into its nest. Its voice that of beauty, its face straight from nightmare.

It drew up its clawed hands to hide from the sudden light, its soothing lullaby voice twisted into a deep screech, a demon's bellow, breaking its song, breaking its hold over her.

Acting on instinct, she turned and ran, popping the camera's flash to light her way, stumbling through the iron grid work of the pier's supporting structure, the thing behind, it's piercing scream echoed out not in retaliation now, but in rage, reverberating around her like an alarm. Her breathing was quick, sharp and jagged as she tried to run back to the freedom of the beach. Faltering on the uneven ground, her ankles bowing on the pebbles, she made it to the edge of the pier. The sound of stomping feet crashed behind her, coming closer and closer.

Squeezing through the last supporting beams, she slipped, clambered, as suddenly a sharp clawed hand swiped through the air behind her, tearing straight through the shoulder of her jacket with a satisfying rip. She let out a glass-shattering scream that almost tore a hole in the night. A cold icicle of pain shot through her, a feeling of being stabbed, the coldness of death spreading over her, her sliced skin jetting with red, warmth sinking into her sweatshirt.

Trapped. She was caught in between the pier's iron supports like a fly in a metal web.

A wet, lifeless hand grabbed her ankle, yanked her backwards. She tried to turn, to flip over and fight. Thinking fast, she grabbed her camera, aimed it behind her and held her finger down, popping its flash off over her shoulder like a machine gun. The creature recoiled, its grasp loosening enough for her to scramble out of the structure.

She ignored the pain as she escaped, adrenaline taking over, pulling herself to her feet and running for her life, the swampy feeling of the sinking pebbles beneath her were no obstacle for her terror-inspired speed. As she ran she heard the shrieking creature again, in its web beneath the pier, furious at its fleeing prey.

* * *

Within an hour, police cars were parked along the seafront, their blue lights flickering like small lighthouses, highlighting the silhouettes of police officers searching beneath the pier with the swaying beams from their high-powered torches.

Up the coast a stretch, in the back of an ambulance, a medic cleaned up Kirsten's clawed shoulder. She stared forward solemnly, cut off from the pain of the stitches that were being threaded through her skin. She had had stitches before, years earlier, as a child, slipping down some old, wet, stone steps and tearing a hole in her side on their jagged edges. She didn't care about the pain, just what she had seen. She wondered how to vocalize the experience. Explain it. The eyes, the claws... She hadn't even been here for a day; she had escaped the problems of London, now new problems had arisen.

Sitting across from her on the fold down seats were Simone and a dull-eyed, make-up smudged, peroxide blonde. They sat watching, wincing, as the tears in Kirsten's flesh were pulled back together like lacing up a pair of flesh colored boots.

'I'm so sorry, Kirst, I'm so sorry, I should have been out with you,' Simone said to no reply. 'You must have seen their face, something? Anything? Who the fuck did it?' she cried, the paramedic, caught in her gaze, shrugged, unable to offer an answer. 'There's all kinds out this time of night. You should think yourself lucky, the amount of missing people around here has doubled in the last month. The police have had their work cut out for them with it.'

'Cut out from what? Sitting in McDonald's car park between twelve and six in the morning?' Simone yelled.

He ignored her and went back to stitching the gouges. 'He must have had some kind of homemade weapon to do this damage. It looks like you were clawed. You were lucky it's only superficial, it's not pretty. It will leave a mark, but you'll live,' he said.

Kirsten shuddered, 'I... I didn't see his fa...' she said in a trance like voice, rethinking her words. 'I don't know… I think he had a mask…'

'What kind of mask? Did you tell the coppers that?' asked Simone.

'I'm making a statement after this, they want to see the pictures on this,' she said dreamily and passed her camera over to Simone and the blonde girl.

They flicked through the images until they both came to a blurry, out of focus picture, the second to last.

The two girls looked at one another. The paramedic caught their exchange. 'Did she get something?'

'Something,' Simone muttered. 'Can't see what it is. It's like… a shadow.'

'Like a shadow?' Kirsten repeated.

'There's something there, some kind of shape.' She clicked to the final image, both Simone and the blonde fell silent, neither sure how to react. Hidden in the blur from her shaking hands, slightly veiled by darkness, reaching towards the lens with unnaturally glowing eyes was what looked like… Kirsten, naked.

'Is that *you*?' the blonde girl asked.

'What the hell were you doing down there?' Simone said, bewildered.

She turned the camera to Kirsten who shuddered at the ghost of herself trapped inside the tiny screen. The paramedic looked at the image, then between the girls, wanting answers but unable to articulate the correct question.

'It's not me,' Kirsten whispered with a shiver.

'It looks like you,' the blonde said dumbly.

Kirsten wrinkled her nose at the obtuse girl. 'Who exactly are you, anyway?'

She shrank away slightly, realizing neither she nor Simone had formally introduced her to Kirsten. 'I'm her girlfriend! You saw me back at the flat, I'm Geena.'

'I never actually got to see your face,' Kirsten replied with an unintentional dry wit.

Simone fired a dirty smile at Geena making her giggle. Kirsten, realizing what she'd said, snorted a tiny laugh, too, changing the entire tone in the back of the ambulance as the paramedic looked up at them, smiling, too, unaware of the joke but picking up the drift they all seemed to be on.

Kirsten had forgotten where she was for a moment and what had happened. Then, checking her jacket, there in its shredded back was hard evidence caught in between its threads – a long, black, sharp talon caught in its torn fabric.

A claw, almost like a big cat's claw, slightly barbed, the thing that had hooked in her skin and left her shoulder a slashed mess. It threw her straight back into the terror she had felt only an hour ago. She touched its smooth, curved form, ending with its razor-like tip, this wasn't any weapon from a masked assailant.

She wondered what to say, whether to show this thing to the others, to the police. She wanted this to be over, she wanted to go back to Simone's and be away from other people. There was a comfortable unity with Simone, she felt like she could just be quiet with her, no signs of an awkward silence just peace. She wanted that now, and to make everything simpler, she closed her hand around the claw, sealing its existence away from everyone around her.

Sealed away, just like what she thought she saw under the pier, it was her secret, one she didn't believe herself. One that she didn't know how to vocalize into sense that would make anyone else believe her. The song, the eyes, it couldn't be true. But she'd seen it, and in her hand was the physical proof, the savaging claw of the thing that tried to kill her.

CHAPTER 8

An hour later Kirsten was taken to Brighton police station to make a statement. She slipped the claw into her bag – luckily her laptop and camera had survived the ordeal – and handed all her belongings over to the police.

They led her to a small studio set up, and before she knew it, she was in front of the cameras again, top off, modelling her wounds as a female officer's cold, gloved hands directed her in various positions.

Everything was done with a clinical procedure; it was like being back in London again. Simone stood by watching everything with distain, she had no real reason to dislike the police, but everything about them rubbed her anti-authoritarian streak the wrong way.

At 3 a.m., bored, Geena had left for home, making up a poor excuse about having to get up in the morning.

PC Moore asked Kirsten if she would like Simone present when she made her statement, she agreed.

The interview room was a small, soundproof space. Worn, hardwearing carpet, a single table with four chairs around it, a white, suspended ceiling and bare walls.

'Let's get this done and get out of here,' Simone whispered. 'I hate these bloody places.'

Kirsten nodded.

They watched through the glass square in the door, every now and then the faces of officers peered through, their voices muffled on the other side.

'What do they think this is, a peep show?' Simone sighed.

Kirsten not liking the look in their eyes as they bobbed in and out of view.

The door swung open and PC Moore walked in with another officer, a blonde, built woman, her face as warm as the underside of an iceberg.

'About time,' Simone mumbled.

'Sorry about the wait,' PC Moore said. 'Had a few things to iron out before we started.'

He placed a digital recorder in the middle of the desk,

'This is PC Jones, she'll be joining us with the statement.'

Kirsten looked up at the women and nodded, who made no gesture in response.

'Well, we might as well press on, you happy to go?'

Kirsten nodded again, cleared her throat, 'Yeah, sure.'

PC Moore pressed the machine's record button, logging today's date, time and year, he proceeded to introduce everyone in the room, Simone dully giving her details when asked what relationship she held to Kirsten.

'So, Kirsten,' PC Moore said nonchalantly. 'Can you tell us what exactly you were doing in Brighton today.'

'Well.' She paused. 'I came down to stay with Simone, my cousin.'

'She's living with me now, actually,' Simone butted in.

'Oh,' said PC Moore, so the London address we have is wrong?'

'Yeah, it was a bit of a quick decision, but I live at Simone's house now.'

'What's the address there then?' he asked.

Simone waffled out her address like a petulant child would reiterate something to its parents – uninterested, with an air of arrogance.

'What made you come down to Brighton, then?'

'I just needed a change of scenery.'

'Lot of old ties there you want to break?' PC Moore quizzed.

'Yeah, something like that,' Kirsten replied.

'Anything in particular you're leaving for? Anyone you're trying to get away from?'

'All of them.'

'What?' he asked, wrinkling his face.

'I was sick of the place. I've been there too long, I just needed a change.'

'Didn't have to give anyone notice? Was it a rented room, shared flat you were in?'

'Rented room in a house, it was just a cheap place to stay, no contract, all cash in hand.'

'All cash in hand,' PC Jones said, her cold face never losing its expression, 'better not tell the tax man that one.'

Simone let out a long sigh, eyeballing the woman.

'It was just a cheap place to stay,' Kirsten said finally.

There was a moment's silence in the room.

'Okay, so run us through everything that happened before the attack tonight.

Kirsten cleared her throat. 'Well, I came down from London on a coach. Met Simone from work, went back to hers…' Kirsten paused. 'Then I went out into town, went to a bar, and went down to the coast after.'

'How come you didn't go out with your cousin tonight, seeing she came all the way down?' PC Moore asked Simone.

'I was spending the night in with my girlfriend.'

'And you didn't all want to go out?'

'Let's just say I was a little engaged.' Simone smirked, bringing her fingers up into a V shape that she stuck her tongue through and waggled.

PC Moore stumbled. 'Just for the record, Simone – Kirsten's cousin just…' He pondered on her gesture. 'They had an intimate night in together.'

'Yeah.' Simone laughed. 'That's the one.'

'Come on,' PC Jones moaned.

Simone rolled her eyes.

'So, did you drink tonight?'

'A few gins, I was on my laptop in a quiet pub near town, I was doing some work, sending out some emails.'

'Tying up a few loose ends?' said PC Moore.

'Yeah, basically.'

'What do you do? Modeling is it?'

PC Jones' eyes seemed to slant at this.

'Yeah, well, used to. I'm a photographer.'

'That's why you had the camera with you?' PC Moore asked.

Kirsten nodded.

'Did you speak with anyone in the pub?'

'The barman, that's it, no one else.'

'How was he with you?'

'Just friendly, normal.'

'Can you remember the name of the pub?'

Kirsten described the area roughly; the look of the place, PC Moore knew the pub and named it for the record.

'Then you left for the coast? On your own?'

'Yeah, I just went to sit down there, to get some peace and quiet, it's been a long day, you know?'

'Yeah, I get that,' he replied.

'Can you show us your camera please?'

Kirsten stumbled on his question for a second, took her camera from her bag.

'Can you take us to the last two photos please.'

She scanned through the images, landing on the picture of the shadowed figure under the pier, a quick breath passed her lips, a slight terror appearing on her face as she passed it to PC Moore.

'For the record, we've taken copies of Kirsten's camera's memory card. The picture I'm looking at now is of a dark figure, under what looks to be Brighton pier. The time and date of the image matching the time the victim reported the attack.'

'So what happened under the pier, Kirsten?' PC Jones asked.

'I went to sit down, had my camera with me then…' It all replayed in her mind, remembering the yellow, burning dots that turned to eyes, the song, the slashing claws.

She remembered it just the way it was, looked at the two officers' faces, knew the next picture on the camera was the picture of her, a picture not of her, she panicked – then lied.

'Someone just appeared.'

'Go on,' said PC Moore.

'I heard footsteps in the pebbles, someone came towards me…'

'Could you see their face?'

'No,' she replied truthfully.

'Did you hear their voice?'

'No,' she lied, thinking of the song, thinking of how it sang her name.

'Male, female?' PC Moore asked.

'I don't know.'

'Didn't you say he might have had some kind of mask on? Simone added.

'So it was a he?' PC Moore said quickly.

'I don't know…' Kirsten replied flustered. 'I couldn't see under there… I couldn't see him.'

'So you think he was male? Black? White?' PC Moore asked.

'I don't know!' Kirsten became agitated.

'Any idea what he attacked you with? A blade?'

'No!' Kirsten yelled.

There was a pause in the room.

'OK, can you show us the next picture on the camera.'

Kirsten moved the image along one, there it was, the blurred picture of what looked like her, naked, blurred through motion and bad focus.

Kirsten raised her hand to her head, sighed, both officers taking in her body language.

'So who's this?' PC Jones asked bluntly.

Kirsten shrugged.

'For the record, the image on the camera is the last on the card. The image is blurred, but it can be easily made out, it's what seems to be a naked girl, dark hair, same build as the victim, under Brighton pier. Taken fifteen seconds after the previous photograph.

'Did you take your clothes off under the pier? Fancied a late night dip maybe?' PC Moore asked.

'No.' Kirsten replied evenly.

'Is this who attacked you?' PC Jones said, her eyes narrowing.

'I don't know.' Kirsten replied.

'Is it you?' PC Jones held her gaze at Kirsten.

'No,'

'You're sure of that, then?'

Simone snorted. 'She said she doesn't know!'

'What were you doing under the pier, Kirsten?' PC Moore asked.

'Nothing... I just wanted to be alone.'

'Were you alone?' PC Jones added.

'Yes, until... it showed up.'

'It?' PC Jones cocked her head condescendingly.

'Him,' Kirsten snapped back.

'So it was a man.' PC Jones snapped back. 'What were you doing under the pier?'

'Look! I went down there to be alone. Someone turned up, I didn't see them, they attacked me, I flashed my camera at them, to get away and those are what turned up on there. Those pictures. That's all I can tell you.'

Tears started to form in Kirsten's eyes. She had to tell them, even if she was here all night, she had to tell them what attacked her was some kind of... creature.

'What do you want from her? You think she would make something like this up? You're having a laugh ain't ya?' Simone said enraged.

Both officers looked at the girls. PC Moore reached inside his jacket, produced a clear evidence bag, something crumpled and cloudy inside it. He threw it on the table.

'For the record, I have just produced what forensics found in the victim's jacket pocket while she was being photographed for her injuries, a small, clear plastic bag, remnants of cocaine on the inside...'

Kirsten's face dropped, Simone sighed and closed her eyes.

'That's not mine it's...'

'It never is sweetheart.' PC Jones smiled, her iceberg face melted by a huge grin.

Kirsten's 'That's not mine,' was the truth. It wasn't. It all came back to her in that second. She was at a house party – six months ago – above a Tesco Express in Soho. She was told about it by another model, who called herself Daisy Chain.

'You have to come to Tesco Disco on Friday night,' she said in her upper class accent, passing Kirsten a photoshopped flyer. 'It's going to be so good!'

The Tesco Disco played out until 4 a.m. and it wasn't long before the police came banging on the door. Kirsten and Daisy were snorting coke on the bathroom tiles as the flat's owner yelled around the door – 'Police are here!'

Their noses worked like dust busters, making the white powder vanish in a flash.

Daisy took the wrap the coke was in, slapped it in Kirsten's hand. 'Quick, get rid of that!' she said, rushing out the door, like the good friend she wasn't.

Kirsten panicked, popped it into the front zip-up pocket of her jacket and followed her. Knowing the second she stepped out the bathroom, what a stupid thing she had just done.

Why didn't I throw it out the window, why didn't I throw it out the window. Repeating in her mind.

The police, already in the flat, just about to come in the bathroom, eyed the girls like the officers were doing now.

But unlike then, as they ran into the streets – scot free, now began the quick fire questions, the accusations she'd avoided all those months ago. Ridiculous, fictitious scenarios were now being thrown at her.

'How do we know that you weren't having a drug-fueled sex session under that pier, met some bloke off the internet and it went wrong?'

'How do we know, you weren't under that pier snorting coke and had a freak out, cut yourself open on the iron works under there?'

'How do we know that you haven't come down here to live with your cousin to escape a man – escape your dealer?'

They warned her they were checking her blood sample for drugs, she should tell them the truth of what happened, tell them everything – EVERYTHING.

And that's how it went on and on until dawn.

CHAPTER 9

She hadn't planned on spending her first night in Brighton with the police.

They threatened her with charges of possession, Simone screaming, 'Prove it's hers, maybe she picked it up in panic under the pier.'

The officers hammered Kirsten for wasting police time that could be spent on the disappearances.

Ultimately they believed that she had been attacked, didn't believe her intentions of leaving London, and knew that coke wrap was hers.

Threats were made – 'seven years inside for possession, that's class A love,' PC Jones bragged, loving every minute of it.

Simone back pedaled for her, said she was in a shared house; anyone could have put it there. Pinching Kirsten's leg to go along with the story.

After an hour of this – not wanting the paper work – they gave her a warning. Knowing they had made her suffer enough, satisfied under pressure what she said was true with her attack, the story never changing.

Released, Kirsten and Simone barged out, two unseen policemen smoking by the entrance passed judgement as they went.

'Seems a bit suss to me. Girl on her own down there at night?'

'Well, she's not drunk. She's been breathalyzed.'

'Probably just off her rocker on gear and fell over. Came down from East London, you know what they're like – everything's just a bloody drama.'

Kirsten shrank inside.

Simone drove her home, a quietness between them all the way.

Not crashing on the sofa as planned, she instead shared the

double bed with Simone and uncomfortably laid on her front, keeping the five long gouges in her back upwards and away from her own weight. She had never really been one for sleeping this way; naturally it was an obscure and uncomfortable position to lie in. But as the soft, white cotton pad covering her wound began to re-decorate itself with itchy, crimson stripes, she quickly became used to it.

Simone laid next to Kirsten still wearing her clothes from a day ago, her denim jacket, her rolled up jeans, even her old, worn Converse. Simone curled in her oversized outfit, like a child dressed in grown up's clothes, reminded her of times upstairs watching cartoons on old VHS tapes at family parties, while the adults downstairs droned on about things that didn't matter.

It was a decade since they last shared a bed like this, ten years of growing up, growing apart and in the last 24 hours coming back together again.

Everything was just the same in a way, Simone leaving an off the air recorded VHS tape playing late night TV from the mid-nineties, two clunky old films, *Octaman* and *Satan's Cheerleaders*. The entire situation felt like a remake of the past.

'I'm sorry, about tonight,' Kirsten said quietly.

'Don't worry about it. It's over,' Simone said in a sleepy voice.

'You believe me about everything right? Under the pier?'

'Yeah, it's over though, you're safe, that's all that matters.'

They stared at the TV for a moment.

'Not sure I believe you about that coke wrap though.' Simone coughed out a laugh, 'Got away with that one, Kirst.'

For the first time all night a smile drew over Kirsten's face and under the TV's rays, they began to giggle.

They did this for a few minutes until both fell asleep.

* * *

The next morning, Simone entered her living room to find Kirsten already up, sitting in the old, black-framed director's chair by the window. She had a steaming cup of coffee and was staring at a giant spider's web that had appeared across the center of the bay window in the night. A huge conker-sized spider had started stockpiling moths and other night crawlers around the side of its web, victims for a good draining.

'Are you going to be okay by yourself today? I've got to go into work,' Simone asked, groggily, slipping into a paint-stained blue jumpsuit.

Turning to face her, Kirsten slapped on a fake smile. 'Yeah, of course.'

'I'm so sorry about last night.'

'It's not your fault. It's cool. I've got some work to do here, anyway.'

Simone watched as a small gust of wind knocked the oversized spider's web, its arachnid maker shooting to a poised, alerted position. 'They'll catch the fucker that did this, I promise.'

Kirsten said nothing.

Simone thought for a second. 'Hey – some good news. I had a word with my friend who runs a gallery and she might be interested in commissioning some of your pictures.'

In actuality, she hadn't asked her friend. Tiffany ran a local gallery in the Lanes of Brighton. But she planned to ask her this morning. She knew what Tiffany liked and that she would most likely take some of Kirsten's work.

She owed her one for some neon signs she'd knocked up on the cheap.

Kirsten looked up at her, a glazed expression on her face. 'That's cool.'

Simone pulled a melancholy smile back. 'No worries. I'll see you later then.' She reluctantly turned and went to work, leaving Kirsten alone.

Kirsten sat for another hour, pouring a second cup of coffee, watching the spider and thinking of the images from under the pier.

Not the images on the camera; they made no sense at all. The camera, just like the TV, had the uncanny ability to lie when regurgitating the images it had captured. She thought of the images her mind had captured.

The glowing eyes. The flash of talons as she escaped the pier.

The creature. Yes. It was a creature.

One that had trapped her in its own web of steel.

Suddenly she felt more fortunate than the flapping creatures caught in the sticky web, but somehow just as tangled and trapped.

* * *

Later that day, not turning on a TV or radio, Kirsten moved around the flat in silence, the slashes in her back somehow already feeling better, remembering she hadn't even taken any of the pain killers Simone left out last night.

Getting a spurt of creativity, she put all thoughts of the previous evening aside to set up her stuff. Building a little studio on a knee level coffee table in the corner, taking out her sketchpad, jotting down ideas.

Searching YouTube on her phone, she pulled up a synthwave music mix she hadn't listened to and put a pair of headphones on. Shuffling through some papers and sitting crossed legged, it didn't take long before she was lost in her work.

She put together a PDF document of her photos for Tiffany.

It was like constructing a symmetrical puzzle, each image fitting together with the last to create a feeling for her style and tone.

After a while of drifting into a cavern of her own mind, subconsciously she began to move back to the night before.

Memory began overriding the thread of creativity, polluting it like a thick, black tar. She drifted to another place, not noticing what she was creating, her hands instinctively moving back to the note pad next to her, jaggedly lining a black ink patch that started to grow all over the page. She whistled gently and eerily under her breath, reproduced what she had heard under the pier; that dreamy, romantic song that had drilled into her soul.

Her movements became more frantic. Her mind flashing back to what she had seen last night. Suddenly, a shock of pain went through the five long gouges on her back, she winced then stopped.

Realizing what she was doing, she looked down at her drawing. There on the page, surrounded by a scribbled darkness, were the eerie eyes and reaching talons of the thing she saw under the pier – the creature – a two-dimensional image unconsciously drawn from mind to page.

A dulled vibration of fear rattled through her. She grabbed her camera. Looking at the blurred images from under the pier, she flipped forward to find the one that troubled her, the female figure that the police thought was her.

In the blurred, overexposed image, the girl standing on the other side of her lens did in fact look like her. She had seen many a dud image in a file of proofs from her life as a model, images where she had moved too soon, where the focus was out or synchronization between subject and photographer was simply off. She knew what she looked like out of focus and over exposed, and right now she was looking at one of those images.

She reached for her back pocket, pulling her gaze down to the claw she had found stuck in her jacket, inspecting it with both hands. Three inches long and as dark and sleek as a panther, she imagined its density and sharpness to be equal to that of a wild animal, a jungle predator.

Its tip felt razor sharp as she prodded it gently, another jolt of pain hit her scratched shoulder.

Then, staring back at the desk, she glanced at the contents of her bag, the paperback the woman in black had dropped at the bar, the last page she had read marked by the business card with her address printed in small, Times New Roman font.

She had never been one for superstitions or supernatural mumbo jumbo, but what she'd witnessed last night went beyond her understanding, but on her camera, her own ghost was captured in an image.

Washing down three painkillers with a shot from a bottle of Simone's vodka, she slipped on her brown bomber jacket, the slashes still in the shoulder and left to return the paperback to its owner. Hoping, maybe, to find some answers to the odd image the camera held.

CHAPTER 10

It was a miserable, overcast day; the evening's last sporadic bursts of sunlight broke through the grey clouds. Kirsten put Melissa's address into the map application on her phone and followed the directions, only getting lost briefly when her mind wandered. After thirty minutes or so of walking, she had finally arrived. There above her, on a neglected Victorian house in Kemptown, was an old hand-painted sign.

'Melissa Clarke – Clairvoyant'.

The sign had a faded grandeur, much like the way that the barman had described Melissa herself. The swirling gold letters on the sign were highlighted by a deep red background, they brought visions of a long ago big top circus opulence, a splendor and magnificence that tied to the old saying 'All the fun of the fair!'. Now weather beaten, rough at the edges and fading. The sign hung with a sideshow creepiness that had naturally seeped in with neglect.

Only a week ago, in fact even a day ago, Kirsten would have laughed at the thought of seeing a psychic, but remembering the woman who had rushed out the door of the pub, a woman she saw only for a brief moment in time, she identified something authentic in her, something that for some reason she felt compelled to explore further.

* * *

Inside the old building, on the top floor of her converted studio apartment, Melissa Clarke sat at an old desk in the middle of a barely lit room. Long velvet curtains shielded her from the outside world, just the way she wanted them to.

Music from a distant carousel played outside. Inhaling a cigarette through an old fashioned black holder, she read a letter the postman had just delivered, one that brought the news she was dreading.

Her husband's insurance wasn't up to date; one mistake with a monthly payment and the whole policy wasn't worth the paper it was printed on.

Of all the piles of documents she had been through – enough to keep the fire at his cremation going for a month – this single letter was the one she had hoped would never show up. This flat, and the home they shared, were legally in his name, like most of the things they had bought.

She had never been the best with money, so she let him deal with all the finances. Life was easier that way, she could be carefree, and she didn't have to fill her head with all of that formal nonsense. But by doing that, ignoring the legalities of life, it had left her with nothing after his death.

Of course, she could fight these things, of course, with a solicitor she could try and tie up the inevitable, could try and swing it round to her favour, but she simply couldn't face it. Not after dealing with Jake in hospital, his body crushed from the car crash on the M23, she wondered how much fight she had in her to deal with bureaucratic pencil necks and their condescending questions.

She reached for the bottle of rum at her side, poured a glass and knocked it back.

There was a tap at the door, her attention snapped back to the present.

Looking up, she tried to see who was on the other side of the frosted glass. She made out a female figure. Maybe the wolves had already found themselves to her door, ready for their pound of flesh. A few seconds passed as she held her breath and waited for the figure to leave, it didn't, and she knew she had to respond.

'Who is it?' she called aggressively.

'...It's err, my name's...'

Melissa butted in, annoyed with the girl's awkward reply,

'You want a reading? Is it business?'

'Yes?' the voice replied.

Melissa stubbed out the cigarette and pulled out a dog-eared pack of tarot cards that she placed next to a fingerprint smudged crystal ball on the table. She quickly lit some candles and incense, doing her best at short notice to create some sort of atmosphere, then wiping the mascara from under her eyes she called out, 'Come in.'

Slowly the door creaked open and Kirsten appeared, peering around in trepidation. Her eyes locked on Melissa sitting in amongst the candles, looking like a séance in an old cliché horror movie.

'Sit down,' Melissa said evenly to the pretty, dark haired girl before her and obediently Kirsten lowered herself onto a threadbare velvet chair at the table.

'What is it you're interested in? Cards? Palm? Crystal Ball?' Melissa asked.

Swallowing hard Kirsten reached into her bag. 'I just wanted to bring this back really,' she handed over the paperback.

'This isn't business then?' Melissa said sharply, making a flush of awkwardness show on Kirsten's face.

'I didn't know I'd lost this,' she took the book back from the girl, turning it over in her hand. Maybe there was still some honesty in the world, she thought.

'I suppose you think I should have known it was missing in my line of work?' she said to the girl, no signs of humor showing on her face.

Kirsten shrugged.

Melissa put her book on the table, her eyes fixed closely on the girl, then reached across and took Kirsten's hands, giving her no option in the matter. 'You've been drawing things,' Melissa said in a quick, authoritative tone.

Kirsten's eyes widened again with sudden surprise, her mind popping back to the two eyes in the scribbled darkness, wandering how this woman could know?

Turning over Kirsten's hands, Melissa ran her soft touch over Kirsten's right index and forefinger, where two black ink patches had seeped into her skin.

'Pen marks,' she stated, her eyebrows raised, condescension in her tone that deflated Kirsten's awe.

'It doesn't work the way you think it works, sometimes it doesn't work at all,' she said, looking deeply into Kirsten's eyes. 'But I know you take pictures.'

Kirsten nodded, not wanting to react, not wanting to show too much, trying her best to listen, not tell. Maybe she remembered she had had the camera next to her on the bar when they first ran into one another, maybe not. Melissa reached under her table producing a black metallic box, a donation box, and held it in front of her.

'So, is it business?' she asked.

Kirsten nodded again.

Something inside Kirsten told her to stay put, to hear what this woman had to say. If nothing else, this should be a distraction from the real problems, something to take her thoughts away, a quick laugh or a quick groan.

Reaching for her pocket she dropped some money in the box, it rattled as it hit the bottom. Melissa looked at the cash unimpressed, keeping the box open her eyes met Kirsten's who didn't understand at first but quickly got it, and dropped more money inside, this time it rustled. Melissa snapped the box shut.

'So, what do you want?' Melissa asked.

'I'm not sure?'

Melissa nodded at the bracelet on Kirsten's wrist.

'Give me this.'

Kirsten passed her the bracelet and Melissa focused on it. A long silence drew between them, the carousel music outside endlessly twinkling over and over.

'This has been in your family for years. The person who first bought it isn't here anymore. But she gave it to your mum and then she gave it to you.'

Kirsten nodded, anyone could have guessed that, it was like saying does anyone know an old, grey-haired lady you called Grandma, possibly who may or may not be dead.

'You're not from here, are you? You come from somewhere busy, fast, noisy... You don't like it...' Melissa said.

Kirsten said nothing, trying not to show emotion either way.

Putting down the bracelet Melissa reached across the table, took Kirsten's hands, squeezing her palms.

A long silence hung in the room.

'There are people who just want you for how you look; they don't know you. Not many people do. They want you for your face. You stand in front of cameras?'

Trying to hide the pang of surprise, startled how right this woman was, Kirsten nodded again.

She wondered, like the pen on her hands, if there was some kind of sign on her, some kind of badge that said, 'Yes, I am a model.' Maybe it was potluck; maybe it was as simple as Melissa saw something in her, just as the agencies in London did.

'You need to show people what you can do, work, work, work. That's what I'm seeing, photos, photos, photos. Then you'll get everything you want. You...'

Melissa thought hard, flinched slightly.

'You're on the wrong side of the camera.'

A truth touched Kirsten, caught in the woman's words, she replied, 'That's right! That's all I try to do, work hard. That's why I model, for money, so I have time to do what I want.' She kicked herself, breaking her personal promise to keep wrapped up about her life.

But the woman's words agreed with things in her life that needed some kind of clarification, some kind of guidance and shaping, a simple pat on the back and kick up the arse to say, 'Yep, you're okay, don't worry about it, get behind that camera again, just get on with it!'

'Like I said,' a seriousness broke Melissa's flat tone, 'they want you for your looks not for your eye, not for your brain, not for what's in here.' Melissa pointed to her temple, then to her heart.

She rubbed her thumb over Kirsten's palms again. Suddenly her face dropped. A confused concern poured over her, deep furrowed lines appeared from nowhere on her brow, a slight flush on her face, sweat quickly flourishing from her pores.

Now and then, when Melissa had read someone, when it hadn't worked, she would fill in the blanks; make things up to keep a narrative going.

That hadn't happened with this girl.

The girl in front of her was like a traced image on a piece of acetate, a simple ink outline of a character, a distinct, understandable form that, with concentration, she could fill in with a defined detail as she read her, pops of color filling the empty parts, the color of her of life, her essence, her aura.

Then everything she saw in the girl was gone.

Melissa shuddered as something else was projected into her mind. It moved towards her, seeping into existence like an ink patch, turning and rolling, a new, dark landscape that washed everything else away like a tidel wave.

There was a new figure moving in the murk of her mind. Distant, hidden, submerged.

'There's someone else who wants your face, who wants to be the only one with your face… It… it… it…' Melissa mumbled, distracted, staring at the thing moving towards her, it was a dark silhouette. It somehow moved like the girl in front of her… somehow felt distantly like the girl in front of her… but somehow wasn't. Like a flash of lightning in the night, an epiphany, an image exploded in her mind, clear and vivid. Rusted iron beams, noise from above, the sea rolling in, and pebbles beneath her feet.

For a moment she was taken aback, she had known as a child that she could see things, knew things this vividly, but it was usually only this clear when it was about herself.

She could remember a time in particular, a day before a school trip, when images passed through her mind like a worn piece of 16mm film, she and her school friends all running up a hill, stopping at the top and looking down at a dense woodland, before running down into it.

The next day, exactly that had happened. Jumping from the coach, they did run to the top of a hill, and at the top she froze, feeling her friends dashing past as déjà vu washed over her, watching them all run into the same woods that had appeared in her mind the day before.

Her precognition had come and gone throughout her life, mostly gone when she left her teens. It was something she played on now, she knew it hardly worked, but pretending to be a psychic was an easy gig. Any telepathic power she may have had was now something that was turned more off than on. But since this girl entered the room, that old switch had started to spark those unused sensory cells that had lain dormant. Now neurons bolted to life inside her again, showing her things she knew to be true, just like all those years ago as a child.

'What happened underneath the pier?' she asked Kirsten bluntly, with concern.

Opened mouthed Kirsten replied, 'I don't know… something… I don't know.'

Melissa became more serious, her eyes focusing on the place beyond the room they both sat in, a place only she could see. The dark, dense landscape in her brain rushed towards her, engulfing her like a dyed flood. It was a deep black dread that passed from the girl sitting opposite, it smothered her, drenched her in negativity.

Her breath taken away, her eyes bulging with a sudden drowning lack of oxygen, Melissa gasped out, 'You need to stay away from the pier, from the sea, Kirsten, stay away from it.'

'Why?' Kirsten cried.

'Just do it! *Just stay away*!' she screamed.

Kirsten started to pull her hand from Melissa, but her grasp was vice like, the intensity in her eyes growing.

'What have you been doing Kirsten? What have you seen?'

A shudder passed through Kirsten's body, knowing she hadn't told this woman her name. She pulled her hand free, Melissa gasping for air, the darkness in her mind rising up around her

Kirsten thought for a second, Melissa knew things it was impossible for her to know; her own questions from last night, impossible to answer.

Maybe she could tell her what she saw last night, what had attacked her, what... *the creature* was.

An idea reverberated through her. She reached in her pocket, taking out the smooth talon and silently placed it in Melissa's hand.

A perturbed look ran over Melissa's face, she had become an expert in filling in the blanks, the bare spaces that dropped in the conversations she had with others. But here the gaps were overflowing with information; they seemed to ooze from the girl's psyche.

Now with the claw in her hand, the silhouetted figure pressed closer. No, it wasn't the girl, wasn't Kirsten that moved through the darkness surrounding her mind, a darkness that radiated like a poison gas.

Kirsten had a bright glow of life to her, but the figures inky aura fed on it like a parasite.

Somehow the physical thing in her hand was in a way connected to the dark thing in her mind.

She ran her fingers along the claw. A chill surged from it through her body, to her core, like an electric shock.

Instinctively, words began to fall from her mouth, broken,

staggered and stilted, 'You have to keep away from the pier. You have to go back to where you came from. You have to...'

Putting pressure on her left index finger, she slid it down the black nail, reaching its pointed end. Melissa jolted as she pricked her finger.

A tiny perfect circle of blood begun to pool at the tip, she winced at the pain. Then, instantly, as if something had walked over her grave, a new feeling entered her body.

Internally, in the darkness, a noise began to generate, a song.

It was a faraway soft sound, a cry of innocence, of beauty, a sweet lullaby; it came from the figure that moved closer towards her in her mind's mists.

She had often wondered what it would be like standing outside the pearly gates, and this tranquil sound matched what she would have imagined would seep from in between its bars.

She turned to look into her crystal ball, in her eyes, rather than being a solid glass mass as it always had been, it became a watery globe of white light that began to glow, to flash, giving three quick pulses.

Kirsten watched, not understanding what the medium was doing, not seeing the vision of the crystal ball she did.

Melissa started to feel an uncomfortable panic rising up to her mouth, slowly choking her.

Staring deeper into the ball, its glow became solid, then quickly, something polluted its inside, plumes of blood red and tar black contaminated the crystal ball with a clouded oil-slicked darkness – it matched the cloud in her head.

The beautiful song only she could hear began slithering into another sound. Uncontrollably, it grew like a twisting vine, turned to a distant shriek, like far off screaming at the end of a tunnel, it was a sound she couldn't get out of her head, couldn't escape from.

Silent and shaking she turned to look at Kirsten; sweat started pouring down her ashen face.

'What's wrong? What is it?' Kirsten asked in panic.

Melissa opened her mouth, the paralyzing sound, the shrieking in her head, now possessing full control of her movements, stopping her as still as a mannequin, paused and frozen in place like a deer in headlights.

She tried to speak, with desperate eyes she stared at Kirsten, a fear and helplessness taking her over. A trickle of blood poured from her hairline, escaping from some unseen place, hitting the crevice of her eye socket, falling down her cheek like a tear.

She saw the outlined figure now; it was repulsive, foul, slick, oily and inhuman.

The scream belonged to it, her skull being used as an acoustic echo chamber, the endless shrieking reverberating, having nowhere to go, nowhere to escape to, rolling over and over blasting its bellow back on itself, bouncing off of her skull's bone walls.

It was inescapable.

Growing louder and louder, coming to the forefront of her conscious it amplified to a point where she couldn't take anymore.

The dark figure stood in front of her now.

A pair of glowing eyes opened on its face, they shone at her like a fox in the night.

Its cold, black lips endlessly screamed out in an ear-splitting, eye-popping, frenzied roar. Melissa screamed, holding her head, trying to stop it from exploding from the inside out.

Shocked, Kirsten fell backwards to the floor, watching as Melissa's eyes rolled back in her skull, turning pure white. More blood pumped from under her hairline, her entire face became a bleeding, pale ghost of the woman she once was.

Through a gravelled voice, she whispered in a long, drawn-out breath, 'Kiirsssteeeeeen.'

Bringing herself straight up to her feet, pulled like a marionette by unseen hands, she stood like a gaping-faced ghoul. A vicious, deep glugging rose in her throat, something pushed up inside her neck, expanding it out from either side. She gagged, her lips drawing apart impossibly wide as a rush of filthy water spewed from her mouth. Kirsten reeled backwards, unable to find balance to pitch herself to her feet, falling gracelessly to the floor.

Melissa shrieked out the sound of the creature from the night before, the creature in her mind, her own voice gone, as a foaming bile-like seawater poured from her mouth that opened like a burst dam, an endless river of rabid phlegm.

Impossibly, pieces of seaweed, pebbles and sand mingled into the liquid as it pooled at her feet. The smell of it hit Kirsten's senses, a dull, muted, sweet stench, the lining of a human stomach mixed with a rotten oceanic reek that made her gag.

Small sea creatures began to fall in to and flail around in the foamy mess, tiny crabs, small urchins, things that couldn't possibly be inside this woman, shouldn't be inside this woman.

Now a new pigmentation entered the growing pool of sickness. Thick blood pushed the pool's parameter out further, washed towards Kirsten, turning its foamy spume red.

Finding her footing, pulling herself up and away from the moving mess that was creeping towards her, she screamed, looking at the petrified frozen face of Melissa, throwing up an ocean's worth of water and viscera.

Kirsten turned to the door, gasping in panic. Throwing it open, she ran out. With the absence of Kirsten in the room, Melissa's possessive trance broke, her screams returning to normal, her vocal cords ripped to shreds as they became quiet, her eyes rotating back to position. Losing her balance, she fell sideways to the floor, landing in the bloody puke; a smothering weakness clung to her bones now.

Stranded and alone, not able to follow Kirsten out the closed door, she watched with dull, exhausted eyes as the rippling red mess came to a standstill around her on the polished wooden floor. Weak, every part of her in pain, she could do nothing but lay there and think. A connection had been made; she was somehow plugged into the dark energy that followed the girl, it now tried to consume her, too.

She had seen something else inside the vista of her mind, visions of the future, of the girl, Kirsten's future... and her own... one that she hoped with the little energy she had left, for both of their sakes, would never come true.

CHAPTER 11

Darkness shrouded the streets with coal-black shadows shaped by silver moonlight. Night was here and the fear of unseen things hidden in every corner made the hair on the back of Kirsten's neck stand on end. The world around her rotated like a fairground ride, lost in panic and disorientation, tears began to stream down her face, the image of the psychic's pale, gaping face burned into her retina, an image she couldn't escape.

Her scream, *the creature's scream*, haunting her.

Having no understanding of where she was as her legs, working on autopilot, pulled her forward. She reached into the pocket of her jeans mid-stride, feeling for her phone. It was the old routine she did every day, keys, phone, cash and cards. There was nothing.

Keeping stride, she reached into her handbag, fumbling anxiously, but no phone could be found.

She knew the shape of the phone by heart; she could even throw out texts covertly in her handbag by knowing the familiar layout of the flat, glass screen. But now, that shape was gone, the device that made life so easy – where to go, where to meet, how to get out of trouble was a thing of the past, dropped on the floor of Melissa's apartment when she fell from her chair.

The swing of her camera made the strap slowly tighten around the leather of her jacket, causing flairs of pain to fire through her. Sweat began to escape her body, her T-shirt sticking to her back in grey patches, her jeans painfully rubbing against her thighs. Eventually running out of steam, her exhaustion getting the better of her, she stopped.

Her heart beating hard and fast in her chest, the image of Melissa, the endless bile, the foaming blood, her eyes wide open with a thousand watts of fear.

That scream.

A gust of wind hit Kirsten's face. In it, the distant salty sea air touched her senses. She gagged, remembering the stench of the rolling red vomit, reaching down to hold her knees she spat on the floor, feeling her belly turn like a roulette wheel, food jumping from red to black, red to black, choosing whether it was going to stay or go. Standing up she sucked in a lungful of air and swallowed it down, trying to suppress the urge to vomit.

Gaining her bearings, she looked around at the area she was standing in, she recognized nothing. Two, wire, diamond chain-link fences cordoned off either side of a still road.

Industrial areas surrounded her, concrete buildings with silent smoke stacks sat to her right, the sea to her left.

Walking forward, amber streetlights highlighted thick networks of web-like cracks winding along the tarmac path beneath her. Looking up, a seven-foot rectangular structure stood further down the side of the road. Realizing what it was, an old BT phone box, a spark of salvation went off in her head and she scrambled though her jacket pockets to find the business card she'd taken from the front of Simone's shop.

She found it.

Running towards the box, uttering, 'Please, please, please,' in a pleading panic, she flipped through scenarios in her mind. The receiver lead cut, the coin slot filled with glue, no phone at all – ripped out.

Throwing open the door, the stench of urine hit her, she grabbed the receiver as the door slammed behind her.

She held her breath when no sound purred up the old line. Then sighed in relief when, with two pumps on the receiver's cradle a crackling dial tone could be heard. Smiling, she jammed the receiver between her chin and shoulder holding it in place.

Finding a pound in her pocket, she dropped it in the slot and entered Simone's mobile number with trembling hands, preying she would pick up.

The line dropped to silence, then she heard the beginning

of a voicemail service. Fearing the answering machine would cut in fully, would take her money, she slammed down the receiver's cradle, not quickly enough, the pound credit was gone. The phone box was a pressure cooker of flustered sweat and exhausted body heat; she fumbled, searching her pockets again, hoping she had more money. She found a shiny 50 pence coin and, shaking, she pushed it hard into the slot, this time ringing Simone's work number.

This time the phone rang and rang.

Simone was in her workshop, working on a commission that should have been finished yesterday, far away in her own world. The hiss of the blowtorch in her hand and the loud bass line pulsing from the stereo next to her, cutting her off from any outside interference.

Her answer phone kicked in, 'Simone... are you there? Simone! Please pick up, *pick up*!' Kirsten cried, begging and pleading, hoping her cousin would be there, to reassure her that everything was fine, needing her to guide her back home. But there was nothing. A far off triple bleep filled the receiver's small speaker, the digits on the phone box's display disappeared as the line cut off and Kirsten continued to shout into dead air.

'Shit!'

She reached around her pockets, searching for money and only finding pennies, useless shrapnel the phone refused to take. She slammed the phone back in its cradle.

Turning and looking through the booth's worn plastic window, she sucked in air, tried to calm her nerves. But before she could fully exhale, it caught in her throat. There, across the road, towards the view overlooking the sea, the shape of an obscured man stood watching her.

In the darkness he had no distinguishing features; no vivid defining physical traits.

Then, suddenly, his eyes shimmered, illuminated with light, as if they belonged to a night-time creature you might spot in the woods, eyes of a savage unseen thing that would hide itself before pouncing on its prey... like the thing that shrouded itself under the pier.

The creature.

A chill rose in her as the figure now walked towards her with slow, calculated steps. Instinctively, her legs began to work independently, recharged from standing still the last few minutes. She slipped out of the phone box and onto the street, tore away from the bright-eyed figure that was coming towards her at an ever increasing pace.

CHAPTER 12

Kirsten's breathing was heavy again; her heart beat echoing through her body. Hoping the man wanted to use the phone box, that he wasn't following her, she turned to look. He was still behind her, like a shadow. His physiognomy a mystery in the darkness, as if he was buried in a deep bank of fog.

She needed to escape the streets, needed to escape the stranger that followed her. There was a hole cut into the chain link fence ahead, a human size hole that some vandal had made for an illegal, late night access that was now an escape route.

With a stumble, she pulled herself into the darkness beyond. What felt like a million thin tendrils brushed against her face – overgrown grass taller than herself. Recoiling for a moment, she piled straight forward, tried to form a geographical pattern in her mind back to town.

The head-high blades whisked against her skin like the striking ends of a flogger's bullwhip. Her eyes adjusted to the low glow of moonlight above as she reached a clearing and jarred to a stop, searching for the figure of the man. There was nothing.

Heaving in two puffs of air, trying to calm her lungs, she couldn't afford more than a moment. Smoke stacks belched their polluting fumes into the atmosphere, glowing unnaturally from huge, industrial security lights that beamed in the distance, beer and spray cans littered her feet. She sprinted on, lost, scared, and trembling.

A sudden sound made her freeze and hold her breath. The long grass ahead of her rustled, its blades thrown back and forth as a hidden figure pushed its way towards her. Crouching down, trying to hide herself in the dense foliage, a slender woman slunk like an oversized grass snake in an industrial Garden of Eden. She, too, had the inhuman eyes of the creature under the pier, glowing in between the quick swish of grass blades like the flicker of an old zoetrope.

Kirsten bolted, sprinted off in the opposite direction.

The tangle of grass around her became plain, dusty earth. No longer having to squint to protect her eyes from the slicing greenery, the cleared view of her surroundings revealed a dilapidated old factory. It would be easier to hide in there from whomever – or whatever – was chasing her. She ran for it.

Moving past old, iron walkways, graffiti covered walls, and broken windows, she entered through a gap in a smashed red brick wall, her feet faltering on unseen debris. The building's insides were surprisingly light, beams of moonlight and a still working security lamp reached a huge, shallow pool of leaked water that rainbowed with the contamination of oil. Racing up a spiral staircase to the first floor, she grabbed the hand rail, tried to lift her feet as she went, making them as light as possible to avoid the dull, vibrating thuds of each step.

At the vantage point from above, she watched, wide-eyed and covered in sweat, through a shattered hole in a frosted window.

For a second the outside world held nothing, just the swaying long grass and a sky filled with banks of factory smoke. Staring for an amount of time that felt too long, too silent, drawing towards the building was what looked like four fire flies. Fire flies that, with a simple blink, reformed into the shining eyes of the shadowed figures, walking in unison towards the building, searching for one thing: her.

Silently and stealthily she moved back into the building, fading away into the darkness.

A sudden moment of realization slapped her, of where she was and what she was doing. It was only a day ago when she thought of how much things could change in twenty-four hours. Now, another 24 hours later – how things had changed again. She, the girl that the photographers of London wanted to flash their cameras at, now being stalked by lights of a different kind.

Moving as quickly and quietly as possible, she could see this was once an old textile mill, rows of cobweb covered sewing machines that stood untouched. Moving down another stairwell, putting one foot in front of the other as quietly as possible, she tried to search deeply into the shadows around her, as if her eyes could beam out light into the darkness, too.

Stepping through the oily pool of water, a quick glow caught her eye from its ripples. She paused, looking down at her own wavering image, a frightened girl that for a moment she didn't recognize stared back. Brimming with fear, Kirsten peered around the old factory, aware that the things behind her must be closing in, not noticing that her own rippling reflection below her feet didn't follow her actions any more.

It had become its own autonomous thing, one that shifted its gaze upwards to look at the girl who once owned and controlled it. The reflections eyes slowly transformed into glowing vortexes, eyes that matched those of the things outside, a luminescent power surging through them.

Kirsten shuddered for a moment, feeling for some reason as if she was having an out of body experience, as if her soul had jumped from her skin. Then the water below her feet exploded upwards in a thin geyser of violent spray. Her reflection inverted in on itself, breaking all laws of physics, as it leapt upwards grabbing the owner it disobeyed, pushing her backwards into the black pool of water, screaming the same hellion cry of the pier creature. Her reflection, escaping its watery prison, was trying to swap places with the original that walked freely in the world.

The original Kirsten, the real Kirsten, the girl who had tried everything to not give herself away to her pursuers, now screamed in pure terror.

Her reflection, now on top of her, pushed her down, its hypnotic glowing eyes reached for her with smoky beams of light, invading her line of vision, locking her in place. Here was the thing from the previous night; the glowing-eyed doppelgänger from the blurry photo. Impossibly, it had come to life, born from her own reflection, escaped from the camera's screen, trying to straddle her, trying to push her backwards into a puddle that was only seconds ago a few inches deep, but now, somehow, became an ocean that she sank into.

Its scream stopped, now in complete control, wrapping around her like a sensuous serpent. She felt a tight grasp on her hair, clutching hands reached up from the shallow pool around her. Rough, scaled hands with more of the needle-like claws that grabbed at her hair, grabbed at her arms, mauled her from behind, grasped her in vice-like grips as the glowing-eyed double pushed down on her from the front.

It was like a gang rape of her identity, pulling, clawing, wanting to be inside her, wanting to be her.

A scream burst from her lungs, a scream touched with the situation's madness. Looking up into her own face she could see the slightly nonchalant, slack jawed expression she had pulled a thousand times in front of a camera now looking back at her. Its eyes flickered with excitement as its mouth widened, opening in a grimacing yawn that turned to an endless shaft of light that spilled over her face like the beam of a flood light. The dreamy, lullaby song echoed from its gullet as if being sung from a deep, far off place, echoing up and into her senses with its hypnotic lilt.

She fought the woozy feeling, remembering the night previous, remembering the way she made the creature recoil. The pinching hands from below restricted her reach as she blindly grabbed for her camera, thinking of its powerful flash and how it had saved her. But what good would that do now? She was saturated, caught in this gloomy pool, and was sure the camera would now be the same, its small circuit boards a washed mess of frazzled electronics. But something else within reach gave her an impromptu plan B. Going for her bag, she managed to slip the grip of the watery hands below and frantically searched inside, finding what she needed. Lurching up, pulling against the thing that held her back, she doused her double straight in its gaping face with a hissing canister of hairspray. Its eyes and mouth snapped shut, poisoned by the chemicals. It howled, this time in pain as it pulled back, folding in on itself into the filthy puddle, turning back into what it was, what it should always have been, a mere reflection. The tight grip below her lost hold, as her mirrored manifestation retreated.

She saw her chance.

Crawling on her hands and knees, she screamed at the madness of the situation, at the nonsensical hands that reached for her, at being attacked by the one thing she always thought she could rely on. Herself.

Wet from the pool, wet with sweat and wet with the piss she had leaked in fear, she ran off into the night, back onto the streets, not stopping as she tracked her steps frantically all the way back towards her cousin's home.

CHAPTER 13

Almost an hour later, she burst through the front door to Simone's flat. Making sure it was shut, she fell hard against it with all her weight, quickly locking it with shaking hands. She was out of breath, filthy and wet through.

Simone, on the phone in the hallway, froze, open mouthed at the sight of her cousin.

She had been determined, strong and unrelenting as she ran home, pushing her body to limits she never knew she was capable of. But now, seeing herself through the eyes of Simone who went from laughing on the phone in the hallway to shocked confusion, the horror of what she had just endured hit her all at once.

'Yeah, yeah, wait… I gotta go,' said Simone as she abruptly ended her call. 'What the hell's happened?'

Exhaustion catching up with her, Kirsten found herself unable to speak, her mouth dry and her throat feeling like she'd swallowed something that was blocking her airway.

Eventually she managed, 'Something… this thing, this… there's something, something tried to…'

'Hang on, slow down who tried to what?'

'No, I don't know,' she wheezed. 'I mean, it was a person but it wasn't.' Kirsten, babbling around her own short breath inhaled deeply. 'It's trying to kill me!'

Simone's face slackened as she slowly moved towards her cousin, a deep concern growing on her face. 'Tell me what's happened?'

Gasping again, Kirsten blurted out, 'I went to see that psychic…'

'What?' A new confusion flooded her face.

Kirsten realized that after everything that had happened the night before, she had neglected to mention to Simone what had happened in the pub.

'Before, last night, I met a psychic in a pub in town, I went to see her today...'

Simone rolled her eyes. 'Ugh, what did you do that for? After last night that shit's just gonna fuck with your head, innit? What's the point of going to visit some old piss 'ead that thinks she can talk to spirits?'

Kirsten stayed silent, annoyed with Simone, unable to muster the aggression to scream at her, to yell at her and make her understand the things she still didn't understand herself.

'Jesus, don't tell me you believe what some old crank from the bloody pub told ya?'

Kirsten swallowed, taking a huge breath and holding it for a few seconds before exhaling slowly. She needed to try to explain again.

'It was real!' she screamed at Simone's myopic ideas. 'She started telling me about myself and stuff from the pier... and then today I was chased to a warehouse... by things with glowing eyes...'

'Glowing what?' Simone grimaced.

'And... and... she knew, Simone, it's fucked up. She threw up everywhere... and she told me I should leave, that I shouldn't be here.'

Kirsten's words, now out loud, sounded ridiculous to even her, they held Simone for a second, she processed them in her mind into something she could understand and comprehend in her short, callous way.

'Hahaha! You're telling me you're freaked out because you went to see an old alky "Psychic"?' She threw her fingers up into patronizing inverted commas, paraphrasing the parts of Kirsten's story that ridiculed its authenticity the most. '"and she puked," – Brilliant.'

Kirsten gritted her teeth and shouted, 'It wasn't just that, look at me, *look at me!*' She held up her soaked arms, the bomber jacket a sad, sagging affair on her body now, presenting Simone with her filthy, dirty, piss stained outfit.

'I've been chased tonight by something with glowing eyes, like the eyes in that picture that looked like me, I've been running around some old fucking factory trying to get away from it!'

Simone stared at her, breathing out a slow, condescending stream of air, then looked away, not knowing what to say, slightly embarrassed.

'You know what,' Kirsten yelled, spittle shooting from her rabid mouth, 'I'm done! I shouldn't have come here. I'm sorry, Simone, but that's it, I'm leaving.'

Kirsten pushed past Simone, barging into the front room, frenziedly packing her bag. Simone went to strike back, to lash out at the girl; it was her nature to bluntly tell Kirsten she was being a moron, to sort it out. But she stopped herself, knowing deep down she didn't want to cut the last tie to the past, a tie that meant so much to her, more so than her own words could express.

Emotionally, over the years, Simone had become a closed book. Emotions, in her experience, had always got in the way. Instead of saying something real or heartfelt, instead of letting herself fall into a deeper part of her personality, she tried to rationalize with Kirsten, to ignore the absurd story and focus on the coherent and logical.

'No – no – no – no… come *on*, let's just think about this for a moment.'

Kirsten ignored Simone and continued packing. Simone grabbed Kirsten's arms, drawing her around, forcing her to stop and listen.

'Look, I told you my mate runs a gallery, she's interested in seeing your work, might even commission you for some new photos. If you wanna leave, just wait and come with me tomorrow night to meet her, see what happens, then decide if you want to go. Yeah?'

'You don't believe me, do you?' Kirsten cried, 'You just don't want to know what happened?'

'Babes, after last night, I expect you to be freaked out! I expect you to be like this, but you gotta let it go!'

Kirsten pulled away from Simones's grip and dropped down cross-legged to the floor. Feeling foolish and alone she looked up at her cousin. 'Just tell me something. Do you believe me? Do you believe me something strange is happening?'

Simone sighed, dropping down next to her. 'Yeah, I believe something strange is happening. I don't know what, but I believe it.'

Kirsten doubted this. She knew that she had been inarticulate in her breathless state, but did Simone even give her a chance to explain fully? Maybe all this time alone, away from anyone who she cared about or anyone who cared about her, had ripened her cousin into such a hardened bitch that she was completely unable to find real words to express herself in any close or intimate way.

Kirsten stared into her cousin's eyes. Already exhausted by the whole evening's horror, she was now exhausted by Simone. Kirsten gave in to her cousin's plea, taking small comfort in that, physically, she was not alone. She was away from the thing that had attacked her. For a moment, she questioned the authenticity of her own memory of her experiences. Then felt a cold shiver rush down her spine, the sting of the slash marks on her shoulder, and any self-doubt quickly dispersed.

'Can I sleep in your bed again tonight?' she asked Simone, flatly.

'Yeah course you can, Kirst, just stay a bit longer yeah? I do want you here.'

Kirsten thought about this for a second then nodded, threw her bag back into the corner taking out some clean clothes and then went to shower. Before long, the two girls were back in bed with one another, the old TV set playing the same tape from the night before as if the entire day had simply been a slip in time. Shallow entertainment wasn't a distraction for Kirsten tonight though, nor was sleep. She stared intently at the ceiling, seeing past it, through the grey roof tiles and into the night sky. She thought of the pier, of Melissa, of the factory and her own reflection going AWOL. Although safe with her cousin, a deeper instinct told her that whatever was happening wasn't over. The instinct told her that leaving Brighton was indeed the best choice. Even though she had tried to explain what had happened today, she was actually the only one who really knew the horrifying truth. She knew the thing that attacked her would be back again, but when and where she had no idea. A wave of dread passed over her exhausted body as she became aware if it did find her, what it was going to do? What did it want?

CHAPTER 14

With the window slightly open and the roller blind keeping the day's sunlight hidden, Kirsten and Simone slept in until noon. From the distance the sound of the sea drifted up with the breeze, filtered in like a lover's soft caressing breath, skimming across their exposed legs.

Simone put off work that day, and with an effort that could best be described as a genuine attempt to show sensitivity – an emotion that seemed to be alien to her these days – she spent the afternoon making sure her cousin thought of anything but the events of the past two days.

Simone knew the importance of first impressions, especially the first experiences of a new place. She herself had made a concerted effort to make her first few months of living by the sea memorable. Going out, soaking in the carefree culture of Brighton. Indulging in promiscuous encounters of either a sexual or a narcotic fueled nature. She knew Kirsten well enough to know that she wouldn't emulate her own idea of a good time. From what she understood, she had that good time in London and now was the time for change, the time for exploring more sensible pass times.

The world was full of two things in Simone's eyes, workers and shirkers. Both had had their time shirking, but here, by the sea, tranquility and peace filled the soul and the work became anything but that.

They hung out for the day, watching movies on some of Simone's old VHS tapes. Blurry versions of *Devil Girl From Mars* and *Midnight Movie Massacre,* taped from late night weekend television nearly thirty years earlier. Simone made off the cuff comments towards the screen and laughed at the films' cheap, cheesy B movie effects.

After the films, Simone convinced Kirsten to get her portfolio together, so that when they went down to the gallery, Kirsten could talk to Tiffany, the curator, about her work. Kirsten wasn't particularly enthusiastic about this prospect; instead she just drifted around the flat in silence. Simone tried to keep her distracted, acting like the jester in Queen Kirsten's kingdom, just like she did as a child, always over the top and larger than life. She went through Kirsten's work, making suggestions for what she should take to Tiffany. The world that her cousin had created through a lens looked like pictures of the world that Simone had created for herself in her flat and her own work. Retroactive backdrops, hot colors, vivid designs, all decorated with attractive, strong women.

The day soon turned to night as Simone noticed a nervousness taking over her cousin. Turning up the volume on her old, silver boom box, the pair got ready like a montage sequence in an old film, wandering around in towels, waiting for a turn on the hair dryer whilst doing their nails. The mood had been successfully changed as they played and messed about and the steely atmosphere that Simone had fought to alter was all but gone, melted away by their laughter.

Kirsten took a swig of vodka from an almost empty bottle before they bundled into Simone's old, rusty, yellow VW bug and drove off into the night. As they pulled up outside Geena's house, she was already waiting outside, hopping back and forth on the spot in the cold evening air, chewing gum. She looked good, fishnets with a black denim skirt with matching jacket. Her hair was combed over to one side, the opposite side to Simone's making the pair look like a pair of blonde bookends.

Simone flashed the headlights towards her; Geena waved and tottered over to the car on stilettos, making little 'click, click, clicks as she went.

'Let me in, its cold out here,' she said climbing into the back seat.

'Why didn't you stay inside until I turned up?' Simone asked.

'Dunno really,' she replied dully, talking immediately and incessantly about things that seemed to float into her head at random. Brain filler talk that added to the distractions Simone needed for the night.

Geena lived a privileged life, she wanted things and she got those things. Much like her old friend from her private school days in West Worthing – Charley Reynolds, the pair never thinking an education or hard work was anything important when you had parents you could hold your hands out to whenever you desired something, parents who would immediately fill those hands with pound notes when prompted.

When Geena heard Charley's dad had bought her a flat, she made sure she got one, too. It was all a game. Who could have the most things, things that they stockpiled, just to say they had. Neither had to work, neither had to try, all they did was receive.

All this made Geena the way she was. When she had to, when the gears of intellect had to be ground into forward motion, she could hold a conversation with anyone, babbling the right words that matched the tone of the subjects spoken about. But empathically, Geena was a bubblehead. She had no relation to anything deeper than her own handbag. Boozy nights, boozy days, her life was a social whirlpool of vacuous meetings with other people who were as useless as herself.

Simone wouldn't normally keep company with someone like her, but Geena had one thing she liked. She was hot. Simple as it may seem, as vacuous as anything the girl herself might say, she was arm candy, plain and simple. How loyal a piece of arm candy she was could be debated. One thing was for sure, if you let her walk all over you – she would. The old, 'But, Ohhhhh I want that,' attitude she used on her parents was still prevalent in her arsenal today. Simone used some good sense though, knowing if you kept the bitch on a short leash you could get what you wanted from her. It was all mind games, it was all fun, but it was never, in Simone's eyes, going to be anything serious.

They liked each other, they were opposites, it was what it was, and right now that's all they both needed from one another.

Simone drove them to a multi-storey car park that overlooked the sea. Spirits still high, laughing and joking, Kirsten almost forgot her problems as they walked up the promenade, the sounds of high heels scraping on concrete mixed with chatting and laughing as they moved beneath the small, sparkling lights strung across the lampposts above.

At the gallery, there was a small gathering of people, all intellectual, artistic types, people Kirsten and Simone could fit in with, but also felt no warmth towards. The curator of the gallery, Tiffany, a tall woman with dark, poker-straight fringed hair, had that old Essex twang in her voice, something Kirsten found that put her at ease when they spoke.

Kirsten looked around the gallery. It was a red-bricked room with spotlighted canvases and prints, all with a distinct style that Kirsten knew would complement her own work. Tiffany flipped through Kirsten's portfolio on her iPad and a smile spread across her face.

'Now these are great. Simone sent me some picture messages of your work taken off a computer screen yesterday, but these look amazing.'

'I bet she did,' Kirsten said with a pseudo put-out voice, knowing it was a sneaky thing done in her best interest. Looking around she saw Geena staring gormlessly at a huge canvas as Simone, half way through a drunken conversation with another patron, nonchalantly took an ice cube from her vodka and coke and slipped it down the back of her jacket. Geena turned, squealing, trying to find a culprit, as Simone kept a straight face, looking at her, pretending not to understand the girl's noises, then staring around the room looking for the fictitious guilty party.

How could she be mad at Simone for sharing her work? She felt like a burden with everything that had happened since her arrival, but all Simone had done was try to make her happy. Simone was family, real family, and Kirsten knew she had made the right decision to come here.

'We are having a display of fashion-oriented black and white photography in two month's time. How would you feel about being commissioned for four original pieces? Full size, six feet by four, real film prints?'

Kirsten smiled. 'I think I feel…'

She stopped, distracted, as out of the gallery's window, in shadow, a pale-faced girl stared in with absent eyes. She didn't take her gaze away from Kirsten, her curly, red hair saturated, dripping down her face, water catching on her fine features, pooling gently at her slightly open mouth.

Something stirred in Kirsten looking at this wanton specter staring through the window

'…That's a great idea,' she finished in a distant voice.

A passing car moved behind the girl, its lights quickly flooding the front of the shop, reflecting from the window back into her face. For a split second the un-flinching eyes of the girl flashed back at Kirsten with a glow that drew out all of the feelings she had tried to suppress.

'That's great! Welcome aboard!' Tiffany said, looking at the final picture in Kirsten's portfolio, a sexy brunette staring straight into camera in amongst a webbing of shadow. 'There's one thing I know people always want – a good face. And that's something you can do better than anyone else by the looks of it.'

There was a truth in these words, one that jarred Kirsten's attention back onto Tiffany as she passed the portfolio back and walked over to talk to Simone. In truth, there were more things than just people who wanted a good face right now though.

In Kirsten's mind, she was back under the pier again, she was back inside the images she had tried to forget were on her camera. The girl in the window. A girl Geena would have recognized as her old school friend if she had looked out and seen her, the only girl as spoilt as herself. The girl from the missing posters that Kirsten had seen plastered on the wall only the night before. She had become a shell, an avatar for something else, for something that had pulled her into the south sea the day she went missing after leaving Dickhead Darren.

And as Charley Reynolds moved away from the window, her stare turned to a glare. All the good feelings from today, shattered, as the ominous, eerie girl faded into the night. Kirsten felt trapped. As if she was trying to escape a web that she had unwittingly walked into. A web, she thought to herself, maybe she might never escape.

CHAPTER 15

Less than a mile away, huddled like a pile of ragged, discarded clothes, Melissa stared out to the sea through the dirty windows of her apartment. A gaunt and sickly mess, her face was as pale as the full moon that was shining in. Her sea-spray-like vomit had congealed to the floor in a wide, sticky, treacled mess. The renegade sea creatures that had spewed from an unknown part of her body had all turned belly up, their once scuttling legs facing the sky like antennas of death.

Slowly, with trembling hands, she fed herself headache pills and copious amounts of booze. Although lucid, her actions were stilted and jarring, as the force that had entered her now gripped her body. Inside her head the phantom screaming still echoed, it slithered around the inside of her skull like a leech.

Her finger still throbbed where she had punctured her skin with the vicious looking claw. Somehow, through that prick, her limited clairvoyant ability had been magnified; a thread of consciousness had been born between her and the girl who had come to see her. But the connection wasn't a single line. It was a triangle. She and the girl were now connected to something more powerful than them both, something from the supernatural world, nothing like she had experienced before – a Siren.

Melissa was used to seeing vague visions, echoes of vaporous spirits, but this new thing gave off the same neuron tingling sensation she had from successful readings, only stronger and more solidified. And although the creature wasn't in the room with them, somehow it was. Somehow a part of its essence had wrapped around Kirsten and polluted part of Melissa, sucking her life force, draining her soul.

A surge of pain coursed through her body, the glass shattering pitch in her head started again, making her feel as if her eyeballs would blow out the front of her skull.

Deep, trembling vibrations pulsated uncomfortably through her bones, making her feel heavy.

Helplessly staring out of the window, the wail of the creature grew in her head. The pain made her brow furrow and weakened her to the point of a sudden, violent nosebleed that poured over her top lip in thick, unrelenting streams.

Since the girl came to her all she had managed was to crawl around the flat, reaching up to the surfaces for basic provisions. The thing inside her skull had reduced her to an invalid, literally dragging her down to her knees from the inside out.

But slowly she was growing a tolerance to the thing that she was incubating within her mind, forging an understanding with it, feeding into it mentally as much as it was feeding into her physically.

Drained, beaten and weak, the thing's connection within her had rewired her brain in such a way that she, too, could travel the triangular wire the three were now tethered to. Little by little, she had come to understand what the creature was, what it wanted, and what she must do to eradicate it from her head. She had entered some kind of telepathic unity with it.

It showed her things, told her things. Everything in her mind's eye had to play out now, in a way she knew how it had to end, and tomorrow she would play her part in the bigger scheme of things.

People thought that being clairvoyant you must know the inevitable future, that it was one singular, guaranteed thing. People liked the guaranteed, the black and white. But from past experiences, Melissa knew the future could be a road of many turns, and this situation had now reached a forked path. A decision had to be made, either by herself, Kirsten or the influences of the people around her. Kirsten's life had become a coin flipped in the air, suspended in time until tomorrow, when a route was to be chosen, a one-way trip with no going back was to be decided. But in Melissa's mind one thing was clear, before fate was to intervene Kirsten had to survive tonight.

CHAPTER 16

The thing wearing Charley Reynolds skin wasn't trying to hide what was truly inside anymore. Her night-time eyes flared brightly as she stood in shadow, looking out to sea. The moon, luminous and full, glinted through the clouds and shone on the waves. Sucking in a lungful of air, she peeled back her lips and screamed with an aggressive, abnormal might. Her voice quickly broke from that of a human girl into a shrieking siren wail. A sound that called out, beckoning to the waves.

Suddenly, from under the old pier, dark, creeping figures rose from the water and moved into the twinkling lights on the promenade, their skin slightly grey and slightly off, just like her own. The creatures' movements were odd, calculated but slow; their eyes glowing like headlights, shining up from the beach in silence. With a shared telepathy, they moved towards the town, dripping wet, bedraggled. The clothes of the bodies they wore skin tight with salt water.

The streets were quiet and moody as they advanced only in the shadows of back alleys and the lanes. One of them walked past a collection of missing posters, stopping to look at them, noticing one in particular. It had her name on it – 'Alyssa Keenan'– a name from the past, an old formality that meant nothing anymore. Its eyes shone, staring at the posters printed visage, the smiling girl it now wore. A rage shuddered through it. Raising a hand, five, curved, black talons had replaced human nails. Slashing out, it clawed the poster, completely destroying the missing girl's face – its own face. The stolen lips curved into an evil grin.

There was an odd coldness in the air, a mist now rising from the coast line, as the creatures moved together towards the old car park where Simone had left her VW. They followed one shadowed figure that spearheaded the pack. It was not the replicate of Charley Reynolds: she was just a scout. It was a form much more familiar to the girl it sought and the friends she surrounded herself with. A wintery chill had come over Brighton this summer's night, and Kirsten's siren had come with it.

CHAPTER 17

Leaving the gallery, they walked down a stinking stairwell to the car park. Simone didn't notice Kirsten's mood, but she wasn't supposed to. Kirsten held a permanent fake grin on her face, nodding along with their conversation when she had to. In a way, she acted no different to Geena, whose gaze was now doubly duller thanks to alcohol.

The girl at the window had spooked Kirsten and had brought all of the awful memories of the last few days flooding back. She jumped as the lift Simone had just called let out a loud ping as it arrived at their floor.

They chatted drunkenly and loaded inside, its metal doors taking too long to close, and awkwardness filled the air. Geena said something half-baked as usual, something that made Simone's childish laughter ring out around the enclosed space, making her double over as she held her knees in hysterics. Kirsten clenched her fists, thinking about just getting to the car and getting back home, neither of which were coming quick enough for her jangling nerves.

Finally, the lift doors clumsily rattled across their runners and shut. But before they pressed together, slowly and eerily, the girl from the shop window – Charley Reynolds – stepped from a dark corner. She was staring intently at Kirsten. The girl's eyes returned no depth of soul, no human quality. A drip fell from the girl's hand and it hit the floor where a small pool of water had formed around her feet. She wanted to tell the others, wanted to grab Simone and twist her head towards her, but the image of the girl was abruptly cut off behind the closing doors and she disappeared from sight.

Now trapped in the lift, Geena drunk and staring at the ceiling, Simone staring at the floor, Kirsten backed towards the cold metal wall feeling the vibrations move through her body as it creaked downwards.

The mechanical drone of the lift seemed to grow, like a menacing, low growl. Uncomfortable, Kirsten wanted to leave, wanted to escape, to get away from this confined situation. She stayed silent and began to sweat, feeling her clothes under her jacket stick to her body; the metal container they all stood in as claustrophobic as a closed coffin.

The lift doors opened and Kirsten heaved a sigh of relief as she stepped out behind her two companions. As they walked back to the VW she was constantly looking over her shoulder, checking behind and looking into the night's mists that had started to reach from the shore into the car park.

A loud metallic smash came from ahead, Kirsten shuddered.

'Shit!' cursed Simone as she bent over to scoop up her dropped keys from the floor, struggling with them in the VW's lock.

Kirsten fixated on Simone's hands, her heart pumping with each failed fumbling attempt to unlock the car door. Geena hopped from one foot to another again as the cold touched her legs, her high heels letting out a loud clicking beat that echoed out in the car park like a metronome. Kirsten's throat tightened, the click-clack rhythm of Geena's shoes filled the air as the mist pushed in further.

Paranoia touched Kirsten from all sides and she could feel the adrenaline making her legs start to shake. None of them noticed in the car park's shadows, dark figures moving in and out, staring in their direction.

All of a sudden, with a loud pop, the VW's door creaked open like a door in a haunted house. The girls all climbed inside, made themselves comfortable, Geena in the back and Simone behind the wheel, trying to insert the key into the car's ignition barrel. Kirsten threw herself into the passenger seat and locked the door fast. Finally managing to plug the key in the ignition, Simone turned the engine over, Kirsten praying that this car wouldn't fall to the horror film cliché of not starting. It didn't fail them and Kirsten jumped as the old bomb roared to life.

The car went to pull away but suddenly jerked to a stop.

'I can't drive – I'm pissed!' Simone exclaimed.

'You said you only had one,' Geena said.

'One too many, fuck it we'll get a cab.' She reached for the key, went to turn it. Kirsten's sweaty palm slapped down on her wrist.

'I'll drive,' she said with intense eyes.

'Are you sure? Didn't you drink…?'

'No, I'm fine,' Kirsten said bluntly. 'Come on let's swap.'

Kirsten pushed over onto Simone, swapping seats. Simone took her hand from the ignition, forced to do the same and slip underneath Kirsten, both clambering over one another.

'Oi, watch where you put those hands,' Geena said flatly.

'She's my cousin, you twat,' Simone said disgusted.

Kirsten revved the car, now in control.

'Let's fucking do one!' Simone laughed as the VW lurched forward, her and Geena chatting again. Drunkenly, Geena lit up two cigarettes and passed one to Simone in front of Kirsten, who gripped the VW's old, worn, steering wheel with white trembling hands.

Fear swelled as they drove around the dark pillars of the car park, some of the old phosphorescent strip lights flickered with age, creating abstract shapes and shades that fed into her imagination. She thought back to the ghost train that she rode at the local fair as a child, being a captive audience, waiting for something to pop out from around dark corners like the one's she swerved around now. That old childlike anxiousness had come back to find her again, giving her a quick pinch with its terrorizing grip, turning into something more tangible than a memory, thickening with authenticity with the experiences of the past two days.

'Oi! Space case!' Simone yelled, 'What do you think? Shall we go to a pub or what?' Kirsten, who was zoned out of their conversation, was instantly beamed directly back into it again, put on the spot by Simone's grinning face. 'Come on, Kirst! It's time to celebrate. You got commissioned, babe!'

A cold hand reached around the back of Kirsten's neck and she jolted, Geena leaned over the seats massaging her neck like a boxer's personal trainer, limbering her up for the big fight ahead.

'Yeah! Let's celebrate!' she yelled.

The drawing mist looked like a thin, rippling white sheet draped over the world in the car's headlights. A loud boom echoed out as the bottom of the car grounded out driving up the spiraling concrete exit ramp, sending a quick rumble through its chassis and deep into Kirsten's body.

Simone and Geena turned to Kirsten waiting for a response; awkwardly, she tried to compose herself, wondering what to say, forgetting what the question even was. Suddenly, the car skidded to a stop.

Geena flew forward and screamed, 'Fucking hell, Kirsten, what ya playing at?'

With a wrinkled nose and squinting eyes, Simone stared into the veil of mist ahead.

Kirsten's mouth turned dry. The situation she was experiencing individually, away from the other two girls, was suddenly unified, it opened its dark robe and invited them under its skeletal wing for the night. They all stared ahead; watching something cutting through the mist, a menacing figure came into view. There, walking down the ramp, was a half-naked male silhouette. The girls froze, stunned, unable to comprehend what they were seeing.

His open shirt, partially torn to tatters, wet and dripping. With no trousers on, his cock slapped against his damp legs with each step. A tramp? Simone and Geena thought. Some kind of junkie stumbling down to try and find somewhere to crash?

Kirsten's mouth opened, inhaling a long, chilled stream of air, sucking out the entire easy-going attitude that had filled the car only a moment ago.

The figure emerged fully from the mist, moved straight towards the VW.

'What the fuck is his problem?' Geena muttered as he moved nearer to the dumbstruck girls.

'Fuck sake!' Simone exclaimed, leaning over, hitting the horn, its sound crudely echoing out around the confined surrounds of the car park. It did nothing, the man ignored it as he continued moving towards them.

His eyes started to beam from his skull, reflecting the bright beams of the car's headlights like mirrors. his head a carved-out Halloween pumpkin. 'Look at his eyes! Look at his eyes!' Geena screamed, and somehow her outburst solidified the situation's reality.

Simone snapped a look at Kirsten, instantly sober, knowing that everything her cousin had experienced and tried to tell her was true. And in that tiny moment in time, the bond they had always shared was reinforced by a slash of fear across their two worlds, immediately making them one.

Kirsten pulled the car into reverse, taking it back into the car park. More jack-o'-lantern headed figures appeared, their eyes blazing from the shadows.

Geena began to panic. 'What's going on, Simone? What's happening? I want to go home!' She reached around to grab Simone who shrugged her off, her attention as sharp as a pin to the threat around them.

'Go up the downward ramp, Kirsten! Just go the wrong way!'

Kirsten crunched the bug's gears and followed Simone's instructions.

Moving up to the next level, another dark figure lurched out towards them. Kirsten swerved as a hand swiped past her, it caught the back window with a high pitched 'Shrrrieekkkk!' that made Geena flinch away, five long slashes, claw slashes splintered the glass. Geena shook, lips immediately trembling, tears leaking from her eyes.

More figures drifted from the darkness, all moving towards them, homing in on their prey. Kirsten looked out of the back window, a whole herd of glowing eyes, all mounted in hanging faces, moved in their direction.

Geena followed Kirsten's petrified gaze. 'Oh no!' she cried, 'what do they want? Simone? What do they…'

'Shut up!' Simone screamed back. The fear on Simone's face sent a bigger shiver through Geena than the creatures surrounding them.

Driving for their lives, Kirsten narrowly avoided the structure's squared concrete pillars as more figures seeped like living shadows from the darkness. The car park had turned into the ghost train from Kirsten's memory, pop-up bogeymen lurching out, injecting terror into her veins.

Geena held her head, the warm swimming feeling of being drunk now turning into throbbing sickness in her gut as the old VW spiraled up the concrete ramps of the car park.

'What do they want?' she screamed, 'what the fuck do they want?'

'Go to the roof, Kirsten! We can double back down,' Simone instructed.

Kirsten did, she fired the chugging old car up the down arrowed ramps, kept moving up until the encasing concrete roof disappeared, and the black night sky appeared.

With a gasp, Kirsten let her foot off the accelerator and skidded to a halt. There, under a light, above the pay and display machine, stood a female dressed in wet, black clothes, her back to them.

Kirsten slowly pulled towards her, nowhere else to go, their options limited and rapidly running out. The image of the figure through the steamed up windscreen looked surreal, slightly distorted, strange and peacefully out of place in the madness that surrounded them.

The night breeze blew the figure's dark hair as Geena peered from behind Simone's seat and whimpered.

The figure slowly turned to face them, its eyes glowing. There, highlighted like the star of this macabre performance, like the main attraction to the ghost train's spook show, was Kirsten's doppelgänger, the creature from the pier and the picture's on her camera.

Simone sat open-mouthed, staring out of the window at her cousin who wasn't her cousin. Her cousin who stood outside the car, but also sat next to her inside it.

Kirsten shuddered. It felt as if her grave was being trampled, not just walked over. Then, on the wind, she could hear it, that haunting song. The same one that Kirsten had heard under the pier. It wound its way into the car, somehow not just coming from its mouth, emitting from the longing, lascivious look in its bright eyes.

The song's cadence washed over them.

'Let's go, Kirsten,' Simone said seriously, turning to her cousin who was hypnotically staring at what looked like herself.

'She looks like you, Kirsten... She looks like *you*!' Geena screamed.

The doppelgänger's face turned into a mask of hatred, screwing up into an expression that the original version could never make, a contorted reflection from a hall of mirrors. Sharp, pointed teeth pushed down from her gums over the human teeth. She opened her mouth wider and let out a deafening scream. Kirsten jerked awake as the girls recoiled in their seats, a shiver shared between them like an ice cold cut of wind. Slowly, the creature moved towards them.

The VW moved backwards as Kirsten frantically reversed away from the creature.

'That's what I saw under the pier and in the warehouse. I saw that... *I saw that!*' Kirsten rattled out, her face deathly pale.

Geena, peeling her gaze away from the seductive sway of

Kirsten's double, looked out of the rear window. 'They're behind us, Simone!' she cried, as a crowd of glowing eyes emerged from the shadows and moved towards the car.

Simone, screamed, 'LET'S GO KIRSTEN – NOW!'

Kirsten jammed her foot onto the accelerator and they flew past Kirsten's double, its eyes flicking wide, intense, fixated on its original version as the VW rolled out of its view. Its mouth wide, exposing its sharp teeth.

Kirsten roared back down the opposite exit ramp, the things lunged for the car as they moved past them, reached out with razor sharp swipes, scratching the VW's windows and paint work.

Geena having a mental breakdown in the back screamed in an endless breath, 'Keep going! Don't stop! *Don't stoppppp!'*

Making it past their assailants, Kirsten fired the car out of the exit, escaping the overrun car park that had become a living nightmare.

* * *

Back in Simone's flat, Kirsten stared into her bathroom mirror, her face splashed with water, her brain dulled into an almost catatonic void. She shivered, reacting to the argument behind her. Simone and Geena screamed at one another trying to make sense of what they had experienced.

'Call the cops! We gotta call the cops!' Geena yelled, her face streaked with tears.

'What can they do? *What can they do?* What do we say? That it was her? That Kirsten and her fucking gang attacked us? They're not gonna believe us – *they didn't before!* What do we say? *You tell me what to say! Because I don't understand! I don't fucking understand!'*

Kirsten's face held a non-expressive stare while everything around her broke down into chaos. Now they knew she wasn't mad, that she hadn't dropped into their lives and brought a whirlwind of crazy problems with her. The problems were real, they had experienced it, too. As Simone and Geena continued to cry and argue, the same solemn, lonely words that had turned over in her head the last few days were now externalized by her cousin and her girlfriend. The same frightened questions of what was happening echoed out from their mouths, interweaved with a shared terror. Kirsten continued to stare at herself, at her own face. A face that had seemingly become a mask worn by another, who, for some reason, wanted that mask to belong to them and them alone.

CHAPTER 18

Morning sunlight poured through the living room's wooden blinds, making shadowed bars fall across the girls who all slept huddled together beneath a duvet on the sofa. They had only been asleep for a few hours, the fear of glowing eyed figures in the night kept them locked in insomnia. Geena and Simone had argued for hours, Simone trying to drill into her feeble-minded girlfriend's head that whatever they had encountered wasn't going to be stopped by a simple call to the police.

Imagination played tricks, the rows of street lights outside the flats darkened windows sent waves of terror through them. Thoughts of glowing eyes swirled through their minds.

Now that peace and sleep had ensued, an undisturbed tranquility had flooded in with dawn's first rays, eliminating all things that dwelled in the dark.

Suddenly a noise penetrated their ears, a noise that put them firmly back in the situation they were in last night.

At the end of the flat's long hallway, a chair and chest of drawers barricaded the front door; a slow deliberate knock came from the other side. Their eyes opened in frozen fear. Like tinned sardines they turned over and faced one another, mouths agape and eyes bulging. Jumping up, sending a quick, cold draft from the duvet across the other two girls, Kirsten in a T-shirt and knickers backed away to a corner, grabbed the old baseball bat Simone had put there. Geena, still fully dressed, petrified and silent, lay like a victim in wait, her face a mask of dried and flaking make-up.

Simone stood up with the sleekness of a stalking cat, also fully clothed, her make-up streaked and ruined, too, but unlike Geena's, with her hard and serious face, it looked more like purposeful war paint.

'Stay here,' she said in a dry, low tone, moving to the kitchen and taking a 14-inch knife from its wooden rack.

Geena drew back into the duvet like a rabbit cowering in its warren, watching with fear and a slight admiration as Simone walked down towards the door, her soft steps creaking on the dark, laminated floor.

'Who is it?' she called out. Silence. No reply.

'Who's there?'

Silence.

Simone heard a creak behind her, turned her head to see Kirsten with a serious, all business expression behind her, baseball bat in hand.

With a nod, an unsaid partnership was formed. Simone pushed the chair they used as a barricade to one side, Kirsten stepped on it, bat over her head, firming up her grip, ready to pulverize whatever was there. Simone pushed away the heavy chest of draws. The doorway now clear.

She swallowed, looked up at Kirsten and nodded at her again, she nodded back, biting her lip. Slowly she reached for the door's small lock, turned it slightly, paused, poised herself, then threw it wide open, knife gripped tightly in her hand – held up to one side like the killer on a poster for an old slasher film – ready to plunge it into the shadowed figure the other side.

But the figure didn't move, didn't flinch or show concern to the knife pulled on it. As from the darkness of the communal hallway, the figure moved forward, it was a woman, her face that of a ghost, only slightly visible in the limited light.

'Is this where Kirsten lives?'

'Who the fuck are you?' Simone shouted back, loud enough to knock the waif like woman from her feet.

Kirsten dropped down into view from the chair, the voice familiar, staring into the corpse like face of the clairvoyant – Melissa Clarke.

* * *

Geena hid under the duvet, sneaking peeks at the disheveled, ghostly woman, her face gaunt, an ill color that reminded her of the ninety-year-old aunty she had to visit in hospital as a child, a feeling of death floating around her like a cloud of dry dust, the same feeling haunting the woman in front of her now.

Melissa perched on the small table Kirsten used to set her work on, holding a cup of hot tea steaming in her shaking hands, Kirsten sat adjacent to her, watching how Melissa tried to stop the cup rattling in its china saucer, anxious and aware of eyes on her.

Simone, like an interrogator in an old cop show, slumped in the bay window, staring at Melissa, her face covered in a thick, grey veil of smoke from her cigarette.

'So what's the story then?' she sneered, 'pub not opened yet?'

Kirsten shot daggers at Simone, who rolled her eyes back at her.

Melissa composed herself for a moment, concentrating on holding the cup still, then looked up over its steaming lip with vacant eyes.

'You've seen it again haven't you?'

Kirsten stayed silent, the same way she had before at the reading, wanting Melissa to give her answers before she shared the questions.

'It's like I said, sometimes it works, sometimes it doesn't. But that thing you brought me, the claw, when I cut myself on it, what I can do, what I can see, it was amplified.'

Melissa raised a scrawny trembling finger to her temple, her eyes squinted into a grimace as the siren cry quietly echoed in her brain.

'I can hear its call. It's in my head and I can't get rid of it,' she whispered.

Simone bluntly snapped in, 'Oh yeah? What is it then? What are they and what do they want?' She took a drag on her cigarette, annoyed, then pointed at Kirsten 'And why did it look like her?'

Melissa ran her hand through her greasy hair, trying not to touch her sensitive head. 'They're things from the sea, things that have started to come up to the surface. Trapped for years.' She looked up at the girls, trying to gauge her audience's response. 'We let them out; they were sealed away, buried where they belonged…'

Simone sighed disbelievingly, Melissa swallowed, stared at her, annoyed, then continued. 'They're some kind of… parasite. They want faces, human faces, so they can use them to draw others in, so they can feed on them. Once they see the face they want, with a scratch, they take it. Your face becomes theirs.'

Kirsten squirmed uncomfortably. Feeling the slashes in her back again.

Melissa continued. 'They lure you in with that song, it gets in your head like some kind of pheromone, then they scratch you… then somehow…' Melissa began to stutter, doubting her own words that instinctively she knew were true, before continuing. 'They pour inside of you… merge with you and become one… they…'

Simone cut her off. 'Ha! I can't believe I'm hearing this, this is fucked up! What exactly are you trying to tell us? Things from under the sea take your face with a scratch and a song? You must…'

'I'M JUST TELLING YOU WHAT I KNOW. You heard that cry, the song, the scream… They're some kind of… sea siren. Using others identities like a mask, using people's faces to lure you in.'

Everyone listened as a cold silence filled the air, Melissa started to become more aggressive with her words.

'It will only come at night for now. But it will keep coming until they can drag you into the sea like the others they've taken, until there's only one of you, Kirsten. It's connected to you now, you're like a beacon, it knows where you are, where you're going, and it won't stop until…'

Simone jutted in with a condescending tone, 'Until?'

'This is real, isn't it?' Geena cried out from over the duvet.

Everyone ignored her.

'Until what?' Kirsten said. 'Tell me what you see.'

Melissa stared intensely into Kirsten's eyes and concentrated before drifting off into a vision.

'I can see you, falling backwards, falling, falling, falling…'

'Sorry, but how are we supposed to take this serious love? You're a seaside psychic! A wind up. This is not real, it's not. It can't be.' Simone laughed.

'Isn't it?' Melissa screamed back. 'Why didn't you call the police? Why didn't you do something instead of hiding away in here? Because you have no idea what you're dealing with, because you saw it has her face, because you know that this isn't something you can explain. I'm part of this now; I hear the cries from that creature in my head, IT WON'T LEAVE MY FUCKING BRAIN!'

Everyone sat in silence watching Melissa, her face contorting as she held her head in pain as she screamed out her words.

'So what can I do? Can I kill it?' Kirsten said desperately. 'There can only be one of us right? This thing's going to come for me, and it won't stop until one of us is dead. That's what you were going to say, right?'

Melissa said nothing.

Simone snorted out another laugh. 'Yeah, you're the psychic. What are the odds, then? Are we gonna be able to stop this thing or what?'

Melissa looked down to the floor, then up to Simone then to Kirsten, holding her gaze, replying with a cold simplicity. 'No.'

Kirsten raised her hands over her eyes, a slight groan seeping from in between her fingers that turned to a quick sob.

Simone's lid was finally blown, jumping from the bay window, grabbing Melissa and rough housing the feeble woman back down the hallway. 'Get out you dried up old bitch! Get the fuck out my house!'

Pulling at each other's hair, at each other's faces, Simone wrestled her back out the door as Kirsten, drying the quick burst of tears, followed behind them. Melissa swayed on the top step of the stairs; both Simone and Kirsten thought she was going to topple down them, that she would be the one falling backwards like in her vision. But she turned, steadied herself and stared at Simone as a trickle of blood dripped from her nose.

'I'm getting this thing out my head, with you or without you Kirsten...'

She wiped the blood stream with the back of her hand across her face, staining her pale visage with vivid, red stripes.

'I'll see you soon, Simone.'

'Let me guess, psychic, you already know when, right?'

'Actually...' she said with a slight, pained smile, 'I do.'

Simone watched her leave, following her to the front door, making sure she'd gone, wondering for a second if anyone in the living room had actually said her name? Maybe Kirsten had told her at her reading? Maybe that's how the old weirdo knew it. She soon tossed these thoughts aside, putting her level head back in check and walked back up the stairs. Suddenly, something moved, a figure in the darkness of the upstairs landing moved towards her, reached out to touch her.

CHAPTER 19

Simone felt sick with fear. Remembering that she still had the knife in her hand, she raised it up quickly in front of her, a glimmer of light catching its blade as she snarled. Raising his hands in retreat, Mickey lurched out into view.

'Woah! What are you doing?'

'How long have you been standing there?' she screamed.
He didn't answer, stumbling over his own words, not knowing what to say or do.

'You hear all that?'

'I just came for my mone...'

She grabbed him and pulled him inside to the living room.

'Sit in here with her!' she screamed pointing to Geena, still under the duvet. Simone beckoned Kirsten over to her and they both walked out of the room and closed the door behind them.

Snuggling under the duvet Geena beckoned Mickey over then began to cry, reaching out to hug him, pulling him beneath the sheets with her, creating a fort beneath the covers, away from the terrors of the outside world.

'What happened?' he said, confused, trying to keep his voice down.

'We were attacked!' Geena sniveled.

'By who?'

Geena, streams of tears running down her face, poured out everything. She threw herself onto Mickey, explaining with jarring gasps in her base way the events of last night.

* * *

In the hallway Simone and Kirsten sat in silence with their backs against the wall, listening to the cries of the girl next door.

'Do you believe what she said?' Kirsten asked.

'Fuck what she says, she can go…'

'Do you believe what she said?'

Simone shrugged and a miserable look fell over her face.

'Can you make any sense of what happened last night?' Kirsten asked.

'Sea sirens… No. I'm sorry, but no.'

'I need to leave, I need to get out of here,'

'Where you gonna go though, Kirst'?'

'Back to London. Nothing good has happened since I've been here, what the fuck is all this? Seriously?'

Simone sighed. 'I don't know. But I don't think it's just going to go away. '

Kirsten held her head in despair. 'You don't have to get involved. I've just brought this shit to your doorstep. I can deal with it.'

Simone stared at Kirsten and gently shook her head; she wasn't going to let her cousin face this alone. She knew her part of this story wasn't going to end here.

* * *

Under the duvet, in the front room, Geena had just finished the story of last night, of the car park, the figures, the glowing eyes, Kirsten's double.

Through the quilted tunnel they had made between themselves, she stared into Mickey's eyes, hoping he could read the sincerity in her face through the absurdity of situation.

'Are you serious? It looked like her?' he said.

'I was her, Mickey! Just not her! Do you believe me?'

He nodded.

'That woman that Simone threw out. She reckons they're sea sirens. That one of them has taken Kirsten's face. I'm scared Mickey.'

He stared blankly, taking everything she said in, processing the absurdity of it all.

She made her eyes wide and vulnerable, a cheekiness washing away her intensity and fear. 'Have you got a cig cig I can have, Mickey?'

He pointed upwards, gesturing to get out from under the duvet and passed her one. As he did, she looked down at his wrists, noticing something she had never seen before. Two vertical lines ran along the inside, scarred slits, suicide cuts the right way, the way if you mean it.

'Why?' she asked sadly.

He flinched awkwardly as she touched the raised pink lines. Her face dropped, then, reaching for his lighter, she smiled at him, ruffling his hair quickly.

'You don't have to tell me.'

He shrugged.

She wiped her tears away and smiled, reaching up to his hair again, stroking it, then running her hand down his chest, placing her hand on his thigh. A warm sensation rushed to his groin as she did, her hand stroking slowly up towards his crotch.

'Mickey...' she said, directing his attention to her face, her blue eyes twinkling like a spring sky, '...we need your help,'

* * *

Back in the hallway, their options exhausted, talking in circles of what they should do, Simone began to reminisce, talking honestly about the unspoken parts of their relationship.

'Remember when we were kids, your mum and my mum. They never trusted me. I've always been the odd one out, just because I didn't do everything the same as them.'

'It's not true,' Kirsten said, the sadness in her voice that said otherwise spread up to her eyes.

'It's true and you know it. That's why I'm here, that's why I had to get away. I was always going to be one thing in their eyes, the thing they wanted me to be. The fuck up.'

Kirsten turned to her, sorrow in her gaze.

'By the sea I can be anything I want, just like you can. That's why I wanted you here, you're my cousin, and you're the only one who didn't treat me like they did. You're the only person from that life I want in mine now. Your problem is my problem,' Simone said as she wiped at her eyes quickly, not wanting to outwardly show emotion. 'I love you,' she added flatly.

Kirsten smiled. 'Same.' She rubbed her eyes looking to the floor.

Simone took a deep breath, cleared her throat, 'But what are we gonna do?'

'We're gonna make sure this is what we think it is. Make sure it's real. The cops didn't believe anything I said about what happened under the pier. They're not going to believe this. Let's end this together. Me and you?'

'Me and you.' Simone smiled.

Kirsten reached out her hand, Simone did the same, meeting her touch then holding her hand. The two girls, strong in unison, at the perfect time when one needed the other the most. Suddenly the hallway door pushed open, Geena, wrapped in the duvet like a druid at a sleep over, stood there with Mickey behind her.

'I've told him everything,' she said imperatively. 'He believes me.' She smiled.

'Keep your mouth shut!' Simone warned.

'No! He can help! We need him!' Geena squealed in defiance 'He can protect us if we're not calling the police.'

Mickey looked awkward.

'You like Simone; you want to help her and her cousin right?' Geena asked him.

Simone rolled her eyes. Kirsten was confused, not understanding what was supposed to be going on.

'Jesus, Geena, what are you babbling about?' Simone said.

'He can help, with the… things. Tell them!'

Geena grabbed Mickey's arm and drew him in closer.

He swallowed hard then began to speak. 'Well, it's not me, it's my dad, he's away but if he finds out…'

'What are you talking about? In simple English!' Simone scowled.

'A gun! His dad's got a gun!'

Kirsten's attention pricked up. 'He does?'

'Yeah!' Geena yelled. 'He's going to bring it round for us! For you, Simone and you, Kirsten!'

Geena pulled Mickey in close to kiss his cheek, leaving a big red smear on his face, making another tingle rush downwards.

CHAPTER 20

Fumbling with the keys and opening his dad's gun cupboard, Mickey reached in to take out the high caliber Remington 700 rifle. He had always known where his dad had hidden the keys, knowing that maybe one day, if the depression that ate at him inside became too much, there was always a way out.

Passing it to Kirsten, she held it awkwardly, eyeing the barrel up and down, not knowing exactly how to use it, but knowing instinctively this was the thing that could solve her problem, the thing that could bring equilibrium to the situation.

Mickey had a deep worry about this. He didn't know the girls that well, but he had always liked Simone and Geena, both as people and in a way a teenage boy would be attracted to two, hot, twenty somethings. But for some reason, on his own instinctive level, he had trusted the story about the new girl Kirsten's problem to his core.

It wasn't just the sincerity or the fear that radiated from her that made him believe, it was the story itself. He had always thought there was more than the reality that surrounded him, a reality he liked to disconnect from. He felt there was too much of it everywhere he went. Reality stank. He hated school, hated the confines, the rules. It felt like a makeshift, junior loony bin. Everyone clawing and pawing to be popular, to have manufactured things and to show off these manufactured things to each other.

He also hated his home life; he hated his dad. Where school was the loony bin, home was a prison. Holed up with the warden, a man who would come into his cell. His mood dependent on his experiences at work that day, screaming and shouting if things were bad, snarky remarks if things were good. Silence was golden, but silence was indeed as precious a thing and rare a thing as gold itself at home. Maybe if his mother was alive things would have been different, he would be happy, his dad would be happy and his wrists wouldn't have the memories of trying to escape emblazoned upon them.

But the girl's story, the experience Kirsten was having with a creature, something that sounded like it came from a comic book or a movie, shattered all of the banality of life into boring, grey, concrete chunks. He knew there had to be more than the mundane, the routine, now maybe he would get a chance to experience it himself.

Simone took two boxfuls of bullets, loading them into the pockets of Geena's black hoody, seeing trepidation and cowardly terror in the girl's eyes as she did so. But with one swift look at her that yelled 'shut up' Geena kept her whines locked inside.

Looking at Mickey, Simone said, 'You're a gardener, right? You've got tools?'

He nodded and before long they were rifling through Mickey's car boot, taking hammers, screwdrivers, a crow bar, an old chainsaw and anything else that could be used for defense against the creatures.

Walking from Mickey's house to the VW, Simone pressed in close to Kirsten, sandwiching the gun wrapped in an old sleeping bag between them both.

'So, what are we going to do? Are we just going to sit around your flat and wait for those things to find me?'

'No,' Simone said, bluntly.

Mickey felt awkward; he stared at the gun, wondering if he had done the right thing. Geena sensed this, squeezed his arm and smiled at him, her full, cherry lips soothing any second thoughts that had begun to close in on him.

'She told me there were at least twenty of those things?' Mickey said.

'There were,' Kirsten replied.

Simone threw the VW's spare tire out from under the hood and packed everything inside, placed the gun on top, still wrapped in the sleeping bag. Knowing they had completed their makeshift armory, the car's storage compartment filled to the edges, the loud clonking and reshuffling of everything echoed out from beneath the bonnet as Simone slammed it down. A knowing look shared between them confirmed it was time to leave.

'It couldn't have just been some people fucking with you?' Mickey said, inquisitively. 'Are you sure it wasn't?'

'If it was, that's twice now. I want to be ready for the third,' Kirsten replied.

'We will be,' assured Simone.

'We've got about nine hours before sunset.' Kirsten replied. 'If this is what we think it is, sea sirens. Let's do some homework.'

* * *

As the others all flicked through pages of old books, Greek mythology, the paranormal, local superstitions, trying to find information on what the things were, Geena looked around the library, she hadn't stepped foot into one since school. The smell of books was just as she remembered, not that the library was a place that she ever spent much time.

It was a dark old building, not newly refurbed like most were now. Almost cave like, with brown carpets and wood paneled shelving. She'd suggested, *'Let's just search the internet on our phones, see what it says about sea sirens?'* they did and nothing of interest came up. She couldn't grasp, with her limited intellect, why they wanted to come here?

She just meandered around the aisles bored, listening to music through her earphones. Jangling everywhere she went, bangles and bracelets clinking.

The librarian had already eye-balled her a few times and had shushed her once. In a way, she was staggered by the library, how many books it had, how much information they held. It hurt her brain just trying to comprehend people had written them all. All of those words in just one book, all of those words from just one person.

She walked back to the others, all of them engaged in their reading, pulled the earphones out with a quick pop. An idea jumping in her head like a light bulb in an old cartoon.

'You know all these books right?' she blurted.

Simone looked up at her.

'Well, it's like this is Google, but in reality, innit?'

Simone looked back at her book. 'Just sit down and shut up.'

Geena slumped down on a chair. She looked at the book Mickey was reading. 'Demon-oogly?' What's that?

He glanced at her quickly. 'Demonology,' he corrected.

Simone rolled her eyes.

Kirsten looked up. 'Anyone found anything?'

'Usual stuff we've seen everywhere else – creatures from the sea, they lure sailors in with their song. Nothing that treats them any different from any other mythology.' Mickey replied.

'Same here,' Kirsten added disappointed.

Time was of the essence today and they were running out of it. Kirsten became impatient, started to bite her lip and dream, maybe winging it was the best idea. It was physical and proactive, it made you feel like you were actually getting somewhere, that you actually had some kind of plan even though you didn't. How could a car loaded with sharp garden implements, a chainsaw, and a rifle not solve the problem?

'Maybe we should have listened to that medium that came round, she knew what she was talking about.' Geena sighed.

'No,' Simone snapped back. 'She didn't'.

A quietness drew between them again, Kirsten's attention not on the page, but on Geena's words. Melissa did know what she was talking about, it had happened like she said...

'Hey, look at this.' Simone threw a book straight into the middle of the table for them all to see. It was a volume entitled

'Ancient English Folklore', a big, brown, hard cover from the '60s. She pointed at a tiny article below the title 'Brighton – Seaside Town.'

'Read that.'

Kirsten pulled it towards her.

'Brighton – South Coast: Ancient legend has it that in the 1800s sailors discovered an underwater chasm in a shipwreck just off the Brighton coastline. Few survived in a small pocket of air, but reported strange singing coming from deep within the core of the structure. After finding rescue, John Ellis – the only survivor to enter the depths of the cave – was found to be possessed.'

Kirsten looked up at them all, a serious look on her face. 'His eyes losing pigmentation would take on a nocturnal glow.'

Geena's eyes opened. Remembering the things that stared at her in the back seat.

'As well as his teeth and fingernails also transforming.'

'Sound familiar?' Simone nodded.

Kirsten went on. 'It was estimated the cave drew back to Devil's Dyke, a nearby town in Sussex where legend has it the Devil himself was trying to dig a trench to try and flood the coast lines churches. The townspeople sculpted a giant stone covering, used ancient diving equipment to seal the cave so no shipwrecked sailor could get in – and nothing could ever get out.'

'Coincidence?' Simone asked.

'What did it say about that stone covering?' Mickey asked as he flipped through another book – 'British Myths'

'The townspeople sculpted a giant stone covering, used ancient diving equipment to seal the cave,' Kirsten reiterated.

'Eighteen hundreds right?' he replied.

'Yeah?'

He opened the book in front of them.

'Look at this.'

In the center of the book, an ancient black and white photograph spread across two pages. A group of people, villagers, all stood around a huge stone suspended upright by rope and chains. Upon it, carved into its stone, was a bald-headed face, jagged teeth and blank empty eyes.

'Jesus Christ,' Kirsten mumbled.

'That's one of them... isn't it?' Geena whispered. Mickey turned the page.

'Look at that,' an old picture depicted ancient diving gear, pipes reaching from helmets above sea level, as a group of men placed the stone seal over the cave.

'Remember what Melissa said? *We let them out somehow,*' Kirsten added.

'I'm having a bit of a hard time with all this.' Simone swallowed hard, looking up at everyone in the room. 'I know what we saw last night. I'm in on trying to stop it but... if this is real... if they were buried out to sea all these years, how the hell did they get out?'

Realization hit Kirsten like a zoom shot in an old film. Pieces from a puzzle she didn't know she was making began to form in her mind. Before they went to hole up, before night fell, there was one more person she had to see.

* * *

Barry the Tramp couldn't believe his luck. Sat at a table in a greasy spoon café, three young dolly birds buying him dinner, filling him with warm tea. Shame the boy was there, he seemed alright though. At least he wasn't one of those poncy estate agent boys he saw always walking around trying to sell houses, he sounded normal, common in a way, like himself.

Dabbing the last of his toast in a worn out fried egg, he smiled at Geena.

'Good in here ain't it love?'

She nodded back at him trying to breath through her mouth rather than her nose.

'So come on…' Kirsten said, an annoyed tone in her voice. 'You said, you knew what happened out there on that oil rig. You said you were there, what the hell happened?'

Barry didn't take his eyes off his plate as he ran a black finger around the remaining yoke and brought it to his chapped lips.

'Another tea wouldn't go amiss,' he blankly said, making good use of their kindness while he could.

Mickey gestured to the waitress, a sneer appeared on her face, not wanting to go near the stinking man on the table who had made any other nearby customers leave.

She brought the tea over and placed it down in front of him. He winked at her, she sprayed air freshener in his direction and left.

'Cheeky cow,' Barry muttered.

Simone leaned over the table, 'You've had your free feed, now talk to us. You're wasting our time, and I'm not wasting any more money on you, you fat pr…'

Kirsten held her hand up.

'Wait a second. Look, I don't know what you were on, but you admitted to us you were on that rig. Maybe you don't remember? Maybe you were too pissed to even realize what you were saying. But you told us you were there. It was the one from the paper wasn't it? Where everyone went missing?'

Something passed over Barry's face and she knew she was right.

'We know that, and if you don't tell us what happened. We go to the cops. We tell them you were out there.'

'Yeah, working cash in hand, were you?' Simone sneered.

Barry's face dropped. 'There's no need for that girls, that's just nasty. What you trying to do, get old Barry's giro stopped?'

Mickey leaned over the table. 'Come on, mate, what happened on that rig. Just tell us!'

Barry looked at his plate, went to sip his tea then didn't. He looked awkward, wanted something, anything to distract him so he wouldn't have to talk. He hadn't had a drop of booze that day and had suppressed the memories by his own will somehow. He had done a good job of it, kept everything on the outskirts of his mind. Now the images of the past that haunted him popped open like the ring pull of a can of beer.

'I... I wasn't supposed to be there, girls. It was just a bit of cash. You know me, old Barry ain't got much. Money's money... But, yeah... something happened... I saw it.'

'What?' said Kirsten intently. 'What happened?'

'Well, it was like, they were digging down. Foundations for one of those wind turbines like. But they hit something and it broke the drill, done it in proper.'

'Hit something? Did you see it?' Mickey quickly added.

'Dunno, must a been some pretty strong stuff. Ground everything to a halt, whole operation ended. Saw some bits of stone and stuff on the drill when they brought it up.'

Everyone threw glances at one another.

'Is that all you saw?' Kirsten asked.

Barry rebelled against the images in his head again, saw them, didn't want to describe them.

'I saw... I heard sounds, like a scream and then, I dunno... like it came from under the sea, like.'

'And that was it?' Kirsten uttered, a slight sweat boiling on her skin. 'What the hell happened to everyone?'

Barry turned his head. Looked out of the cafe's window. Finding something to distract himself with.

'I just need to go check on my box, make sure no one's nicked it.' He went to get up.

Reluctantly Simone grabbed his filthy jacket and pulled him back down. A foul tackiness stayed on her hand when she let go.

'You ain't done yet. What happened to all the people?'

Barry looked down at his hands, he saw a momentary flash

of the blood from the blonde he had used as a shield to escape.

A tear formed at the corner of his eye, as the deep sadness he tried to forget consumed him.

'You girls seem nice...' he said in a broken voice. 'You, too, mate.' He nodded at Mickey. 'But don't go messing round out there, or down by the coast. There are things out there, things that will hurt ya bad, things from under the sea. Old Barry got away, he did. Hot footed it like you wouldn't believe. I had to do what I had to do. Old Barry don't want to talk any more, old Barry is like... ashamed. ' Two tears fell down the filthy man's face, no hope with his encrusted grime that that would ever leave a clean mark.

He brought his tea up, sipped it, looked at Kirsten.

'Don't go looking for trouble, love. You got your whole life ahead of ya. You look like a lovely girl, you could have the pick of the fellas...'

Kirsten nonchalantly nodded.

'What I mean is, old Barry did wrong once, maybe now, if you listen to me, he can do a bit of right.'

He went to touch Kirsten's hand, a gesture to reassure his words, he saw his own black finger nails and stopped. Thought of the blonde and stopped. 'Just be careful, all of ya.'

He slipped out from the fixed chairs, took a step forward then turned back.

'You don't want to be like all those others.'

'How's that?' Kirsten asked desperately, her heart beating hard in her chest.

Barry smiled, something sincere broke through the grime, a sad glint in his eyes. He did the sign of a crucifix with his heavy hand, ending it with solemn thumbs down.

At the table, everyone's stomach dropped.

'Better go check on me box. Thanks for the grub girls.'

They watched him walk outside, his precious box folded flat against the café wall. He checked his pockets, looking content as he produced a roll of packing tape.

Quickly, he spun round to the door, pulled it open, held the stained box up to them, and shouted inside.

'Better than a mobile home ain't it. No road tax or insurance.' Then he turned and wondered off back to the underpass where he slept.

'So what do we do?' Geena asked, finally breathing through her nose again. 'Do we tell the police?'

Simone sighed. 'Tell them what? A pissed psychic and a pissed tramp think sea sirens want to kill us. The old bill are useless.'

Kirsten watched Barry cross the road out the window, a man who had given up. She wouldn't give up. 'It's up to us now,' she told them, 'and all we can do is kill it.'

CHAPTER 21

Driving along the motorway, any spare space in between the car's passengers was now filled with provisions, sleeping bags, junk food and spare clothes. Simone kept the speedometer's needle firmly to the limit, not wanting to get pulled over with their cargo on board. Kirsten stared out of the window as Geena, who was on the backseat, nervously chewed the toggles on the oversized hoody she wore. Reaching out, she put her arm around Mickey, lolling her head vacantly to one side on his shoulder, the afternoon sunlight turning her dyed blonde hair into a golden corona. Not sure how to respond, he awkwardly put an arm around her, reciprocating the gesture, feeling the ends of her hair touch his face gently with the cool breeze that ran through the car's slightly wound down windows.

Looking up into the rear view mirror, Simone paused, watching as Mickey comfortably, too comfortably, pushed his head into her girlfriend's hair and placed his temple against hers closing his eyes as he did so. Raising her sunglasses, Simone's cold, blue, unimpressed eyes stared at Mickey, holding her harsh, steely gaze on him. Sheepishly, he looked back, a flood of embarrassment running through his body, getting the gist of her piercing look as he quickly withdrew his arm, disturbing Geena who was unaware of the eyeballing from her girlfriend up front.

The sunny sky outside disappeared as the day became draped with streaks of dull, grey cloud. Kirsten became aware of her own reflection staring back at herself in the car's window, staring back at her as if it had its own intelligence, the eyes seemingly not her own. Just like the face of the creature that stalked her.

After an hour of driving west along the coast, Simone pulled the VW off road through an old, rusted, chain-link fence, moving up an old, stony, dust road. In front, sitting perched on the cliff line overlooking the sea was a dilapidated three-storey building. Victorian in design, beautiful in its architecture, once a flamboyant hotel, its pastel paintwork deteriorated into hard, worn flakes, colored bunting had now become dangling, faded vines that moved in the wind.

Everything here had once been light hearted, a family holiday spot, an appealing getaway, now it had become dark, gothic, run down, covered in graffiti and saturated in casual menace. Its upper front windows were smashed, with jagged glass left in the frames, glass that had become sharp teeth for the ghoulish lips of hideous creatures spray-painted around them, creatures that looked like neon gargoyles.

'Could you have picked anywhere creepier?' Geena whined. 'If we're out here alone, they can do anything they want.'

'So can we,' Kirsten said, as the icy bite of the wind and banshee shrieks of seagulls made their way into the car.

Pulling up, Mickey passed out the weapons, giving Geena a garden fork from the trunk and keeping a hoe for himself. Simone grabbed the chainsaw and Kirsten took the gun.

'How come you get that?' Geena said, looking at the chainsaw.

'Because I won't end up cutting my leg off if I use it,' Simone replied. She watched as Geena went to say the same dim-witted thing to Kirsten about the gun, moving quickly to stand in front of her bubbleheaded girlfriend before she could open her mouth. Simone, with sincere anger on her face, slowly shook her head. Geena paused mid-step, understanding. She tightened her grip on the garden fork, nodded awkwardly, turned and walked away.

Climbing through a knocked down wall, the darkness and stench of the old hotel engulfed them. Corroded rot and damp drifted on the sea breeze that reached inside, blowing the old papier maché decorations with its steady, cold breath. Their eyes adjusted to the juxtaposition of the harsh darkness and vivid shafts of white light that beamed through the holed ceiling. They were standing in an old, long, dance hall. The room felt like being trapped in a dead giant's decaying mouth, the throat like-length, the deathly smell, its floorboards burnt, ripped up and raised like rotten teeth.

An oppressive atmosphere grasped all of them as they walked around exploring, kicking spray and beer cans, prodding and poking at the ramshackle furniture that had either been broken or burnt.

It was a place that smelled like people used to smoke here, nicotine mixed in with the damp, claustrophobic air. Kirsten, acting strong and focused, walked away from the group exploring the shadows on her own. But Simone could sense the fear inside her and consciously made sure she was no more than six feet away from her at all times.

'How do you know about this place?' Kirsten asked.

'Some of my mates used to come here to graffiti it up. No one ever comes here now though. Used to be called 'The Grand' back in the day. Don't think it'll ever be that again,' Simone said as she pulled the old, wooden door to the kitchen jarringly open with a screech.

'So, how are we going to do this?' Mickey asked.

'Lock this place down, we stay in, those things stay out,' Kirsten said nodding at Simone.

'Exactly. Let's just lay low, see what happens.'

'I'll get my toolbox, I've got hammers and nails. Let's try and get this done before the evening.'

Bringing in everything from the car, they boarded up all the doors downstairs, using old sofas and shelving to barricade themselves in. The hole they came though was covered with an old table top. Unable to fix it to the wall, Simone reversed the beetle, pinning it in place and climbed back through a window. The wedged table was sealed from the inside to the smashed wall, glued shut with two tubes of No Nails. Kirsten and Simone worked at a feverish rate, the sound of hammering never ceased once between the pair.

Crowbarring some internal doors from their hinges, Mickey and Geena stabbed old knives from a dusty cutlery drawer straight through them, attaching some of the kitchen's drawer handles at either end of each door's length, turning them into makeshift spiked, battering rams.

He checked around the kitchen, almost everything that could be of use was vandalized beyond repair. Geena, dirt on her hands, wondered where to wipe it, hands bobbing from jeans to jacket while she scrunched her face, trying to make the decision of what garment to encrust with the hotel's filth. A quick, high-pitched serpent's hiss, shot out behind her, she spun, gum popping from her open mouth.

Mickey poked his face around the pantry door, 'Look at this.'

She tottered over, stared up at him reaching behind a high shelf, an adjustable spanner winding the bolted end of a nub of pipe shut.

'They left the gas on.'

'Fuck sake,' she blurted, holding her chest in shock, 'what you gonna do, make us a fry up?'

He shrugged and went back to work.

Their phones were out of signal, but Simone had guessed that this might be the case and planned ahead. She passed out some old '80s walkie-talkies, things bought for their aesthetic value, now being used again for a practical one in this cut off place.

As the sun went down, they walked the hotel's hallways on old ruined carpets as crispy under their feet as spilled cornflakes. With the hotel completely boarded up from the inside, an air of safety surrounded Kirsten, this feeling marred by another feeling, the feeling of being entombed. Trapped inside concrete walls, with death all around.

The hotel had a flat, open-plan roof that in its prime would have been described as a cocktail area, for its guests to enjoy their drinks with the nuance of a romantic sea view.

Simone had packed four sleeping bags, some torches, and

had picked up enough Papa John's pizza to last them the night.

Mickey showed Kirsten how to load the gun, aim up the sights, and the correct way in which to keep it cocked in her shoulder as not to dislocate it when it was fired.

He took some of the rifles rounds and made what he called 'surprises', super gluing a bullet to the business end of three hammers, turning them into high powered close range weapons.

Simone was right about the place. They were left alone, living as nomads, holed up. Like the lost boys in Peter Pan, it was their own make-believe world, away from the one outside. A world set in the husk of long dead grandeur of the derelict hotel, a building whose long shadow grew as the sun began to set. Simone and Geena checked the last few remaining rooms, making sure latches and locks and the pounded in nails were doing their job. Now everyone was ready for nightfall. As a tense silence filled the air, each of them silently prepared themselves mentally for what to expect that night. Prepared themselves to find out if the previous attacks weren't just random, if it was all going to happen again. Prepared for the sirens to return.

CHAPTER 22

The sun had all but disappeared and on the roof of the old hotel, lounging in a pair of old foldaway chairs overlooking the sea, Kirsten and Simone shared a cigarette while Mickey and Geena walked around the concrete perimeter side by side.

Geena, chewing bubble gum, stopped and spat it out over the roof's edge down towards the ground below, hitting Simone's VW bonnet with a low, metallic thud.

'Bullseye!' she squealed, making Mickey grin.

'I didn't think you were going to get involved in this,' she said.

'Why not?'

'Because I don't want to be here, but I don't have a choice really.'

'I don't know...' He shrugged.

'How come you know how to use the gun?'

'My old man used to take me hunting.'

Geena scuffed her heels to a stop. 'You killed things?'

'No,' he said turning to the girl. 'I always missed.'

'On purpose?' she asked hopefully.

He nodded. 'Yeah.'

'Good boy,' she said, stroking his shoulder, leaving her warm grip there slightly too long, an amount of time meant to mean more than a simple, glancing touch.

'You're a good boy, Mick, Mick,' she said as she popped in some more gum.

Strawberry, he thought, he could smell it as she let the wrapper fall to the floor, carried away on the breeze in quick arcs. She offered him one and he popped it in his mouth.

'How old are you, Mickey?'

'What?'

'How old are you? I've never been able to work it out.'

He swallowed, looked away, then uttered, 'Fifteen.'

She paused for a second, stopping dead in her tracks again and processing his reply.

'What? You're fifteen? But you've got a car?'

He stared at her for a long second, contemplating his answer, not knowing if he wanted to beat his feet down Truth Street, not knowing if he had already said too much.

Seeing no other way out of the tight corner she had put him in, he thought hard and replied, 'It doesn't mean I have a license.'

She thought about this then continued chewing her gum in acceptance.

'Why the fuck do you do our gardening for money?' she puzzled.

'I don't,' he said with a quick raise of his hands, 'she hasn't paid me yet,' he thumbed over his shoulder to Simone.

'Oh. Yeah,' she quizzed, 'but why do you do it? You come there during the week? What about school?'

'...I don't go,'

'Why?'

'Got kicked out,'

'For what?'

'For not going to school,'

'Oh,' she said dully, accepting his answer.

'I got expelled last year for truancy, so my dad said I have to earn some money in between.'

'I hated school, I went to one of those private schools. It was just all about fitting in. Getting a job's not much better.' Geena sighed.

'You have a job?'

'No... I got sacked.'

'What for?' he asked.

'For not going,' she quickly responded.

Mickey smiled and Geena, having another excuse to touch the boy, pushed his shoulder playfully. 'Ain't we a pair?' she smirked.

Slowly, his smile fell and the lighthearted tone of their conversation left the expression on his face. Something deeper grabbed hold of him, something that had dwelled beneath the surface of his existence for quite some time now.

'I'm bored,' he blurted out, his own honesty seemingly hurting him. 'Bored of everything, already,' he paused with a seriousness. 'My old man sent me to a psychiatrist. Been going all year. Apparently, officially, "I'm not happy." He breathed out with an ironic melancholy laugh. 'I could have told him that without the bill.'

There was a pause between them. The information about their lives released into the world slowly digested by one another.

'Why aren't you happy?' Geena asked genuinely.

'I don't even know the answer to that.'

'Simone makes you happy,' she said with a lascivious smile.

He looked at her, the old awkwardness between them she thought had evaporated when the conversation began was back again, all over his forlorn face.

'Don't worry, its obvious mate. It's true through, right?' she asked matter-of-factly.

Silence hung between them, not an awkward one, but a thoughtful one. He liked the fact that he could talk openly with the girl next to him. Her basic, uncomfortable question and answer routine getting to the ground zero of the things that haunted him in life.

'Have you ever got laid?' she blurted out.

His eyes widened with shock. He went to reply but all he could do was sigh in embarrassment.

'It's normal,' she said with a wink. 'Don't be so uptight about it.'

Geena stopped, grabbed Mickey's hand and pulled him close to her. She looked over at Simone in the chair, talking to Kirsten, assessing the distance between them, making sure it was safe to talk.

'You made me happy, you got that gun. I told them to call the cops and they didn't. You're here helping us and you don't have to be. Do you promise that you'll look after us, protect us if it kicks off?'

'Yeah.'

'Promise?'

'Yeah, course.'

She paused, looking deeper into his eyes with a more penetrating gaze, a gaze that reached inside him to a deep place. 'When are you sixteen?'

He swallowed. 'Two months. Why?'

'I like you, Mickey, how about… let's say if you look after us tonight. Make sure we're all safe and use that gun if we need it, in two months' time, I'll give you a birthday present?'

He looked at her not understanding where this was going or what Geena meant.

'Do you fancy me, like Simone?' she said. His eyes widened, squirming in his own clothes at being asked such a blatant question.

'I'll take that as a yes,' she said with a dirty grin. 'How about on your birthday, instead of giving you a present, I take something away from you?'

He looked confused, not following what she meant. Winding the strawberry gum around her tongue, she closed her mouth with a wet chew and licked her lips gently, making them glisten with saliva.

'Something like… your cherry?' she purred.

Speechless, he stopped walking.

'Yeah, I thought that would make you happy.' She reached over and squeezed his hand, pulling it away from him and towards her body, rubbing it against her warm midriff under her sweatshirt.

Moving closer to him, her strawberry lips an inch from

touching him with their kiss, she whispered in his ear, 'That's our secret. Promise you'll look after us?'

He nodded. She threw him a wink, turned and ran back to the other girls, sprinting like a blonde pixie across the roof's cracked concrete, happy to have a life insurance policy in place, its payment as simple as a quick wink and smile.

A warm flush moved through Mickey. He had watched porn films on his computer where people violently smashed faces and fucked hard, and had been turned on by it. But the simplicity of what Geena had just said and done, the slinking seductiveness of it blew all internet understanding of sex out of the sky with one giant hot load. He reached down, feeling a hardness swelling in his pants. Picking up a stone, he threw it down to the ground below. The sun was gone now, and in darkness a smile broke over his face, an expression that was a foreign one to his features these days.

'Yeah, that makes me happy,' he whispered to himself. 'That makes me really happy.' He threw his own chewing gum off the roof where it landed on Simone's VW Bonnet next to Geena's. He smiled again.

CHAPTER 23

Night had fallen. A few miles down the coastline the darkness of the sky had seeped down, blackening the ocean to match it. The lonely, remote cliffs overlooking the sea were wrenched from their tranquility as an old, orange Escort skidded to a standstill in front of them.

'I thought you said we were going back to your place?' said the young girl, her face plastered with make-up, her hair peroxide white in an attempt to make her look older. 'I wouldn't have left me mates in the pub if I knew we were coming up here.'

Next to her, Darren – the pretend mechanic, the real bin man, and still holder of the nick name 'Dickhead Darren' by the family of his ex-girlfriend Charley Reynolds – sat, cracking open a bottle of beer he pulled out of a flimsy blue carrier from the back.

He had picked this girl up from the local pub; this girl named... he couldn't remember now. What did a name mean anyway? She didn't need a name. He had gotten, in his own words, 'pissed off', at the police and Charley's parents involvement in his life.

She had disappeared after their last fight, vanished like all those others that had been disappearing over the last few weeks.

The questions, the accusations, the pointing fingers and harsh tones. It was all too much for him; he wanted a simple life, a simple life to match his simple outlook.

The police had kept him in two days. Missing work he'd had to grovel to get his job on the bins back. Crying, pretending to actually care that Charley had gone missing.

Charley's dad had even tried to get him out of the flat, had confronted him, but having all his mates with him at the time, drinking and smoking, he simply laughed, 'Squatter's rights innit, fella?' at the man who paid for the place, then slammed the door in his face.

Tonight was different. Some of his mates were holding the fort, making sure the old bastard didn't try to get in. That's when he met… the girl next to him.

The mates who were in the pub with him had tried to warn him as he left, 'You ain't gonna drive like that?' as he staggered from the bar. 'You ain't leaving with her are you? Do you know how old she is?' as he dragged the young blonde he had been chatting up away from her friends.

Bollocks to them all, he thought. All he wanted was that simple life again, and nothing could be simpler than beer and birds.

She looked outside the window at the endless dark. Then checked her phone – no signal – she sighed.

'Look, I forgot,' he mused. 'I left two of the lads at mine, what kind of bloke would I look like if I would have just brought you back for them to eye up.'

'S'pose,' she said, vacantly.

'Look,' he said trying not to slur, 'you fancy me, right?'

'S'pose.'

'Well, I fancy you. We wanted a bit of privacy and I've given us that. I'm like one of those hunter-gatherer types ya' know, like a caveman.'

She smiled slightly, a flicker of excitement filling her eyes. 'Like a caveman?'

'Yeah!' he shouted, seeing her slight amusement, then beat his chest like Tarzan, he yelled out of his open window, hearing it echo out into the nothingness.

She laughed harder this time, he smiled.

'So, you think I'm funny then, do ya?'

'Yeah, a bit,' she coyly shrugged.

'Well, don't be cold, come over here then.'

They stayed looking at each other for a second. She was trying to pluck up courage, having only done this once before, the other time with a boy her age, one just as equally awkward as she.

In her eyes, Darren was a man, an older man with a car. Part of her wanted to be near him, another part – a bigger part – wanted the luxury of being driven around in his car.

Forgetting her hang-ups she moved into him, pressing her soft, lipstick caked lips against his, feeling his thick, ridged tongue penetrate her mouth like a fish as it wriggled around trying to find a space to escape.

It took exactly six seconds for the kiss to last before his probing fingers tried to rotate round her knickers to get to her groin, exactly ten seconds before he made her rub the modest, hard lump at the front of his jeans.

After a minute of exploring each other, a synchronicity she took for them being compatible joined them.

He wasn't shy like the other boy; he knew what he wanted and how to do it. And to him, she was just what he needed, a little pick me up. Who cared about her age? He knew she was young, but his excuse if anyone came asking would be, 'well I met her in the pub, innit fella?' It would work, he knew it would; the other day he'd read a story just the same in The Sport.

After a few minutes of rubbing and pulling, smashing faces and groping at flesh, the girl spoke up.

'It's a bit uncomfortable in here,' her legs spreadeagled, one on the dashboard the other in the back seat.

'Oh come on,' Darren barked, 'let's just get on with it.' He realised then how drunk he was, his vision betraying him, nearly calling her Charley for a second. Gathering his thoughts, hearing the annoyance in his voice, he quickly flipped it around.

'We'll go outside!' he said passing her his beer. 'Loads of space, loads of space.'

She looked at him wearily. 'It's cold out there.'

A strain of annoyance grew in him; this time he caught it, suppressing it, down below the surface.

'I've never had a girl on the bonnet before,' he murmured.

'I've always thought about that, would be nice if it was like... if it was you.'

She smiled, thinking of the car, the act making her somehow part of the car in her mind, combining her with him and the car in physical contact like some kind of bare-backed cyborg. It was like it would be her chance to put a claim on the car. Oh, and Darren, too, of course.

'Yeah, I like that,' she said.

'Me, too.' He grinned, the nameless girl becoming officially the eighth he'd had on the bonnet. 'Jump out and I'll meet you by the front.'

She did, checking her make-up and slowly getting out, giving him enough time to snort a cheeky line of coke from the glove box off his finger. Young and fun she might be, but worth a line of his coke? No chance.

He turned the headlights on – illuminating the grass that led towards the cliff edge – then jumped out.

'Romantic, innit?' he said to no reply.

They kissed and he positioned her where he wanted her, him sitting on the bonnet, her in between his legs.

'I thought I was going on the bonnet?' she said.

'You will,' he replied.

He made her reach into his pants, take out his throbbing cock and begin to stroke it. Holding the back of her neck, he tried to push her down there, reluctant at first, then giving in, an act that let the suppressed rage flare inside him again.

'I've never done this before,' she said, meekly, her age showing in her eyes as she did.

'It's alright, I'll help,' he said, pushing her down all the way so she could take him in her mouth.

He reached for his beer, listening to the waves in front of them. Yeah, he thought, this was the simple life.

Enjoying her mouth working on him, he closed his eyes. Another noise caught his attention. At first, he thought it was a whistling on the wind. Then it started sonically slinking around him, held him, froze him, it was a slow, caressing, female voice, seductive and soothing, an eerie soft singing.

It spoke to him, 'Darreennnn, Darreennn.'

With it, he became slightly harder in the girl's mouth; she became more aroused, too, her movements quicker, the wetness in between her legs doubling.

He enjoyed this moment, wanting to raise the beer up, wanting to drink, but was unable to. Their dreamy states did not allow them to hear the creeping footsteps from a small path on the cliff face, inhuman footsteps.

The song got louder, nearer. Then suddenly it stopped. Darren opened his eyes, staring at what looked like two lights in the distance, two lights he realized were closer than that, two lights that were directly in front of him.

Suddenly the lights blinked and disappeared into the darkness, his newfound hardness slipping for a moment.

He went to speak, but words never left his slack lips as the girl continued to do her work.

Maybe he was more pissed and stoned than he had known. *Fuck it*, he thought, enjoy it. 'Keep going, girl,' he told her, 'keep going.' She did, just thinking of being had on the bonnet, of having the thing in her mouth between her legs.

He heard more steps, the sound of something almost dropping down to the floor; he opened his eyes again, looked around, but his vision was a blurred mess, his head was thumping. He saw nothing, just the girl doing her deed, kneeling in the headlights and her shadow behind her.

His mind cleared for a second. The shadow didn't fall on the grass, nor did it ripple over its blades. It was sitting upright, kneeling right behind the girl like a blank double.

Before he could say or understand anything, the young mouth that was serving him so well was wrenched off, his length left throbbing in the wind.

A piercing cry came from the girl as he helplessly watched the three-dimensional shadow reach across her chest and rip it open into four flowing lines of hot, red blood.

She shrieked out a sound he thought no person was capable of.

But then, his drunken eyes failing him in ways he couldn't have imagined, played an old fantasy out. There, on their knees in front of him, were twins; blonde twins. He tried to refocus his eyes, tried to sharpen his brain, each betraying one another with the substances he had put in him.

Did he have two of them on the go up here? Had this somehow slipped from his mind?

But this wasn't any porn movie come to life, this was a porn movie filmed with a horror filter. The new twin grabbing the bleeding, screaming one, covered her mouth, and fell backwards from the cliff's edge to the water and rocks below. The girl's piercing cry disappearing before being cut off by an engulfing splash.

He stood mesmerized. It was over in less seconds than it had taken him to find his way into the girl's pants. He shivered, scared, fear covering him.

The darkness from outside the car's windows soaked inside his system like the coke and alcohol, biting on his bones, demanding terror to generate there with each cold chomp.

Reaching for his beer, he knocked it off the bonnet, hearing it thud and froth on the floor. He shivered, trying to work out why he was now alone, what had happened and what to do, when from the darkness a face emerged, one he recognized.

There, wet and bedraggled, was Charley Reynolds, his Charley.

He froze, caught red-handed, literally with his pants down.

'Babes!' he said pulling the most charming, gormless grin he could.

She did nothing, just stayed still, looking at him. He thought he saw a flicker in her eyes – just like the two bright shapes he had seen a second ago – as she slowly moved towards him.

'Everyone's been looking for you, babes, where ya been?'

Too scared to move, too worried he had been caught to do anything else, he watched as she dropped to her knees and crawled towards him.

The song started again. 'Darreeennn, Darreeenn, Darreennn.'

Unsure, he pulled his buttocks close to the bonnet, but a part of him told him otherwise. 'She loves it,' it said, 'just like all those slags in The Sport. She loves it.'

He stood proudly, thinking she must have been turned on seeing her man with another woman, thinking she was here to show the nameless blonde bitch how to do the job right.

He flinched as she took him in her hand. Her eyes looking up at him glowed to match the cars headlights. He smiled. 'Yeah, that's it, babe, glad ya back.' She smiled too, with a mouthful of razor sharp teeth, the last thing he remembered before she lunged in and bit his cock off.

CHAPTER 24

The black night had hidden everything, the sky was a tie-dye wash of moonlight seeping through grey clouds over the hotel roof. They huddled like kids on a camping trip, sharing cold pizzas and warm cokes with only a couple of LED lamps to illuminate them. The sea smashed from the surrounding darkness, invisible by sight but loud and clear with its monolithic crashes against the rocks on the tide line, a sound that would be treacherous at sea, but soothing up and away on terra firma.

Curled up in a sleeping bag and chewing on a slice of ham and pineapple, a fear wrapped around Geena with the bleak atmosphere the hotel held at night. She took a sip from her coke and realized her hand was trembling slightly, the warm bubbles washed down her throat uncomfortably, only making her unease worsen.

'Did we have to come all the way out here?' Her eyes watered as the fizzy drink went down the wrong hole.

Simone looked at her, bored of her idiotic attitude. 'Well, we're going to find out what's what if those things do show up here,' she snapped shortly. 'If there's been some kind of mistake or if they really are... you know...'

'If they're coming for me,' Kirsten said coldly.

There was a moment of silence, the chewing and drinking stopped as they glanced at each other.

Kirsten's gaze fixed on Simone as she brought up the rifle so it's long, sleek barrel leant against her shoulder. 'If they do, at least I can use this thing out here without drawing any attention.'

'Do you really believe what that psychic told you?' Mickey asked, throwing a crust into the pizza box. 'Sea sirens?'

Kirsten thought for a second, staring forward at nothing but seeing a greater distance than what was before her, trying to understand what was happening.

'All I know is, I've seen some strange shit since I've been here.' Kirsten pushed her hair from her eyes. 'I've cut this up in my mind so many ways. What was happening, why it was happening. Last night you two saw it, too, and all I know now is I'm not crazy.'

Geena threw back the last of her Coke, swallowing it hard and letting it sink down into the dull lump of fear that grew in her stomach. 'You're not crazy.' She wished she didn't have to agree. Wished that all of this wasn't happening, remembering that moment in the back of the VW, a cold, hard fear drilling into her body, hearing the car's paintwork whine as the sea creatures' claws slashed across it.

Simone sighed. 'Hopefully this is just something random that's got out of control, maybe we're thinking too much into this.' She looked at Kirsten, 'But maybe not. But we know what to do if they do turn up. You all got your radios?'

Mickey reached around to the back of his jeans, pulling the radio out and holding it up. Kirsten nodded silently, looking at Simone with distant eyes.

Geena's face displayed a dawning horror. 'Shit... I've left mine downstairs somewhere.'

Simone looked at her with disgust, knowing deep inside that the only reason she had kept this girl in her life so long was because of her good looks. As if telepathically understanding what passed through her girlfriend's mind, Geena looked disappointed and sad.

'Come down there with me to find it,' she pleaded to Simone.

Simone kicked her empty coke along the floor in a quick burst of fury and yelled at her, 'Fuck sake, come on.'

She picked up the saw and swung it around her back on its old worn strap. Reaching down in annoyance, she pulled Geena to her feet, who grabbed her garden fork as they marched back down the stairwell into the bowels of the old hotel.

Kirsten and Mickey watched them leave, Geena padding

behind Simone like a little dog following its master, lost in life without her.

'Simone really cares about you, doesn't she?' Mickey said.

'I care about her. I hadn't seen her for years until a few days ago, nothing's changed though. We used to be best mates, proper friends. You can never change some things in life, no matter how much time goes by.' Kirsten smiled thinking about her cousin, then looked at Mickey. 'Thanks for helping us, thanks for –' She rattled the gun. 'It's a pretty big thing.'

He shrugged.

'Do you think I'm crazy?' Kirsten asked.

'No,' he replied immediately.

Kirsten looked down at the LED lamp in front of her for a moment, staring at its small glowing lights, her mind floating towards the glowing eyes that seemed to follow her everywhere at night. 'Why?' she asked.

Mickey drifted into his own mind, his own life and the problems it held. 'Because it makes sense. I hate living here with my old man. I hate my job, I hate the things I have to do to keep a roof over my head. He wants me to be the perfect son, doing everything he tells me to. It's like I'm living a version of life he doesn't want.'

Kirsten distracted from her own thoughts stared sorrowfully at him.

'He thinks somewhere in me another version exists that could live his idea of a perfect life. Sometimes I worry that one day I'll wake up and there will be this other version he always wanted in my place, ya know? Like what Geena told me was coming after you, some kind of... double... a replacement... some kind of subordinate that does the job of being you... better than you. I don't want to change.'

A cold shiver crawled down Kirsten's back.

'If there is this thing, this siren, this double... I just wish I could get rid of it just as easy as shooting it,' he said.

An uncomfortable silence punctuated the conversation. Kirsten understood his words in a way she thought she never would. They solemnly stared off into the darkness that surrounded the hotel, a darkness so intense that it made them feel as if here, next to the small LED lamps, they were sitting on the last place to exist on earth, their island of light surrounded by a vast, alien ocean of oppressive nothing.

* * *

Simone and Geena wandered around the dark, dank smelling building, moving from darkened room to darkened room, trying to retrace Geena's steps looking for the walkie-talkie.

'I can't believe I just put it down somewhere,' she whined.

'Really?' Simone replied in an unimpressed tone, her head clouded with annoyance, completely believing she could.

Walking down a long, dusty corridor, with silver moonlight creating bars through the rows of boarded up windows, Simone paused. 'Hang on, did you leave your radio turned on?'

Geena stopped, the gears in her mind almost as audible as those on a burnt-out truck. 'I don't know…'

Simone rolled her eyes. 'Just be quiet,' she said with a sigh, taking out her own walkie-talkie, tuning it to Geena's frequency, turning down the volume and pressing the small Morse code button on its side. She turned to the empty old hotel and listened.

'You don't have to get moody with m—'

Simone grimaced and raised a finger. 'Shushhhh!'

Further away a low, peeping sound could be heard, distantly bleating to itself.

'You found it!' Geena squealed. Simone looked at her, unimpressed again, a nagging feeling at the back of her mind, knowing that once this was over Geena would soon be referred to as an 'ex-girlfriend'. Simone didn't even want to look at the girl. She just wanted to retrieve the radio and get back to Kirsten.

She walked off further into the shadows, Geena trailing behind again. You knew in your heart when a relationship was over and, in the last few hours, Geena, her brainless piece of arm candy, had solidified that place for herself on the scrap pile of ex-girlfriends. All Simone wanted to do was be back upstairs with Kirsten. That's why they were here in the first place and now she was running around babysitting Geena, moving further and further into the old hotel. Her sense of the possible danger around them nulled by the irritation she felt with each slap of Geena's feet behind her.

* * *

As they moved further through the building, above them and out of sight in darkness, the hotel's old corroded water tank – situated in a small loft space – began to bubble.

Its ancient pipes came to life, animated with jarring movements, vibrating themselves from the mounts that held them in place, moving as if something were travelling through them, snaking up inside to find its way out.

Dust from decades before erupted into the air highlighted by moon glow that the shattered roof tiles let in.

Suddenly the silence in this undisturbed room was broken as an overflow tap began to squeak round, undoing itself as if turned by invisible hands, relieving the built up tension behind it, freeing the unseen thing that rattled its copper bones to life, ready to let it check into the old hotel.

* * *

On the opposite side of the building, on the flat concrete roof, Kirsten's mouth widened to a yawn. 'What's the time now?'

Mickey, nodding off, threw his head back up and widened his eyes, checking his watch. 'Nearly three.'

He yawned, too, pushing his face down into his jacket as a cold night wind blew around them. Tiredness and fatigue were weighing them down and the stillness took away their attention and feeling of danger. Away from what was about to begin.

CHAPTER 25

Barry the Tramp lay in the underpass; he had become a familiar face with the locals in the nearby council flats. The drunks staggering home to their dwellings in the tower blocks had often stopped and pissed all over his cardboard shell. At first he was furious as to how anybody could do this to his home, now complacent, he just let them do it.

The smell of another's urine was no worse than the constant stench of his own. Tonight, as he lay in silence peering from the box's darkness, he watched as an unusual form wandered down the subway, a shapely form, a female form. Not like one of the rounded, loud mouthed ones with a plethora of children in tow from the flats. No, here was a silhouette like one of those Page 3 stunners he used to ogle. Nice, like the one that bought his breakfast today, but with all the curves that caught his eye. Clearing his throat, sounding like a cement mixer as he did, he raised his filth-caked head up, licking his teeth clean and called out to her.

'Alright, my lovely, got a spare quid for an old 'un?'

The girl stopped, her blonde hair moving across her shoulders as she did, and then turned to face the stinking wretch.

Barry the Tramp's heart stopped, his insides turned cold, an uncontrollable jet of piss warmed his soiled jogging bottoms. As this woman, this lovely, turned to him, a stone-cold fact hit him. He knew this woman, he had been intimate with her in a way no other man had. He had embraced this woman, held her, used her as a shield to save his own pointless existence and watched as she died as a result.

He recognized her and now she recognized him.

The blonde from the rig, but not her.

The double he saw in the water next to her.

The one with the ey…

Her eyes ignited, glowing over him. In life, she would have never touched this man, never gone near him. Now, with a hunger for flesh, oh yes, now she would. Now she would do more than just touch him. Now, she peered down, pressing in closer and closer, her mouth opening, revealing sharp teeth, reaching for him with a handful of blackened talons. Barry withdrew into his shell, screaming, hoping it would act as just that: something to protect him. And as she slashed and tore at his cardboard hut, he hid from the moment he had always wanted, a beautiful woman clawing for his attention, their second meeting a role reversal of the first. Now she held him in the special embrace that he had held her, the cold embrace of death.

CHAPTER 26

Simone tried to pin-point the walkie-talkie's location by proxy of its dull beep. She followed it to an open cellar door.

Looking down the stairs, a smile passed over Geena's mouth.

'Yeah! That's right, I left it down there somewhere!' she squealed.

Gaining some confidence and wanting to please Simone, she went to jump down the stairs into the darkness. But as she leaped forward, with a quick authoritarian clasp, Simone grabbed her shoulder and yanked her back.

'What's wro...' Geena squawked, shocked by her girlfriend's strong grip.

'Wait, I'll get it,' Simone cried in a strong tone.

They both looked at the walkie-talkie in Simone's hand. Through its waves of filtering snow and static, a distant banshee like cry quickly rattled distantly through the small receiver.

A cold shiver surged through Geena. The dull fear she was incubating in her stomach felt as though it had pushed up her throat and wrapped its cold tentacles around her.

'Did you hear that?' she jabbered? 'It's them, that's the song from...' she choked as Simone cut her off with a determined hardened tone.

'It was feedback, you moron.' Simone went to walk down into the basement, Geena grabbed her.

'No, don't go down there!'

'Look, I'm not leaving it down there, we've come all this way, just let me go get the bloody thing.'

'No, wait...'

'Look, you were just about to skip down there, but I don't want you staggering down like an idiot and falling on your arse. So just get my back then, turn on that torch and cover me with it,'

'I'm scared, Simone.'

'Go on, move,' Simone said coldly, 'You're really beginning to piss me off Geena, just hold that beam on me, just in case there is anything in those shadows. '

'Don't say that,' Geena gasped. 'That's fucking terrifying, don't say that.'

'Just do it,' Simone growled through clenched teeth. Geena limply raised the garden fork to a fighting position, holding the torch along its length, then beamed it down onto the old, brittle, wooden stairs below.

They stared into its moving circle of light that penetrated the blackness, watched as it passed dusty crates, stopping on the old keg where Geena's walkie-talkie sat.

'See it's just there,' Simone said.

Simone passed her walkie-talkie to Geena, held in front of her face, showing her it was her panicked imagination and just some random interference with the walkie-talkie's signal that had cried out. At the back of her mind, something niggled Simone, worried her, but she ignored it. She'd had a hard time with this bollocks all along, sea siren's, the bloody alky psychic, she had gone along with the stories in the library books… but it was all grating against her now, she just wanted to get back to the others, get the night over with.

'Just keep the torch on me,' she said with an intense stare.

'No! No!' Geena pleaded, her breathing intense and fast, all of her instincts telling her to run, to hightail it back out the door and all the way home. But her trembling legs, like palm trees in a storm, stayed rooted to the ground.

* * *

Upstairs in the attic, the old tap connected to the archaic water tank turned fully, spinning wide open with a quick violent force. Instantly, a filthy black liquid gushed from its lime scale encrusted end, dousing the dusty floor, moving across its weathered boards with a life of its own as it seeped between the joins. It moved with a consciousness, searching and looking for an easy way to escape, a gap or nook to slide between, to move downstairs, seeping through the hotel's irreparable foundations as it reached down with a primal instinct. Down towards the girls below.

* * *

As Geena tried to pull her back, Simone shrugged her off, gritting her teeth, tired of the girl's wimpy disposition as she slowly crept down the stairs. Fumbling and confused, Geena held the torch's ray on Simone, over exposing her in a beam of ancient dust particles.

Halfway down the stairs, she took out her own torch, cutting through the darkness ahead with its powerful bulb, then set the beam straight onto the walkie-talkie. Not wasting any more time than necessary in the damp, stinking pit, she rushed over and grabbed it. Moving straight back to the foot of the stairs, firing her torch's white beam into the deep, cobwebbed darkness around her, a chill climbed her spine that made goose bumps appear over her body. Spooked she turned, ready to run back to Geena, then paused.

'Come on! What are you doi…' Geena cried.

Simone threw a wide fearful glare at her, silencing her with a quick raised hand, making the torch in Geena's hand tremble, its beam flickering over Simone as she tried to steady herself, eyes twinkling in terror. With a hard gulp, Geena, fixed to the floor, unable to move, watched Simone react to something.

'Wha… what is it,' she whispered.'

To her left, echoing towards her, Simone could hear, drawing nearer, the far off cry of the sirens, this time not through the walkie-talkie's inferior speaker, but emerging from somewhere within the room.

Suddenly, an authentic intoxication rushed through her as the sirens' screams shifted in her mind to alluring, soothing voices, female voices that reached out and caressed her, making her head swim and her feet feel like they were levitating from the floor.

'Simonneeee, Simonneee, Simonneee.'

She remembered the word that Melissa the psychic described it as: an aural 'pheromone'. That's exactly what it was, a carnal attack of the senses, the soreness of her last sex session with Geena tingling with a wet pleasure in her panties.

'What are you doing? Come on! Come on! *Come onnnn*!' Geena screamed, the shrill terror in her voice bringing Simone back to reality like a bucket of water to the face.

She pulled back from the songs mystical grasp; felt its sinister dreaminess piling up in her mind, trying to cloud her from rational thought. She quickly raised her torch, trying to pinpoint where the song emanated from while mentally holding the tune and the pleasure it brought from the forefront of her mind, wrestling with it like a giant, thick, wriggling sea serpent that wanted to bore deep inside her brain.

She staggered on the spot, moved over to a stack of dusty old crates piled ceiling high in the corner, feeling a draft coming from the wall behind, slowly peering behind them, she stared at a ragged, broken, brick wall, its center a deep, gaping hole into the nothingness of a long, concrete drainage pipe. The pipe, six feet in diameter and smashed in by vandals long ago, had become a gaping chasm into the outside world, filled with a wet, damp stench, wide enough for someone – something – to come through.

Then, distantly, echoing louder and louder, the otherworldly song began to grow, a noise both bone shaking with fear and delicious with desire. Her eyes adjusted, in the tunnel's depths, moving closer and flickering like a church mass of candles, were pair upon pair of glowing eyes, creatures eyes, the sirens' eyes.

Terrified – solidifying the reality of the situation, of the night previous, of the idea that they were indeed coming back for her cousin – Simone lost all of the confident demeanor she had displayed for the entire day. Trying to move back to the stairs, ungluing herself from the spot, her feet a tangled mess, she dropped Geena's walkie-talkie next to her on the dirt floor of the cellar, buzzing like an electronic hornet, her attention caught by the multitude of bobbing, dazzling eyes pressing ever towards her, closer and closer, bigger and brighter.

Forgetting she had the saw in her hand – her weapon of choice – it suddenly became a dead weight pulling her shoulders, just something else to make her stumble backwards to the stairs, bumping into their first step and reeling backwards onto her arse. Geena, shaking from the seizing fear in her girlfriend's movements, let cold, terrified tears run down her face, still obeying, staying silent at the top of the stairs, but internally screaming the place down to the ground.

Finding a quick power surge, Simone pulled herself up, swung round and stomped at full speed back up the stairs, pushing Geena backwards and slamming the cellar door behind her, holding it shut with outstretched arms.

'Get something!' she screamed.

'What?' Geena rattled out, trembling and perplexed.

'Something to barricade the door with! Now!'

Geena ran to the room next door and pulled at broken furniture, random pieces of split timber, anything that could be used. All the while, only a few rooms down, the black water from the attic had found its way through. Two feet deep and defying gravity, sloshing and swaying impossibly around the lampshade, the ceiling had become an inverted living ocean. Slowly, it poured down the walls, soaked into the torn wallpaper in long, thin streams. Streams that webbed out, reached down like blackened tree branches, forming quickly into spindly arms and long, black-clawed fingers that rose from the two-dimensional patterned wallpaper into a horrifying, living, three-dimensional reality.

CHAPTER 27

Geena dragged an old dresser by one of its drawer-less compartments, stumbling and stalling as it caught on the filth-textured carpet. Bringing it to Simone, she limply dumped it with a loud huff across the door, with a white, expressionless face. Simone screamed at her, eyes burning with a glow of pure fury. 'Well, get more then! Come on, think!'

Spittle shot from Simone's mouth like webbing from a spider's spinneret, falling and disappearing on the floor.

Something began to fire inside Geena looking at the desperate anger on Simone's face. A survival instinct ignited with common sense, accelerating inside her as she began to run on all cylinders, knowing what she must do. Tearing back down the hallway at lightning fast speed, she carried back old chairs, desks, anything big enough to wedge against the door. Within minutes enough destitute furniture was there to haphazardly barricade the door shut, pinning it to the hallway wall opposite.

They worked together, quick grunts and violent groans escaped their mouths as they threw everything into place.

'What did you see, Simone? What did you see?' Geena wailed.

Simone searched for the walkie-talkie she had in her hand only a second ago, patting herself down, trying to frantically find it, not realizing she had dropped it in the room below.

She went to grab her own walkie-talkie back from Geena. Nervously, it popped from her sweaty grasp like a warmed bar of soap in a hot shower, falling straight to the floor, exploding in slow motion, batteries rolling across the rough terrain of the time-worn carpet and into inky black shadows.

'Shit!' she screamed, ready to drop to her knees to try and piece it back together, pausing, as suddenly, the slow, sinister, wet slap of feet made their way up the stairs behind the barricaded door.

Silently, with a gentle touch, something tried to push the door open from the other side, the door frame letting out a thin creek that turned to a shrill timbered whine.

Claws, Geena thought with a tremble, *they're scratching at the door trying to get through*. The sound made her visualize all the things that tormented her mind.

Once they see the face they want, with a scratch, they take it.

'Not my face, not my face, not my face,' she whimpered.

The furniture they had piled up began to fall, slipped slightly out of place with the pressure applied to the other side, a pressure that, with frustration of being denied entry, became quicker and violent.

Ravenous, frantic groans hissed and growled with madness and rage trying to tear their way through, the sound of wood ripping and shredding, as unseen hands slashed with unseen talons.

Simone grabbed Geena by her collar, yanking her backwards as she stood stiffened in fear. 'Come on! Let's go!' she screamed, dragging the stunned girl back with her through the hotel.

* * *

On the roof, the walkie-talkie next to Mickey and Kirsten sat in silence, its frequency tuned to dull fuzz. Only ten minutes or so had passed since Simone and Geena had left, only quietness around them as they looked out to sea, unaware in their cut off surroundings of the horror show unfolding below.

'I think we're going to be okay, only three hours until sun up,' Mickey said, rubbing his face, a rubbery texture to it with tiredness. Kirsten pulled a dour smile, glad that indeed nothing had happened tonight. A gladness that was sullied with the idea that, maybe, nothing would happen the following night, or the one after that. No comfort came with this thought, knowing that the feeling of dread, that constant expectation that something was coming for her, would never go away.

'Torches?' Mickey said, with surprise.

Kirsten turned to him, a cloud of confusion settling on her face, watching as he shifted forward in his chair, staring off at something over the concrete barrier of the roof into the distance.

Making her jump, he pitched forward, a sudden life firing through his veins as he ran to the edge looking down. Kirsten followed behind him, her heart immediately running on overdrive, a new streak of fear working through her with his sudden jerky movements. Now, both hanging over the concrete edge looking out to the darkness, she could see nothing.

'What is it? What did you see?' she asked in panic.

He stared for a second, a new intensity killing off the drab tiredness that had covered his face only a second ago. His eyes grew to twice their normal size. 'There!' he said, pointing his right arm off out into the abyss before them, to the spot where he saw something that she did not.

'There,' he said, 'torches, two of them right down there.'

Positioning herself to stare down the barrel of his arm, squinting and adjusting her gaze to see what he could see. The image caught her eyes; understanding flickered to life, a tightness wound around her. Two beams poured from the tideline, lights that weaved and searched around for something, looking like small spotlights, but they weren't radiated by any bulb or battery, spotlights that were the incandescent eyes of a siren.

Kirsten's mouth popped open, a gasp of warm air escaping into the night. Her vision adjusted to the darkness, watching as the 'torches' multiplied, expanded into an entire flock of projected beams that made their way up from the sea – straight towards them.

It was a small army of sirens, ten or so, their faces slowly revealed by the lights in their eyes, cold, steely faces that seemed to just float in the darkness.

Mickey looked down in confusion. 'What are they doing up here?' His mind reached for the most obvious solution, thinking that these were fishermen coming up from the coast, small lights attached to bands around their heads, probably wondering why there were people on the roof of the old Grand Hotel.

Then the penny dropped. This was it. The story. The creatures. The glowing eyes. It was all true. Excitement and fear was coursing through his body, adrenaline made his legs shake. He went to speak, but before he could, out of the corner of his eye: a slick, black barrel swung past his head like a striking cobra, it was his father's rifle. On its other end, in the stance he had shown her, was Kirsten. Cocked, aimed and poised, her sights set on the figures below.

'Wait!' he yelled, reaching to grab the barrel to stop her, thinking he hadn't even known this girl a day ago, thinking – *what have I done, giving her my dad's gun? What have I done?*

But before he could think any more, Kirsten took quick aim at the nearest creature walking towards them – a brunette girl, a face she knew, a face she had spoken to – Tiffany, the curator who commissioned her – and pulled the trigger. A thunderous crash echoed out, breaking the sleepy tranquilly both had felt only a moment ago. Mickey fell backwards; hitting the concrete floor, his hands up to his ears, tears of fear, of being out of his depth appeared in his eyes. He was now an accomplice, aiding and abetting in the murder of whoever the rifle's bullet had just hit.

'What did you do? What did…' he mumbled in a weak, lifeless tone.

The female siren jolted backwards, the shot entering her right shoulder in a snowy puff of vivid red and black viscera. Hitting the ground, wet hair thrown over her face, the light in her eyes flickered like an internal power cut had caused them to dim.

A shocked awe grew inside Mickey as he pulled himself upright and looked over the roof's concrete barrier to the corpse below.

The brief moment of success that slid over Kirsten's face dropped instantly, as its glowing eyes popped on again, the creature rose to its feet and started walking towards them again, as if the loud, piercing shot hadn't even happened.

Their own eyes widened in shock and horror, skulls of death filling their pupils, making no sense of how this thing could seamlessly walk with a gaping bullet hole.

Mickey watched as Kirsten reloaded the gun, aiming at the girl once more, her wet hair illuminated like a reflective surface by her shining eyes, making her the perfect target in the darkness.

Another shot cracked out, this one a bullseye, hitting the girl in the face, tearing half of her skin away in a fast, ragged lump, exposing underneath the black deaths head of her real form; the sharp-toothed, oily-skinned creature Kirsten saw under the pier. It cried out, bringing its hands up to its face, now a visage split down the middle, half human, half siren. It staggered backwards and hit the floor, now seemingly stone-cold dead.

'Holy shit! Holy fucking shit!' Mickey whimpered. 'It's all real! Isn't it?'

Kirsten grabbed the walkie-talkie, quickly searching for a frequency and punched its button, shouting for Simone. The cry ran through the airwaves, connecting to the walkie-talkie in the basement, the one behind the barricaded door, the one Simone had dropped. All she could hear were the loud, violent smashes as the sirens cried out trying to escape, ripping the door to shreds. Their seductive purrs mixed with their awful cries. Kirsten knew what these sounds meant. That feeling of dread, that constant expectation of something coming for her was confirmed in the gut churning terror of that moment. They had returned. They were back, and they knew that the girl they sought was near.

CHAPTER 28

Simone led the way, tearing along the hotel's hallways, navigating on fear and instinct, rushing through shafts of moonlight that seeped through the boarded up windows.

A loud thump, followed by a winded 'gah!' came from behind her. She stopped, jarring around at whiplashing speed, to see Geena yanked along the floor by her ankles, reaching with no hope for the garden fork she had once clung to. Her loud scream filling the air, as her bottom half disappeared around a door frame. The transmutations of the old water tank – a moment ago black, dripping stains on the old wallpaper – had reformed into humanoid hands that reached around to clasp Geena as she held onto the jamb for dear life. Her lips curled back baring teeth, face as white as bone, her knuckles and fingers, impossibly, even whiter. The mauling black hands reached from the darkness as if part of it, pulling her hair, wrapping her face, covering her features like a tight, wet, cobwebbed veil, trying to pull her backwards. Sharp clawed tips running over her face, her bulbous eyes watching them go, tearfully waiting for them to sink in her soft skin.

Geena cried, 'Don't let them scratch me, Simone! Don't let them scratch me!'

Spasms of icy fear shot though Simone as she ran back to her girlfriend.

The hands caressed her, teased her, each one waiting for the other to do the deed – to plunge into her with its claws. Flesh, warm, human flesh, how long they had waited, how much they enjoyed it in their grasp. How much they enjoyed her fear.

Not screaming now, she trembled silently, imprisoned in their palms as they yanked her backwards. With a forced calm, with a trembling stutter, Geena whispered, 'Help me, Simone... *help me! Please! Don't let them take me...*' the words spilling from her throat in a hiss.

Thinking fast, Simone dropped on her arse, spread her legs either side of the doorframe, stabilizing herself and reached forward, grabbing Geena's wrists, her hands sliding down into Geena's palms. Geena slowly letting go of the rotten doorframe grasped Simone, a grasp usually reserved for making love now used for trying to save her life.

'*Help me!*' Geena pleaded with a whisper, tears running down her face. Simone wrenched backwards, Geena reeled forward, her face pulling away from the slimy, jagged hands, like a fly yanked through the jaws of a Venus flytrap.

'Don't let them scratch me! Don't let them scratch me! Don't let them scratch me!' she cried, touched by insanity, touched by the cold claws of death. Simone pulled her again; she came up closer, the pair almost hugging now. Simone stared over her shoulder into the room behind, reforming sirens stared back at her. A room filled with fiery, glowing eyes that crawled towards them.

One of the creatures lunged forward, reaching for Simone with its dark, clawed hand, grabbing onto a clump of her hair and yanking her face first towards the door. Its force made a small pop reverberate from her neck, a headache instantly spreading, her face slackening in pain. Almost doubled over, Simone screamed in agony, tears falling from her eyes, digging her nails into Geena, who felt them and screamed louder thinking of the things in the room behind, their long black claws.

Once they see the face they want, with a scratch, they take it. They take it. *THEY TAKE IT!*

Then, to their left, fast moving footsteps grew louder and louder. 'Simone!' Kirsten yelled, Mickey behind as she ran towards them.

She skidded to a halt beside her cousin, raised the rifle up and blindly fired off two rounds into the dark room. The siren's wails rang out; the grasping hands let go and recoiled back into the shadows, letting go of both of the girls. Simone clambered to her feet helped by Mickey, they both pulled up Geena who grabbed her garden fork. Briefly eyeing each other, they all took off down the hallway, barred streaks of moonlight flicking in their eyes like strobes.

'Fucking hell, Kirst, the basement, it's full of them!' Simone shouted as they ran.

'Outside, they're coming up from the sea!' Kirsten yelled back.

'I want to leave! I want to go home!' Geena cried, reaching for Simone's hand as they fled.

'We can't!' Simone screamed as they ran like rats in a maze.

'Did they scratch me, Simone? Did they get me?'

'No!' She screamed back,

'Are you sure?'

'Yes! I'm su…'

Suddenly, a boarded up window smashed straight through, two slick black hands reached inside, latching onto Geena's hair, yanking her backwards with vicious, scalping jerks. Looking over her shoulder she stared into glowing eyes that peered through the sheared-off boards, seeing a venomous smile cracking over oily-skinned lips.

Simone leaped forward, swung the saw around on its strap and fired it to life, it growled as fiercely as a wild bear, all sharp teeth and deep bellow. She ran the chewing blade blindly through the window, as blind and as wild as Kirsten's shots into the dark room, hitting nails, board and the creature beyond in a fury of splinters, sparks and blood. There was a repugnant crunch of bone, a cry of high-pitched pain, the deep gouge from Simone's saw more deadly than its own slashing nails. It fell from its perched position on the window sill, fell backwards, contorting though the air in shock before it hit the ground.

Another black skinned creature leaped from the darkness, grabbed Kirsten's shoulder, its claws digging into her leather jacket, spinning her around face to face with its mesmerizing eyes. Disorientated for a second, she stuck the gun's barrel under its chin, instantly unloaded it, an ear ringing explosion went off around them as the creature's head erupted onto the ceiling and walls in a splatter of black gore and bioluminescent light. It fell to the floor and began to try and recompose itself. Reaching around with flailing arms, trying to scoop and mop up the eviscerated parts it was now missing.

Trembling, Kirsten led the way again. Her mind scrambled, she tried to remember her bearings in the dark, hitting her top speed as she ran.

Seeing movement in the shadows ahead, she detoured into the old ballroom. Slamming the door shut behind them, Mickey and Geena threw their weapons down and pulled a pair of old, turned over chairs against them, jamming them under the handles.

'They're everywhere, let's cut through here an…' Kirsten said out of breath, pausing as a cold draft wafted over the beads of sweat pouring down her face. She turned to her left, in a far corner, emerging from the ballroom's shadows, a red curly haired girl stood, calmly staring at them.

Kirsten shocked, stepped back, trod on an old spray paint can and fell, hitting the dusty floor with a thud, she knew her face, didn't know her face, then remembered.

Geena's face erupted in smile. 'Oh my God! Charley! What are you doing here?'

She ran towards her old friend, her old school rival, never more happy to see her.

Charley held her arms out, wanting to embrace, wanting to hold her, a deadly crocodile grin, peeling over her face.

CHAPTER 29

'No! Don't, you stupid bitch!' Simone shouted.

'How'd you get up here?' Geena smiled, feet pounding forward.

Charley silently smiled back, beckoning her forward with her fingers.

Kirsten quickly crawled along the floor, lunged out and grabbed Geena's legs, pulling her face first straight down.

Mickey remembered where they were, what they had left down here from earlier. He nodded to Simone, then at the sidewall, where, lying against it, was one of the battering ram doors filled with knives.

They bolted for it, grabbed it, pummeled full speed ahead, moving either side of the door's length to avoid wild clawing hands.

Geena saw what was happening, the world suddenly gone mad.

'Nooooooo! That's Charley,' she screamed, 'she's my...'

The collection of knives impaled into Charley's midsection, blood erupted from her, she bellowed out in screams no human girl should make, slipped on her own spilled viscera and fell to the floor.

'Friend!' Geena finished, her eyes wide with what she was witnessing.

Mickey picked his hoe up from the floor, moved back to the siren that struggled under the door, raised the worn garden instrument high then pummeled its head in with one wet 'thwack'.

'Nooooo!' Geena rabidly cried.

Simone pulled her saw to life again with its petrol fed cry, walked towards the downed creature, teeth bared, the chainsaw her mechanical roar, then took its blade to Charley's throat. A geyser of blood shot diagonally from the girl's neck.

Words spewed from Geena's mouth, no breath between them,

'That's Charley Reynolds we were best friends at school my dad bought a flat from her dad we used to go out on the pull a few years ago you can't saw her up Simonneeeeee!'

A disgusting pop came from Charley's neck, a head no longer attached to it.

'You killed her!' Geena screamed. 'You killed her!' 'You killed her!' 'You killed her!' Scrambling to her feet running over as if she could save her, looking down to see her decapitated head staring back with glowing eyes.

Geena screamed and fell into Simone's arms, as Mickey teed off with the hoe, and sent Charley's head rolling off into the shadows.

'It's fine! She's one of them… it's fine!'

All of a sudden, another black skinned siren appeared from the darkness beside Kirsten, its arm's darting out to grab her. Then three more sirens were coming towards the girls, closing in, circling them.

The hotel, a place left to decay, was now a place riddled with parasites. Nothing as innocuous as insect life, wood worms, termites or cockroaches, things that would destroy its foundations or revel in their own filth and squalor. The parasites in this house wanted one thing only: to destroy its human occupants.

Mickey ran towards them striking blindly with the hoe, swinging, tearing black, pulpy lumps of flesh from them with harsh swipes, slicing deep cuts across faces, trying to put the lights out in their heads.

'*Come on!*' he screamed in high-pitched, maddened, desperate tones, his face red with fury.

Slowly, the creatures drew back from the girls, their attention placed solely on the boy who was tearing their tarred bodies to ribbons. Now he was circled, now they stalked him, glowing eyes and reaching hands all moving towards him like a slow motion car crash.

'Go!' he screamed at the girls, *'Come on!'* he screamed again in a shrill, despairing tone at the creatures.

Instinctively, he knew behind him was the doorway to another of the hotel's old, dark rooms, jeering and goading the sirens to follow him back through it, to leave the girls alone. Cornered, he moved towards the door, reached for the handle and pulled it.

Nothing. Locked.

Looking up in panic, the sirens drew in on him.

'No! No!' Kirsten screamed, a pang of guilt firing through her body at the thought that the boy she had only known for a day, the boy who was a friend of her cousin, might die because of her.

Her cries sending goosebumps up his arms and pumping pure fear through his heart. He leapt forward making three quick slashes towards the creatures, each swipe contacting with their reaching limbs, causing deep, wet lacerations. He took a run up to the locked door, using his teenage frame as a battering ram, jarring the rotten door open with a wooden crack, yelling and screaming like a loon, the bleeding sirens taking chase behind him.

Desperate tears filled their eyes, a sinking feeling in each of their stomachs, each one wanting to run after Mickey, but knowing they needed to take the opportunity the boy had given them to get to the roof. They pulled the main ballroom doors open, doubling back, evacuating like a blast of air, running back down the hallway they had come from. A cold feeling hung all around them, a feeling that they would never see Mickey again.

CHAPTER 30

As they ran on the east side of the hotel, Mickey ran to the west, stumbling down derelict hallways. Terror coursed through his veins as he moved through the shadows. Quick flashes of graffiti; spray-painted images and words on old wallpaper flashed past him as his feet beat against the old, threadbare carpet. Panicking and desperate he began pulling on door handles, begging, praying to find salvation in an unlocked one. Looking over his shoulder, a horde of glowing eyes flared with fury as they came nearer. Covered in the cold sweat of dread, a sickness grew in his stomach, what would happen if they caught him? What would they do with those claws if they were close enough? All made a shiver bolt through his body.

Pushing those thoughts away, he pulled another door handle, it creaked then jarred, jerking him to a stop as it swung outwards. Wanting to be anywhere other than where he was right now, he dived inside, slamming the door shut behind him. Instantly he was plunged into undiluted darkness, no light cut into the new room. Only a deep, nautical stench attacked his nose, his sense of smell seemingly the only thing of use in the darkness. He held the door handle, tensed and paused, listening to the creatures footsteps pad up to the other side, then stop.

No,no,no,no,no,no, he repeated in his mind, trying to stop the door handle from shaking with as much will as he still had over his trembling hands. Blood pumping loudly around his body, chest pounding, he listened, holding his breath. He could hear inhuman whispers between the things. Carefully pressing his face to the door, his eye found a gap between its boards, a shard of light passed over it, the lights of the siren's eyes beamed around the hallway. With vacant, long faced stares, they turned, looked at one another, communicating with more undecipherable murmurs – his hiding place worked as they turned and headed back to where they had come from.

Letting out a deep sigh, his beating heart seemed to pause for a second in relief. He reached around his pockets looking for his lighter, glad for once he hadn't let either Simone or Geena 'accidentally borrow it' from him permanently. Flicking it as silently as possible, its sparking flint seemed as loud as a rocket in the room's silence. The lighter's small flame exploded, a quick wide burst, illuminating old, wooden stairs beneath him, his trainers only an inch away from the top step.

On the wall next to him was an old, brass light switch, dulled brown through time and dirty hands. He reached for it, down the flight of stairs a single, ancient bulb popped to life, cobwebs pregnant with dust stringing from it to a series of red brick archways under the building.

It was an old cellar, more murkiness than light, obscurity than clarity, everything covered in a thick layer of damp.

Letting the flame from the lighter drop, he pulled two, heavy wooden crates across the door, blocking it shut and moved downwards.

Trapped in this small space, everything suddenly raced through his mind at once.

If the girls were okay. If the creatures would come back. If he could escape.

Calming his breathing and leaning against a red brick arch, he pushed his sweat drenched hair from his eyes, unaware that in the corner of the room behind him, a pool of dank liquid had formed. It was a fault in the buildings foundations from years ago that allowed water to seep up from the sea, destroying the foundations with damp, rotting the wood and plaster around it. Over the years it had stagnated, fermenting into a rancid stale quagmire.

It was a pool that had been still for years, a stillness that was now broken. Quick quivering ripples began to appear across it as slowly, a blackened dome rose up from the center. A siren's head ascended. Standing up fully, outstretching its clawed hands, poised like a stalking cat. It stepped forward onto the dirt earth floor, wet feet creating faded wet footprints, footprints that were slowly leading with each silent step straight towards the distracted Mickey.

* * *

Kirsten, Geena and Simone had made their way into another room. Slamming the door behind them, the rank smell of rot hung in the air around them, it was a thing they couldn't escape as much as the sirens. The filthiest mattress any of them had ever seen lay in the corner, needles and cider cans littering around it.

'We've gotta get to the roof,' Kirsten panted, finding it difficult to catch her breath. 'The ammo's there. I only have a few rounds left. Up there we have the advantage.'

'I know,' said Simone.

Geena went to weep again, Simone threw her arms around her and held her close.

'We can do this, 'she whispered reassuringly,' 'Everyone's going to be okay.'

Simone punched the button on the walkie-talkie's side, yelling into its microphone for Mickey.

* * *

Far off at the other end of the hotel, deep in its old cellar, his radio crackled making him jump. He grabbed it, hearing the broken stilted voice of Simone through a microwaved filter of analogue snow. Unable to understand her words, he punched his radio's own button and shouted her name in response, their distant voices only clarifying to either that the other was still alive.

Excited, his spirits momentarily raised, he turned around

trying to get a better reception, then stopped in horror as he came face to face with the snarling black sea creature.

He froze, mesmerized by its eyes, as if caught in the twin circles of two spotlights. It's fishy stink filling his nostrils. He had no time to move, to run or react. He just watched as it raised its right hand, the glossy claws on the end of its fingers glistening with wetness, lit by the drab bulb above. They plunged down in a quick lighting sweep, slashing him straight across the chest.

With a surprised yell, he fell backwards to the floor, his spine and lower back fully absorbing the impact as he reached for the bleeding cuts. Five long scratches stung like being raked with lava tipped razors, the pain burning all over his body like hell fire.

Looking up towards the siren, he watched as it retreated backwards, slinking behind the red brick arches, only its silhouette against the old, muted light bulb made it visible. It was moving slowly behind crates and barrels, shielded from plain sight.

His eyes grew wider now, seeing that just like that, just like a click of the fingers, it had morphed into a human form, its black oily skin now gone, its claws vanished. Something else was in the shadows now, a boy moved forward, naked, smiling, eyes focused straight on him. A twisted double of himself stepped into the light.

'Mickeyyyy,' it whispered, 'Mickeyyyy.'

* * *

Upstairs, Kirsten grabbed the walkie-talkie from Simone and punched its button. 'The roof, Mickey, come to the roof! Come to the roof!'

Suddenly the door to the room shunted forward. Geena, who had her back braced to it, screamed and pushed back against it with all her might, black, screeching fingers reaching around its jamb.

* * *

In the cellar, Geena's scream somehow travelled down a clear beam of reception, ricocheted around the small, enclosed space, echoing from Mickey's walkie-talkie. As the glowing-eyed doppelgänger stalked towards him wanting the original that existed before it, who crawled backwards holding his tingling, bleeding chest, to not exist anymore.

The double's face grinned a devil's smile, reaching out towards him as the illumination of its eyes intensified.

Its body was perfect, his own scars – his suicide scars – on his wrists gone from this replica.

A thought flashed through Mickey's mind: this was it, the scarless body, the blank, emotionless eyes, that primal instinct to kill regardless. Its complexion perfect, no marks or spots. His words from the roof with Kirsten came ironically jangling back towards him.

This was the version of himself his father wanted, this was the variation of himself that was acceptable in his eyes. If this thing lived and he died, life at home would be different, he could feel and sense it wouldn't just survive in that environment with his mean spirited father – it would thrive in it.

His father pushed him with his own ideals – don't trust anyone, everyone's out for number one, it's you or them. Calling him a 'pussy' because he didn't want to go on hunting trips. Calling him a 'loser' because he didn't enjoy the banality of school.

Saying, 'You couldn't even get that right' when he visited him in hospital after slitting his wrists.

His father wanted him to fit in. Wanted him to be like everyone else – everyone else being just like his father.

But this soulless, empty thing, a thing that based its intellect on parasitic instinct rather than free thought, a thing born of a simple scratch, wasn't his doppelgänger. It was his father's.

From its grimacing face, he could tell it held more traits in common with his old man than himself.

The thing before him was an insult to his very being, to every idiosyncrasy for better or worse that was his own.

This was the son his dad had always wanted.

This was the son he deserved.

Anger surged where fear bubbled only a moment ago.

As it reached down for him, he remembered what he'd made earlier, the 'surprises' and reached for the back of his jeans, taking out one of the hammers with the rifle bullet taped to the end. He lifted it high, swinging it down with all the might he could muster, straight onto the creature's foot.

A deafening blast exploded out, a bright, burning, gunpowder flash blinded him. Rolling to one side and covering his face, the loud whistle in his ears cleared and he could hear the creature screaming in pain louder than the blast itself.

Looking up, watching it recoil, watching 'himself' recoil, he jumped to his feet. Black blood sprayed from the ragged flesh and bones that protruded where toes should be. Mickey clambered to his feet, reached for the other hammer then with another mighty swing, pummeled it into the thing's skull. With a gut wrenching crack and another flash of light, his double spasmodically flinched backwards, a ragged wet hole in its fragmented head, its hair smoldering to burnt clumps.

It brainlessly reached for him again, blankly stumbling forward, trying to regain its balance. Its movements disjointed, oily blackness pouring over its once perfect skin. Eyes flickering like a broken florescent tube in an old bathroom.

The thing, injured, probably dying, held no remorse or understanding. It dragged itself towards him, still powered by a primal craving for human flesh.

Quickly he grabbed for his jeans again pulling out a fourteen inch kitchen knife, then, with no hesitation, with a wild glee, he repeatedly stabbed the creature in its torso, penetrating his own pigeon chest.

It made no attempt to defend itself, it just screamed its banshee wail even louder. The feeling of the knife plunging in sent cathartic waves through his own body. Fuck his old man, fuck his life at home, and fuck this thing. Fuck the teachers at school; fuck the arseholes who laughed at him, fuck everything and fuck them all.

When he had slit his own wrists, he hadn't felt any euphoria in trying to take his own life, but in killing this thing – killing himself – that muted rage that dwelled within was finally released.

The screams, his own and the thing's, echoed out. It fell to the floor trying to drag itself away now as streams of black, viscous fluid fired from its punctured back, and he stabbed, and he stabbed, and he stabbed. Pulling itself back into the pool of water it came from, Mickey followed, ventilating it with fourteen inches of Sheffield's finest steel, still stabbing into its skin as it slid off into the depths of the old pool, its scream a gurgling trail of bubbles as it left a cloud of black blood misting behind it.

He watched, panting, gripping the knife tightly, looking for something to keep stabbing, but unable to find it. Then he turned to the stairs, adrenaline pumped its high-voltage juice through his system. He had to get back to the girls. An idea popped in his mind, he saw red, it flickered in his mind to a crackling orange. These things couldn't live, these things had to die. He smiled. He knew what to do. Knowing time was of the essence and nothing could get in his way he opened the door.

CHAPTER 31

Dark hands reached around the door as the three girls pushed back against it.

'How the hell are we going to get out of here?' Geena cried.

Kirsten, awkwardly beat at the swiping claws with the butt of the rifle.

'After three, we go, just follow me,' Simone yelled, yanked on the chainsaw's ripcord and it roared to life.

'One!' She sank its blade, like a hot knife in butter through the old, rotten door, a cacophony of siren screams sounded from behind as it tore into them.

'Two!' Kirsten gripped the rifle, ready to swing its butt into the face of anything that got in her way, Geena, knowing she had to be brave, collected herself, standing upright and raising the garden fork.

'Three! – Go!' She wrenched the saw from the door, they bolted into the hallway, its faded, antique wallpaper now refreshed with a fresh coat of oily blood.

Following Simone's lead, they ran back towards the roof, chainsaw buzzing like a mad hornet, ready to strike anything in its way.

Geena threw a glance over her shoulder, shadows moved with sirens speeding towards them, eyes burning, cries high pitched, wailing, ferocious, gaining on them.

They followed Simone as she ran up a flight of iron stairs, stairs that they recognized as the entrance to the open rooftop. She got to the top, threw the small metal doors open, stumbling through and falling to the floor on one knee. Managing somehow to keep the ticking saw away from her, she struggled to her feet.

The sirens were swarming up the stairs, hot on their heels, not just the black, oily ones in chase now but ones in human form, some dressed in work wear, formal and blue collar, all uniformed with the same glowing eyes.

Kirsten cocked the rifle and unloaded the last two rounds down into the oncoming creatures, stalling them in their tracks with its echoing shots.

Simone and Geena slammed the door's shut, one either side, throwing their backs against them as Kirsten frantically scrambled to the other side of the roof to get the ammo.

She fell to her knees, frantically searching through the boxes, turning and looking over her shoulder at Simone and Geena, the creatures pounding against the doors, their violent vibrations reverberating through their bodies. Geena froze solid, she was like a stone statue with a rapid pulse, trembling at the sounds of them clawing at the door with fast, metallic slashes.

'Come on!' Simone screamed, a manic tone in her voice.

Kirsten quickly loaded rounds into the gun, the girl's cries making her work at double speed, hot sweat dripping from the end of her nose, hitting the gun's cold barrel and spiraling down its length.

Suddenly, she fumbled, becoming aware of something; a presence that sent shivers the size of arctic shards down her spine, a manifestation that felt jarringly familiar, but alien and distant.

She stopped, closing the rifle's chamber, hearing the soft crunch of footsteps over her shoulder.

Spinning around, she paused, her jaw falling and locking open in awe and terror, face to face with herself, her doppelgänger, the Kirsten siren that took her face under the pier.

* * *

Below them, back in the hotel kitchen, Mickey ran back into the parlor, he looked around for the adjustable spanner he'd had earlier, couldn't find it. No time for searching, no time for anything. Quickly he gathered up some old newspapers, lengths of brittle board and tore up a section out of dried carpet. He piled it all together, laughed, reached for his pocket, took out the lighter and began to flick it. Its flame burst to life again and he ignited the paper, blowing on it, making it catch the rest of the makeshift kindling alight. He reached for a brick lying by the filth ringed sink. Ran back to the parlor and began hammering the gas pipe's valve end. It ricocheted, rumbled, bent and buckled. He pummeled it hard and faster, yelling, flecks of sweat falling from his face, chest aching, anger growing, then, Snap! Sssssssssssssssss. The pipe end was in two, a hollow poisonous hiss bellowing from its end. Gas spilled into the room, claustrophobia clutching him, the fire – now beginning to roar – fifteen feet away, felt like fifteen inches. He turned, jumped the flames, laughing like an escapee from a loony bin, looking like an escapee from a loony bin, and ran for everything he was worth, as the invisible explosive seeped across the room.

* * *

Kirsten's siren slinked towards her clothed in a tight, black outfit, cast away old garments, wet and glistening from the lunar glow above.

She stared deeply into its eyes, mesmerized, partly by its ability to possess someone by their senses, partly because it was like watching a life-size photograph with a pulse. When she was in London, she had studied a full-sized air brushed poster of herself up close, an image to be used for the promotion of a new clothing range.

Her face, lineless and clean of imperfections with digital aids – the thing before her physically dismissing such modern technology – born from a bloody talon with a perfection she could never have in her own reality.

It grabbed the rifle, yanked it from her grasp, throwing it to the side of the roof. Its cold hands grabbed either side of her face.

She reached up, trying to prize them away feeling herself being walked backwards as the creature's mouth gaped open, its gullet becoming a hypnotic tunnel of bright light, its hallucinatory glow forcing her back towards the edge of the building.

Simone and Geena could only scream out, both unable to move, unable to help Kirsten without exacerbating the situation with the addition of a hallway full of creatures bursting through the doors. Both stuck between a rock and a hard place.

Simone, hot headed, anxious and angry, her better judgment dropped, tried to step away from the door. Grabbing black hands and sharp clawed fingers appeared around its jamb making her jump back into position. Geena screamed to high heaven, a scream that made the creatures on the other side push harder, wanting the frightened girl.

Suddenly there was another sound: stomping and clambering up an old iron fire escape on the side of the building, a pair of hands grabbing the lip of the roof. Both of the trapped girls trembled in terror.

Battered, bloody, and bruised, Mickey's hands pitched him up onto their level, he quickly assessed the situation, then ran towards them.

'Her! Her!' Simone yelled, gesturing to Kirsten.

He turned to see the creature frog marching her backwards to the side of the roof, its face glowing from any opening. Instinctively, he lunged towards them, putting his head down like an American football player, running like lightning, hitting the pair like a runaway train, spilling them either side, splitting them apart like a pair of conjoined twins, their bodies crunching as they hit the deck.

Below, the plume of gas rolled deeper into the kitchen, filling the entire space, reaching towards the only opening it could find – the main door, a blazing fire in its frame.

It moved to escape, tried to whisk through, tried to… A deep, white flash opened in the kitchen, a flash more penetrating than a photographer's bulb, a flash louder, more thunderous than any rifle. A bomb was dropped through the old hotel, fire travelling back up the gas pipe, back around the building, blowing every radiator and boiler in the place from the wall in a lapping, holocaustic roar of flame. Every dead room, every dead bathroom, every dead hallway, instantly igniting in a deep, ravaging orange. The entire building shook, everything paused as the explosion cracked out like a nuclear strike.

Geena and Simone jerked from the door, stumbled and threw themselves back against it. Mickey fell, smashing his head against the roof's concrete surround, eyes slowly opening, vision fuzzy, looking up to see two Kirsten's – one dazed, her eyes swimming from the fall, the other slithering to a crouching position, eyes yellowed, nocturnal.

The real Kirsten's mind spun inside her skull, she blinked, wanted to puke, then murmured low but urgently, '...The gun!'.

Mickey, dazed himself, scanned his blurred eyes around the floor. Then managed to focus, seeing the weapon scattered to one side.

'Get it, Mickey! Get it!' Geena yelled frenziedly.

He moved as quickly as he could, feeling winded, feeling broken, he grabbed the gun, slid it backwards along the rough floor, scratches tearing down its slick, black barrel.

Kirsten saw it moving towards her while the siren rose to her feet, staring at the girl whose face it had taken, fury passing over its features.

The real Kirsten reached for the rifle, grabbed it, raised it up but paused for a second at the impossibility of aiming the gun and being able to place herself in its cross hairs. It felt as if she was going to blow a hole in her own reflection.

Tension built in the air.

Simone screamed.

Geena screamed.

Flames leapt from the hotel windows, the spray painted

gargoyles on the building's front breathing fire that lapped the concrete surround of the roof.

Everything ground to a slow motion drawl.

The siren, enraged, leapt forward, reaching out, its fingers as jagged and twisted as dead tree branches. Running straight at her, its eyes blazing like two pieces of coal embedded in its face, vocal cords reaching an inhuman pitch.

Kirsten held her breath, aimed at the evil replica of herself, its reach coming nearer and nearer as it cut towards her through the night air, her target becoming bigger and bigger.

Closing her eyes, she pumped the trigger. A loud crack exploded from the rifle barrel.

The sound of the oncoming double's footsteps stopped.

She opened her eyes.

There in front of her was herself again, this time staggering, with a huge black patch squirting from its chest, its glowing eyes rolling around in its skull.

The real Kirsten ran forward, holding the gun across her chest, using it as a battering ram, pushing the double backwards to the edge of the roof.

With one final push, Kirsten's double lost its balance, fell head first over the concrete barrier, clearing it perfectly, straight towards the ground below.

Its turning body twisted through the air, falling, licked by the flames bursting from windows, screaming its siren's wail before a sickening thud ended its unearthly high-pitched cry.

For a moment there was complete silence.

Kirsten fell to her knees, exhausted, trying to regulate her rapid breathing. She slowly drew herself up, peered over the edge, staring at an image she was never supposed to see – herself, lying crumpled like a stepped on insect, arms twisted impossibly over her head, legs bent in abstract directions that no living person or their foul doppelgänger could ever physically survive.

It was caught up in a thicket of brambles, entwined in their barbed tendrils. She thought back to the spider's web in Simone's window, the doppelgänger now the one caught inside, unable to escape, death was the spider, coming to stockpile it with its other victims. The incandescent lights in the siren's eyes dulled, then, slowly, died.

In the distance the sun began to rise.

Smoke bellowed out, timber popped as the fire did its job.

Simone and Geena felt the creatures' tirade stop, behind the metal doors dying screams ripped from scorching lips, unable to escape the fire that cooked their skin they flailed in defeat, tearing at the inferno that smothered them wildly. Their claws no good now, no hypnotic song now, only the sound of defeated hisses and crackling flames.

Too scared to move, Simone and Geena trembled as they looked at one another, sliding down the doors, their arses hitting the floor simultaneously with a dull thump. They stared over at Kirsten and Mickey, a vacant relief now dwelling where fear once prevailed.

Simone began to laugh, a far off, maniacal laugh, like a female Vincent Price.

Geena recoiled from her, emotionally reacting the opposite way as tears poured down her face. The two girls a yin and yang, a pair of Greek theatre masks, two opposites, as they were and always would be.

Mickey smiled, the pain of the scratches on his chest strangely not as bad as they looked through his ragged shirt as a far off tingle seemed to sew the wound back together, dulling the pain with every stitch.

Kirsten laid her head on the roof's concrete barrier, staring down at the crumpled mess of herself below, veiled with gusts of black smoke.

'Falling, falling, falling…' she whispered, thinking of what Melissa Clarke had said to her, her advice pointless and arbitrary at the time, now resonating a definitive poignancy.

This is what she meant, she thought, *this is how it ends.*

The sea wind cut into Kirsten's face, making her squint, tears welling in her eyes, and for some reason the melancholy sound of the saxophonist back on the pier played in her mind. The drawn-out, lonesome sound mingling with the rolling waves around her again, soothing her, calming her, and making her heavy eyelids close, cutting off the image of her own death.

CHAPTER 32

As the siren lay entangled in brambles, a rearranged mess, the earth around it slowly darkening with its oily, black blood. Down on the beach below, pale and gaunt, life force drained, as weak and fragile as a walking corpse, Mellissa Clarke looked up towards the blazing Grand Hotel.

The creature's cry had grown in her mind, she followed it like walking an invisible beam, and it drew her here – to the girl. She had been here all night, waiting.

When she met Kirsten, her fate was a two-way road, she had given her a chance to try and solve the situation with her, both of them could have solved this together, but the loud mouth cousin, Simone, had sealed her fate with that option.

It was a one-way road now; and she knew what she must do.

She knew Kirsten and her friends would come here, knew how they would try to stop it, knew it wasn't over. She had seen it all on that first day when she visited their flat.

Now, there was only that other way.

As Kirsten, climbed from the roaring hotel, drove away in the old VW with the others, victory in her heart. The siren's spectral cry pulsated in Melissa's cranium once more, making her a prisoner inside her own mind, building a wall on the inside of her skull like a macabre architect she couldn't escape from.

There was only one way to escape it.

Melissa made her way towards the hotel, climbed an old, worn path up the side of the cliff.

Blood began to build inside her nose in dark pools. It gushed over her lips as she held her pounding head.

She knew the way things had to happen. Her clairvoyant instincts told her what had to be done. How this situation would play out now, how it would end this internal agony that had been inflicted upon her.

The siren's cry attacked her brain again like the frozen end of a pickaxe. She fell to her knees, warm trickles of blood snaked from her ears now, muting the soft sway of the sea.

Melissa moved closer to the hotel, moved closer to where they thought the dead siren lay.

Where nothing lay.

She smiled, teeth stained red.

Day was breaking, the pain would lessen – it always did during the day. But tonight she would cut her connections to them. Empty her mind of them both. Two was company, three was a crowd, and she knew it had to end now, no matter the cost.

CHAPTER 33

As dawn broke, two boys kicked a football about the council flat gardens. Kyle and Wesley, both were aged ten, both had been out all night, both not old enough to be out all night, both bored, both not really knowing what bored really was.

'When do ya think ya brother will go out?' Kyle asked.

'Dunno,' Wesley replied, cuffing his nose. 'Think he's got some girl in there, he's gotta kick her out sometime. He'll go.'

'Then we can play on his Xbox, right?' Kyle almost pleaded, his daily intake of recreational radiation from a flat screen TV as much a fix as a junkie craving heroin.

'Yeah,' Wesley blurted. 'I hope he doesn't come back either, the bastard.'

'He still beating you up, is he?' Kyle asked, emotionless.

'He tried to. Mum said she'll take his benefit money away if it tries it again.'

Both stopped kicking the ball, spitting on the floor one after the other.

'So, what do you wanna do then?' Wesley asked.

It was then Kyle had an idea.

'Let's go annoy that fat bloke in the subway.'

'Yeah! The fat prick!' Wesley agreed spitting on the floor again.

'My mum says he's a disgrace.'

'Yeah! A disgrace!' Wesley agreed, spitting on the floor once more.

'My mum was talking to your mum the other day,' Kyle said, ' They were talking about that fat prick, said he's just a ponce, a burden on society a stinking good for nothing.'

'When was that?' Wesley asked.

'Tuesday, when they were both signing on.'

The pair walked down to the subway. All was still with an

eerie silence, but there, in the tunnel's darkened center, were the dirty boxes that the stinking man was always found in.

From a distance, Kyle could see an opening into the boxes, he could make out what he thought was a pale, sleeping face.

'Is he in there?' whispered Wesley

'Yeah, course he is! Where else has he got to go?' Kyle sneered.

'What's his name again? Terry?'

'Barry,' Kyle spat out.

'That's it.' Taking the football from Kyle, an impish, devious grin on his face, Wesley shouted 'Barry! Barry, mate! You stink!'

They both laughed, but no reply came from the boxes.

'He's pissed.' Wesley laughed. 'Watch this…' He ran towards the boxes, threw the ball in the air and kicked it with all his might, straight at the ragged hole in the tramp's cardboard hut.

'Take this, you stinking wanker!' Wesley screeched, a huge smile on his face, Kyle laughing before the ball even hit its mark.

The cardboard around the tramp split away as the ball hit with a cold, wet, 'thwap', rebounding off the ceiling of the subway, hitting Wesley in the chest, and rolling to a stop on the floor. The ball's point of impact was recorded with rounded red stains that decorated the underpass. Bloodstains. Wesley touched his once white football shirt, now dotted red like a Japanese flag.

The sleeping tramp lay lifeless on the cold, concrete floor, his face a petrified mask, his rib cage pulled open, insides on the outside, intestines and entrails falling from his shredded guts like the strings of sausages and meat their mums brought back from the market, all chewed up raw. Barry the ponce, the burden on society, the stinking good for nothing had been eaten from the inside out.

Any boredom the boys had felt previously was now gone. Both crying and filled with terror as they screamed and ran from the bloodied underpass all the way home.

CHAPTER 34

The following evening, Mickey, Simone, Kirsten and Geena lay in a circle of sleeping bags on Simone's front room floor. The downing sunlight poured through the window in a hazy glare, sheering through the slats of the heavy wooden blinds. Each of them bruised, aching and sleeping the greatest sleep of all sleeps. Each of them dreamed, distant unrecorded visions none would remember on waking.

Mickey stirred and opened his eyes, memories of the previous night instantly poured in to his mind and ensured that he wouldn't get back to sleep. He lay awake, his eyes fixed on a time in the not so distant past, only twelve hours ago, when he had literally taken a knife to a copy of himself, he remembered the eyes – the glowing eyes – how he stared into them before plunging it into 'himself'. He thought of the blades heavy blows, the meaty thuds that reverberated up its handle and back into his body, each strike feeling just as sickening as the last, but at the same time feeling good.

It could have been worse, the blood could have been red. The black tar-like substance allowed him to distance himself from the experience, but cemented its more surreal elements in others.

He thought back to when Geena had told him Kirsten's story. About the scratch creating another of you, him seemingly the only one apart from Kirsten falling prey to the creature's strange survivalist cycle.

Hers spread over the course of a week, his finishing in the matter of minutes. Of course, it was dead. It had to be. Kirsten's doppelgänger was shot and thrown from a roof, the rest burned alive, he had personally filleted his own. Yes it had escaped back into the water, but nothing could survive that… could it?

He didn't want the girls to worry. He had kept his encounter with the siren to himself, kept it a secret that it had slashed his skin, that it had taken his form and tried to take his identity.

When they had returned last night he quickly changed his top, putting on a black T-shirt to hide any blood that might seep from his own wounds. But on closer inspection, cleaning the red mess on his chest, it seemed to be more superficial than it originally felt. He felt lucky, like he had gotten away with something. Either that or… either that or somehow it had already begun to heal.

'Is that it then?' he heard a meek voice say, and saw Geena's panda eyes peering out from her sleeping bag as vacantly as his were only a second ago.

Slowly the others sighed their first breaths of the day and awoke, bleary eyed and absent from their surroundings.

It was silent for a moment, then Kirsten spoke.

'It's what she said, the psychic,' she yawned, 'falling, falling, it's either you or that other one.'

'You killed it though, didn't you?' Geena said with a cold timbre present in her voice.

'Nothing could have survived that fire,' Mickey added.

'Hang on,' Geena added, reaching for her phone, searching Google, her mouth falling open. 'Oh my God!'

'What?' Simone said blearily, rustling up from her sleeping bag.

She held her phone out, a news headline, 'Grand Hotel Decimated in Fire' a wide shot of the Grand, now a blackened, skeletal structure, engulfed in thick orange flames.

'There ain't nothing getting out of that is there?'

'Jesus.' Mickey said. 'What's it say.'

Geena scrolled down her phone, quickly digesting titbits of information.

'It's still burning now, they reckon vandals found a live gas main and lit it up.'

Simone huffed out a laugh, looked at Mickey. 'They got that right.'

'We did it,' Kirsten said evenly, 'nothing could survive that. Nothing.'

She pondered for a moment, reaffirming herself.

'It's dead. It's dead,' she added with a deep, thoughtful sincerity.

A silence fell over the room.

'But how do we know, like really know?' Geena wondered.

'Look at that picture on your phone! Do you know anything that could survive that?' Mickey said.

'S'pose,' Geena replied, thoughtfully looking at the image of the burning building.

'Yeah but... what about... all the people... like Charley.'

A somber tone lay amongst them. 'She was my mate once, we used to...' A tear fell from Geena's eye, 'Simone... you... used that saw... you...'

'She was gone!' Simone yelled. 'Gone! Anyone those things got were gone, dead men walking, dead women walking. What I did was...'

She thought about the bloody saw, her trembling hands, the repulsion, the terror of killing another, she had kept her true feelings of this event secret at the time, she would keep them secret now, too.

Simone knew how to be strong, had survived her own emancipation from her family, did it all alone. Now she would survive this, like she helped Kirsten survive this, like she would help them all survive it.

'What I did was... kept you alive, Geena, you're a dick, a complete dick. But I do love you.'

Tears fell from Geena's eyes, 'I love you, too.'

Mickey and Kirsten smiled. 'Look! We're the fucking dream team!' Simone yelled out with a dirty laugh. "We lived, we can party, we can fuck, we can eat pizza until we have waist lines like the fucking Pillsbury Dough Boy! We survived! That's what's important!'

Simone slapped a kiss on Geena's snotty face.

'Errr watch my make-up!' she cried back.

'You need to look in a mirror, it's fucked love!'

Geena panicked, took out her phone and used her camera like a mirror.

They each snorted out a laugh or sigh of relief with the solemn tension broken.

'Jesus Christ, it's over,' Kirsten exclaimed, tears of relief falling from her eyes.

Simone sat up, an almost nipple revealing side boob falling from her vest. A sight that used to be Mickey's dream, a thing that had taken second place to now possibly catching sight of Geena's nipple revealing side boob instead.

'You don't have to cry about it, babes,' Simone said, roughly rubbing her face, think of the material you can make out of this shit for your portfolio.'

'I don't know if that's going to happen,' Kirsten said regretfully.

'Don't be a div, of course it is.' Simone blatted out another frothy laugh and jumped up in happiness, going to the fridge, padding her bare feet on the wooden floorboards as she grabbed some beers, throwing a cold can to each of them.

'Celebration time, lads!' she screeched. Geena snapped back the silver ring pull with a loud cheer. 'Yeah! We did it,' and chugged down a quick rush of Red Stripe lager. Hoping it would take the haunting images away, wanting another before the first sip was even swallowed.

Mickey laughed, popped his own and took a sip. 'I better head home soon. My dad's back in two days. I gotta clean up the house.'

'You can come back whenever you want, Mickey, you're always welcome here,' Geena said with sincerity as she sat up. He nodded, trying not to make too much eye contact with her, thinking back to her cherry-popping proposal from last night.

'Oh yeah,' Simone said after taking a gulp, 'I don't think you're just my gardener anymore, Mickey. You're family dude,' she reached for her wallet and threw him a fifty.

'I can't ta…'

'It's yours bruv, least I can do, and I'm not taking no for an answer.' Simone slammed the fridge door shut like a judge's gavel, to finalize her statement.

He scrunched up the red note and put it into the pocket of his jeans.

'Can I drive you home?' Kirsten asked him.

'Yes please.'

They got up to leave; both already dressed in yesterday's dirty clothes, stinking of sweat and smoke fumes.

Simone, a look of concern pouring over her face, took another mouthful of beer. 'You okay to go?'

'Yeah. I'm good.' Kirsten nodded back.

They held a look. Simone understanding she wanted to be alone, taking a step back from the role of her cousin's guardian she had played over the last few days.

'See you in a bit, yeah?' Kirsten said.

Simone nodded, a slight smile flickering where a serious concern used to lie on her face.

Geena jumped up and wrapped her arms around Mickey, pushing her C cups as far as possible into the boy's chest, then planted her lips on his.

He smiled, feeling awkward, keeping his eye contact arbitrarily in the realm of blank space, trying hard not to look at her tits.

Simone held a slight smile on her lips watching them leave, the grin dropping instantly as the door clicked back into the jamb. Geena turned around, a big goofy grin on her face, her nipples hard beneath her tight-fitting T-shirt.

'What the fuck was *that*?' Simone seethed, making Geena's smile drop to the floor.

Just a few hours ago she had wanted a refund on her dim-witted girlfriend, but tonight, after the stress of yesterday, she could think of nothing better than relieving some tension with Geena in the bedroom, to get her own haunting images out of her head.

'You getting all wet for boys now, bitch?' Simone asked, a huskiness dwelling in her voice.

'Give it a rest, he's jail bait,' Geena replied dully.

'What?' Simone cried.

'Yeah, fifteen, unreal innit.'

'How'd you find that out?'

'He told me last night, we had a chat, I was talking to him about protecting us, bringing that gun. He didn't want to bring it at first, I twisted his arm though.'

'I bet, what did you promise him?'

Geena blushed.

'I can read you like a book. You are a bad girl, Geena.' Simone rubbed her tongue over her lips slowly, 'I think it's about time you were a good girl to be honest,' she said not taking her eyes off of her, swallowing more of the beer.

Geena grinned cheekily and Simone smiled seductively, 'I think we deserve it... don't you?'

CHAPTER 35

Kirsten drew Simone's VW to a halt outside of Mickey's house. Night had all but set in now, the old streetlights splashed down in orange pools.

She pulled up the car's worn out handbrake, the plastic handle almost standing upright like an antennae. The pair sat in silence for a second. Not an uncomfortable one, just a relieved one.

'Why did you go along with it?' Kirsten asked. 'Why did you help us?'

Mickey thought about this before replying. 'It made sense...' he said flatly.

'I always wondered what to do, how to make sure I wouldn't grow up to be like my old man,' he turned to look at his house, 'I never knew if I was strong enough to stop being something I never wanted to be. Now I know I am.'

She nodded. 'I think I know what you mean.'

Silence fell upon them again, before Mickey, almost jumping out of his chair exclaimed, 'the gun! Shit, Simone took it inside. I gotta get that thing back tomorrow or my old man...'

'I'll drive it back first thing in the morning. I swear, we'll bring it back,' Kirsten said. She reached out to touch his hand, the physical connection between them both seeming to work as he calmed instantly.

'Okay, but make sure you do, yeah? It's important.'

'Yeah, course, don't worry. See you tomorrow.'

'Tomorrow,' he reiterated.

She smiled at him as he got out of the car, knowing that she was going to take the long way home, maybe go grab a drive through burger and just sit for a while, let things permeate in her mind for a bit. Give herself some 'me' time for a while, 'me' time that was all her own again, not a time to be shared with anyone or anything or any other variation of a 'me' that existed.

She watched as he went, thinking that only after knowing this boy a few days, he proved to be more of a friend than any of the people she had known for the last few years in London. Would they have risked their own lives to save hers? Highly doubtful.

Letting off the worn to the limit handbrake to the floor in one quick drooping movement, she pulled the car away, driving back down to the coast, that burger she promised herself on her mind.

Mickey walked up to the front door of his house, a panic coming over him as he thought of the gun, the one thing his old man would flip his lid over if he knew it was missing. His mind was away from the immediate, away from the here and now focusing on how he could have forgotten it, how he could have just left it propped up in the corner looking no different to an unused umbrella on a sunny day.

He searched his pockets for his keys, then paused.

There was a sound behind him, the shift of loose boards on the old wooden porch, slow, deliberate footsteps, the sound of something stalking, moving towards him not wanting to be noticed.

He looked up in the rippled, frosted glass window of the front door, seeing the outline of a figure stop in its tracks. Abstracted through the filter of glass in front of him, he couldn't tell if the shadowed figure was male, female… or something else.

A whisper passed his ears.

'Mickkkeeeeyyyyy'

A dark, smothering hand reached around his face, cutting off his vision. More hands reached from the darkness, pulling him backwards, unable to fight, to scream, to run, his feet and arms kicked and lashed, trapped in a prison of fingers, all pulling him towards the pond at the end of his garden, into the darkness of night, a place where he would never return from. As he was dunked backwards into the pond, the other 'him', his doppelgänger pushed down on him, pushed into him, ended him. Now there was only one Mickey that lived – his father's favourite one.

CHAPTER 36

Simone turned on the bath taps. Hot water turned into steaming fog that rose up into plumes of warm vapor around the room. Feeling the heat touch her flesh she stripped off the dirty clothes from last night and closed her eyes, enjoying the solitude behind her own eyelids.

Geena, only a few feet away in the bedroom, dropped the needle of Simone's old Sharp record player onto the first few grooves of a twelve-inch record. Pops and crackles filled the stereo's speakers, low electronic keys mixed with soulful synthetic pads on a Synthwave L.P.

Geena swayed, her musical choice as soothing as the sound of running water in the bathroom, she closed her eyes, slunk out of her clothes and moved from side to side in her underwear. Slithers of last night replayed before her eyes, it was like a slide show of the worst bits – the grisly bits. She held her head, wanted to forget, took a swig from the beer in her hand.

She looked into the hallway and saw the rifle leaning against the wall opposite. Her eyes widened in their sockets. Simone dressed in a towel stepped around the door, a waft of warm steam behind her like an old '80s music video. Staring at her scantily clad girlfriend, a river of desire flipped her internal switches on.

'Simone!' Geena cried, 'what did you bring the gun back in for?'

Just in case, just for tonight, she thought, a shiver causing goosebumps over her body. Her head throbbed, fighting back fear.

'I just forgot it.' She shrugged.

Geena stared at the gun, fear visible on her face. With her eyes still wide, her bright blonde hair, small frame and perky tits, Simone thought she looked like a perfectly drawn Hentai character.

'You look good,' she said.

Geena changed her transfixed gaze into a big, dirty grin. 'So do you.'

'Oh yeah?' Simone replied lasciviously. 'I thought you had bailed and were back into mankind again? Sure you don't want to wait for old Mickey boy to turn legal?'

'Naaaahhhh,' she replied swaying on the spot like an awkward child. 'I'm into you.'

They moved closer to one another, meeting halfway, in the bedroom. With a long, deep, passionate kiss, their bodies tingling with pure desire, they shared this fervent moment. They couldn't wait to explore each other's bodies as they had a couple of nights earlier. They both needed this, needed physical contact, needed to forget... *everything*. This was a moment that they would never share again after tonight.

In the bathroom, the water spewing from the taps began to splutter, just as the old water tank in the hotel had, turning the tub black, thick and polluted with an organic, living tar.

The once tranquil, hot bathwater, filled with the living protoplasm of the sirens, and slowly it took form.

CHAPTER 37

Hot, steaming water poured into the bathtub, misting up the mirror and tiles, turning the room into a humid biosphere. Geena and Simone parted lips, and still breathing heavily, touched foreheads.

'I need to jump in the tub,' Simone said.

Geena nodded towards the bathroom. 'Can I join you?'

'No. I want you dirty.'

Simone pushed her tongue out and licked Geena's lips quickly in a soft cat-like movement, staring deeply into the girl's make-up blotted eyes. They kissed again, now more passionately.

In the bathroom, with a groan of the building's old pipe work, the taps spluttered off. The once clean water, now a thick, tar-like oil, formed a vortex of black, living liquid. Bioluminescence fired beneath the surface bringing life to the mass as it morphed into a dark, humanoid form, non-descript features drawing together on a vague framework.

Simone broke their kiss and turned back to the bathroom.

'Hey!' Geena yelled, reaching out and yanking the towel from Simone and leaving her naked, she twirled it like a baton in victory.

Simone stood, stripped, the coldness of the open bay window caressing her soft skin, teasing it to more textured goosebumps.

She laughed. 'You cheeky little bitch, give it back,' and swiped the towel back from Geena, quickly wrapping it around her body.

As they played flirtatious games, neither was aware that in the bathroom, a dark-taloned hand slithered up from the tub, its ends so sharp it engraved the enamel with five jagged scores.

They pulled in close to one another again, their noses and lips almost touching, Simone playfully made a big biting motion at Geena's face, snapping at her like a shark. 'Mmmm, I could eat you all up...'

'Are you sure you don't want me in there with you?' Geena said, marching towards the bathroom door, unaware of what was lurking beyond it.

Simone reached out and grabbed her arm, pulling her backwards playfully.

'No, I want your arse in there,' Simone said, nodding towards the bedroom door. Pulling a cartoonish frown over her face, Geena slunk onto the bed on all fours, her well-shaped rear end pushed up towards Simone. 'Hurry up then,' she said rolling onto her back and spreading her legs.

Dopey the girl might be, Simone thought, but when it came to games in the bedroom, she knew what she was doing.

Dragging her eyes from the sight of the sexy girl on her bed, Simone walked into the bathroom, throwing open the door. She couldn't see three feet ahead of her, the tiled walls replaced by blank, slowly curling steam.

Pulling her hair to one side, gaining focus in the mists, she walked to the mirror, wiped it clear and looked into it. Her own reel of last night's images played in her mind. She slapped her own face, focusing on her own reflection, it took a moment before she saw that the baths taps were clogged shut, the tub filled with oily black tar.

* * *

Geena put the needle of Simone's record player down on the next side of the spinning LP. Swaying slowly, she sang along to the lyrics to Marvel83' and Roxi Drive's *'Stay with me'*.

'The world is turning fast, it won't wait for us.
Don't hold on to that dream, leave it all behind.
Let it take you far away...'

Dropping to the bed, Geena raised her legs in the air, grabbed her panties and slid them up and off with a quick flex of her knees, slowly sliding her hand down between her legs, making herself wet for the girl in the next room.

* * *

Simone stood over the black bath tub, disgusted with the rippling mess in front of her, pissed off that she might have to call a plumber, she bent down to touch the contaminated water, to free the plug. Then stopped.

Frozen, she felt a presence over her shoulder, a cold dread contradicting the warm plumes around her. She turned, slowly pivoting on the spot, looking into the steam, to the corner where the door was behind her.

Her heart pounded.

Through the steam, a shape, an outline.

Her terrified brain made sense of it.

Glowing eyes ignited and a grisly vision moved forward.

A black, oily-skinned siren.

She gulped at the air, ready to scream but found herself unable to, mesmerized by those deep, glowing, dreamy eyes. A rotten, nautical stink filled her sense of smell.

The figure, like a shadow, moved towards her, pressing itself on her naked flesh.

It wrapped its arms around her, embraced her with a romantic softness, a softness that quickly turned to agony, as ten sharp claws tore at her flesh from her shoulder blades and down her back.

* * *

Next door, Geena writhed on the bed, bringing her hand up, licking her fingers, tasting herself, thinking of tasting Simone, then reached back down between her legs again to keep pleasuring herself. Slowly humming the song's lyrics under her heavy breaths.

'We can't wait forever, we won't survive.
Holding on for something that won't arrive, we have to do this now...'

* * *

Suddenly, as if by some magic trick, instead of the glowing eyed, living shadow standing before Simone, she stood before herself. A perfect square was formed by Simone, her double and their reflections in the mirror. It grabbed Simone's hair from behind, scrunching it up into a rough pony tail. Her towel dropped to a heap as it forced her backwards, down into the bathtub, its hypnotic gaze never broken. An acquiescence pouring over herself as much as the blackened bathwater.

The cords in Simone's neck tightened, preparing herself to be submerged as her blood congealed in her veins.

She had wondered how it all worked, what Melissa had meant when she said, after scratching you, after taking your face that a siren would '*merge into you as one.*'

Now she was about to find out.

It pushed her below the surface, a warm song emanating from between its lips, a song that lulled Simone into a sedated state, unable to scream, or react in any way.

She felt distracted, away from her own being, an outsider watching her double manipulate her body. Breathing in the blackened bathwater, its sour taste filled her lungs in shuddering gulps.

* * *

Geena, on the edge of orgasm, stopped. She wanted to finish it off with Simone, sharing the experience. 'Hurry up!' she shouted over the music, 'I want you in here!'

* * *

Simone heard her, but was unable to reply, was unable to move. The thing with glowing eyes was weighing down on top of her. It melded into the water, dissolving to become part of it, melting and mutating, entering any orifice it could, completing the final stages of its formation into her.

It was like watching her own decomposition, her own corpse disintegrating on a time lapse.

A scream tried to burst from Simone's lungs, but nothing came. She felt like she was being filled with a thick, expanding foam, a dark, slimy viscous that stuck to her bones, building an internal avatar as it plugged into her central nervous system, wiring itself as the dominant force of her soul. Simone felt like she was taking a back seat to her own body, caged inside an ever shrinking darkness, gradually disappearing from existence as now the copy became the original, her view of her own bathroom ceiling becoming filtered through new eyes, eyes that seemed to radiate from the inside.

She heard Geena singing, the lyrics taking on a new meaning as she faded.

'The world is turning fast it won't wait for us.
Just grab onto that light and don't let go.
Let it take you far away.'

The siren was in her now, its physical attributes alive and working under her skin. Slowly the bath tub began to drain, the thick ooze seemingly pulling the plug itself, leaving the newly born hybrid, lying in the black ringed placenta of its birth.

It sat up, looking around, the transformation complete, stretching slightly in its new skin like a man at a tailor's would adjust himself in a new suit.

Suddenly, a voice came from next door making it turn its head slowly.

'Come on! Get in here! I want your face between my legs, you bitch!'

The thing in the bathtub smiled slightly, closing its eyes and letting a soothing, cold song ride from its breath.

'Geennnnaaaaaa...'

Geena stopped touching herself, listening, hearing for a second what she thought was another song, one other than that playing through the stereo's speakers. One that was calling out seductively from the bathroom. For a millisecond she felt drowsy.

The new Simone rose from the bath, eyes glowing.

Stepping out, dripping wet and pooling black footsteps on the tiled floor, it walked towards the bedroom door and pushed it open. Blinking quickly to extinguish the glow in its eyes to make itself look human again. Lips slightly apart, giving it a sexy model look, an expression it knew fit this face, it moved into the room.

Its primal instinct was to be wanted, it gave it the upper hand, it had to feed and what better way to eat than have the food willingly come to you.

'Take ya time!' Geena pouted. 'Now come here... and eat this.'

She spread her legs, her wetness glistening at the thing with Simone's face. A slight smile crept over it as jaggedly it moved like an animal onto all fours to taste its waiting, naked prey.

CHAPTER 38

Kirsten pulled up to Simone's flat. She had done everything she had mapped out in her mind.

She'd driven down to the marina. She'd got a Big Mac and sat looking out to sea.

The waves were highlighted by the blinking lights of a ship, it was just the same as her first night under the pier.

She'd eaten the burger and washed it down with a supersized Diet Coke, her feet up on the dash, enjoying food that any agent, any photographer and any other models would fry their wiring over.

Fuck them, she thought.

She had wasted time in London, caught in a circle, trapped in a loop, revolving around the fashion world's perimeters.

Pointless, vacuous and soulless were words that sprang to mind thinking back to that time. It had all been a miss-step, a time spent walking in someone else's shoes. And now this experience – shared with her cousin and two new friends – made her realize how important it was to walk in your own shoes.

Now the vain version of herself was locked away again, put back in its box and stashed in the chasms of her mind. It resembled in her mind's eye the small, red devil version of yourself that would sit on your shoulder and whisper in your ear, filling you with bad advice, like in old films.

Fuck the past, she thought.

Fuck who you were.

Worry about who you are, who you're going to be.

She was a photographer.

She used her brain, her talent, and one thing she was never going to be again was just another pretty face. Quickly, she wound down the window and puked the burger on the floor, everything that had happened last night having one final jab at her appetite. She needed to keep face, it was over, she knew it was over. It had to be.

Now, grabbing her stuff together, she could hear music blasting in the background, music she knew was Simone's.

She smiled gently, things had returned to normal, back on track to the way they were. She kept telling herself this. Over and over.

Abruptly the music stopped, cutting off with a reverberating echo around the silent streets outside, a sudden uncomfortable shiver rattled her insides.

Gathering her stuff up and getting out of the car, Kirsten walked inside.

Opening the front door, an immediate eeriness grasped her senses.

There were only the pops of a finished LP, jumping like the crackling kindling of a fire. She thought of last night again – pushed it away.

Remnants of steam blasted from the bathroom. It made her nose wrinkle, a dirty smell buried inside it.

Looking down she saw a trail of wet footprints leading from the bathroom, at first her eyes made no sense of it. A smile brushed her face, thinking of Inspector Clouseau following similar prints in the Pink Panther films.

She followed them down the hallway.

The memory of the smell came back to her now.

It was a seaweedy, oily smell, a nautical smell, a smell that had lingered under the pier, in the car park, at the old hotel, everywhere that the sir…

She pushed the bedroom door open. There, with her head between Geena's legs, Simone sat naked. A slow, rhythmic movement in her neck as she went down on the girl.

Embarrassed, Kirsten yelped, 'Oh fuck! I'm so…' then stopped.

Looking around the room, one that before could have been

described as organized chaos, could now be just described as flat out chaos.

The TV smashed, the arcade machine on the fritz, books and videotapes thrown around everywhere.

She drew her eyes back to the girls, noticing Simone's hands, the way they held Geena's legs, her once perfectly formed pink digits now blackened twigs that didn't hold her legs apart seductively, but prized them apart.

Long claws digging into her soft skin causing rolling beads of blood to trail down her lifeless legs. A meaty slop hit a pool of wetness.

Simone sat up, slowly turning her head around, her eyes glowing like headlights in the night, her mouth dripping with red viscera, parts of Geena's genitals, the stringy parts she was unable to digest sliding down her chin.

Awe, fear and sadness rolled over Kirsten like a steam roller.

The calm she felt in the car all gone now.

Looking around, she saw the rifle in the debris at the bottom of the bed, something that it seemed Geena had tried to reach for before her death.

Kirsten, acting on instinct, tried to reach for it, too, visualizing herself doing the unthinkable: pointing it at her cousin, or what had been her cousin, and having to pull the trigger.

She made the move, tried to run to it but jarred backwards as Simone leaped towards her.

Her cousin's mouth pulling to a contorted shark's grin, her teeth sharp razors, stretching her skin like a special effect in a movie as her mouth drew apart impossibly wide.

Kirsten fell backwards out of the room, yanking the door shut as she went, Simone rabidly reached around it, eyes flaring, clawing, wanting her.

The siren wail that had haunted her now escaped through the abnormal mouth that had grown in Simone's face.

She caught a split second glimpse of Geena now, naked,

broken and twisted like a doll contorted by the callous hands of a child.

Bites and scratches covered her breasts, arms and face. The white bedsheets now a crimson mass of gore.

Her eyes made Kirsten shudder the most, staring blankly at the ceiling, buried in a greying face, a distant look of non-understanding permanently fixed in them.

The Simone thing pulled the door wider and wider, its strength more now than the girl she once was. Kirsten, doing the only thing she could, pushed the door back onto Simone, its edge hitting the siren straight between the eyes, sending her reeling backwards onto the bed, next to her cold victim, giving herself a moment of opportunity to turn and run back out into the night.

Momentarily dumbstruck, she was punched with the gut wrenching feeling that it wasn't over, that all the fear dispersed by killing her doppelgänger, the stone like worry that sat on her chest, was now back again.

* * *

Kirsten flew through the streets, back in the car again, back to the only other place she knew to go: Mickey's house. Skidding up outside, she bolted from the car, everything moving at a super-fast speed, like an over-cranked movie camera. Reaching his front door, she pounded on it with open handed slaps, crying out the boy's name. The old Victorian house was as silent as a tomb, the lights off, the windows looking like black sheet ice.

In between a sobbing breath, she caught hold of something, a noise coming from some bushes, a quick, night-time animal rustle, a prowling thing, unseen to the human eye.

An eerie silence followed, one that sent chills into her bones, a far off feeling inside her sensed something had happened here, something like what had happened back at Simone's. A terror pulsated though her.

Suddenly, Mickey's house became the haunted house of a thousand nightmares, a home to unseen things, eyes seemed to watch her, burned onto her from every angle – glowing eyes.

She turned on her heels, gasping at the night air and ran back to the car, plugging the keys in the ignition and firing the engine, she took off into the night.

She drove frantically, speed limits and red lights becoming irrelevant.

The flash of a speed camera making her recoil in surprise.

Brighton's bright lights became a kaleidoscopic blur as she accelerated to her last hope.

Pulling up in Kemp town, mounting the curb, she stared up at the worn hand-painted sign she first set eyes on only a few days ago.

'Melissa Clarke – Clairvoyant'

Running up the stairs, shaking from adrenaline, she hit Melissa's door like a bullet, her hands pounding on it before she had even stopped.

Hoping and praying she was at home, that she would answer after hearing her voice. Maybe she would recognize it, maybe she was already waiting, wanting to help.

Pausing for a second, the door's black, gloss paintwork now covered in the sweaty prints of her own open palms, she noticed a small piece of white paper, folded over and taped to the glass, a single name written on it in black ink.

'Kirsten'

Unfolding it frantically, she read.

'I know what's happened. Meet me on the edge of the pier. I know a way to stop this for both of us.'

Unable to process anything properly, the common sense of why and how Melissa knew anything went ignored.

Kirsten could only focus on the final sentence: *'I know a way to stop this.'*

She let out a cry, a vulnerable rasp, knowing she should have listened to the clairvoyant all along, she should have ignored Simone's skeptical attitude.

Simone... oh Simone...

With a final shred of hope, Kirsten ran back into the night one final time.

CHAPTER 39

The door to Simone's apartment was slowly pushed open by a corpse-white, trembling hand.

With trepidation, a figure walked inside, shuffling like an extra from Night of the Living Dead. Using the walls to stabilize itself as it slowly peered around each corner, it surveyed the state of the flat. The place was still a mess from the carnage that had occurred earlier.

A layer of smoke filled the place, the overturned electrical equipment sparking as the smashed TV infrequently flickered to life on the floor with wild, sporadic strobe bursts.

Pushing open the door to the bedroom, the figure froze looking down at the mutilated corpse of Simone's girlfriend, naked and sprawled out on the bed, the red of her blood contrasting with the whiteness of her skin.

Turning to look at the floor, the figure saw the rifle, pausing for a second as an idea went through its damaged brain. It reached down to pick it up, holding it in both hands, its metal coldness matching the temperature of its own freezing fingers. The figure looked in the bedroom's full-length mirror, now partly smashed as Geena kicked out trying to escape her fate.

Its reflection looked back, taking a second to realize it was herself.

Melissa Clarke.

The woman who was literally falling to pieces now, gaunt, sickly, her face a crimson mask of her thinned, splitting skin, her mind all but overcome by the sirens' song that scratched in her skull.

She knew how this must end and how her part in this story had to play.

Suddenly, as if gripped with a seizure and staggering backwards, her face became a death's head of contorted pain as she hit the wall behind.

Silent tears fell down her face, eyes watering into pools of internal pain.

The walls of her cranium reverberated, the sirens' cry intensifying to a point where she thought her entire head would pop like a crushed grapefruit.

She was done with this now, she had to stop this pain, stop the entire situation from progressing, she knew she had to... open her mind.

Raising the rifle's barrel up to her head, she rubbed it against her temple.

She thought long and hard on the connection between herself, Kirsten and the creature and focused.

Gritting her teeth, she let her hands slide down the barrel's length, and then tensed.

Cold sweat rolled down her face, removing the blood.

Concentrating, letting out a long, pained whine that become a screaming growl of agony, she touched the trigger with a quivering finger, squeezing her eyes tight, knowing whatever happened next was inevitable.

* * *

'Boom!' A loud bang exploded out as Kirsten smashed the VW into a cluster of red metal Biffa bins next to the pier. Jumping out of the car, she popped the bonnet, remembering the tools, and took out a long, flathead screwdriver and a hammer, tucking them in her jeans and ran towards the pier.

Fog billowed the further out to sea she ran, forming a thick blanket that hid her away from the town behind. The end of the pier became a place away from the rest of the world, a small island cut off from everything.

The only sound was her own fast footsteps clacking on wooden boards like a metronome. Almost at the pier's end and past the amusements, she slowed, her hot, sweaty skin losing its heat as the cold night air fought against it, cooling her as she caught her breath.

Now walking, swaying slightly with fatigue, through the fog she saw a silhouette at the end of the pier, it's back to her as it stood looking out to sea.

'You have to help me!' she wheezed, allowing all of the sights she had seen that night to ferment in her mind.

All of her friends – dead.

Alone, scared – no one to go to.

But she had Melissa.

She should have listened to her before, but hopefully now they could work together to solve the problem that plagued them both.

'I should have listened to you, Melissa. They're all dead! *They're all dead!*'

Melissa said nothing as Kirsten drew nearer.

'They're still coming, they got Simone, she's killed Geena! I don't know what to do!'

Kirsten continued forward, desperation sinking into each step.

Behind her a creak sounded, out on the wooden boards.

She turned, watching as two silhouettes wandered through the fog. She gasped.

There, slowly drawing into view, two figures appeared. Ghosts in the night.

Simone and Mickey. They moved sensuously, their eyes illuminated like lanterns from within. They tilted their heads, eyeing their prey, watching her with empty, malice-filled stares, both distracting Kirsten long enough for the figure at the end of the pier – the figure she thought was Melissa – to turn around, its eyes glowing.

Not Melissa. Her doppelgänger. The siren with her face, the thing she had naively believed to be dead.

Kirsten snapped round, face to face with the dark version of herself, the one she shot and threw from the roof, now looking as good as new, its clothes showing signs of their last encounter – a ragged bullet hole in its black top fabric, but no such wound in the pale chest beneath.

She grabbed the screwdriver, plunging it forward, its long, thin, metal end glinting in the muted lights at the pier's end.

But before she could sink it into the creature's skin, she found herself winded, both of her feet taken out from the ground, her entire body taken down as the siren charged into her. Dropping the screwdriver and hearing it hit the boards and roll out of view, she struggled with the creature as it pulled and yanked at her.

Its own face becoming a hypnotic void again, light pouring from its eyes and mouth beaming down onto her. She snapped her eyes shut and screamed, fighting with everything she had left to get away from her.

They began to roll over and over as she tried to escape its grasp.

The Simone and Mickey sirens watched on, slowly closing in like two cats stalking the same prey, fanning out either side in case the human girl tried to make a run for it, keeping her trapped in the bottleneck end of the pier.

Kirsten, kicked, reeled and rolled, both of them nearing the back of the pier, slamming against the iron railing that surrounded it, limbs flailing over the edge, both almost dropping into the black water.

Another creak of board was heard, this time not from the creatures, but from behind them, a noise that took the sirens by surprise.

They turned to see another figure stumble through the same fog they had appeared from. It was Melissa, bedraggled; her face wrecked, blood and tears both running from her eyes. She staggered towards Mickey and Simone who stared at her, eyes burning as they hissed at the human distraction that had interrupted their game, watching as the bedraggled woman swung the rifle up from her side.

She unloaded the gun into Mickey's face first, his human skin exploding in a spray of red, ripping off like a cheap Halloween mask, revealing its true wearer: the black face of the siren.

He fell backwards, his luminous eyes dying like a pair of worn out bulbs.

Melissa turned to the Simone siren. Even in such a state, Melissa remembered Simone's attitude as a human. This could have ended differently if it wasn't for her. She walked straight up to her, pushed the rifle's end against her forehead and pulled the trigger.

A cracking explosion destroyed her entire head in a spray of red membrane and chiseled skull. Her body flailed for a moment, then fell to the ground.

Losing her footing, the psychic sound of the sirens' wail pile-drove through her head again. She had come to understand, the three of them – her, Kirsten and the siren – were united in a triangle of minds, somehow sharing the same mental space together. The creature's mental homing device on Kirsten – the girl it scratched – had somehow become cross-wired through Melissa when she pricked her finger on its claw.

But rather than just receive the creatures cries, Melissa had manipulated its thoughts, had psychically projected back at the thing in her head, telling it to be here, moving the players in this situation like chess pieces, drawing this entire situation to a checkmate.

Now here she was, all the pawns in position, exactly where she wanted them to be.

She had seen the future of others before, but had never been so interactive in someone's outcome.

She knew this was a two-way street, Kirsten was either going to be with her or against her. But now, after losing her husband, after losing her home, her mind was something she wasn't going to let go of without a fight. The future was self-preservation; the future was looking after number one, something that would start right now.

Melissa turned her attention to Kirsten and her doppelgänger, both of them still rolling around as she swung the gun over the pair. Trying to take aim in her feverish state, she placed them in the rifle's cross hairs with delirious precision.

'Hey!' Melissa screamed.

The doppelgänger looked up, its eyes beaming with an animal like glow. Melissa's finger caressed the trigger ready to hammer a round into its face. But quickly, instinctively, it rolled over and over with Kirsten, visually mixing her target with its prey.

Melissa unsteadily managed to hold her aim, followed the pair along the floor, staring intently as they pulled each other to their feet, slamming each other backwards and around over and over against the iron barrier, like partners in a macabre dance of death.

Exhaustion grasped both, beaten, bruised, neither wanting to lose the fight.

Melissa knew time was of the essence, she knew that the final glue holding her insides together was about to split apart and spill everything outside. Breaking their repetitive movements, one Kirsten, with gritted teeth, held the other firmly in place by the throat, squeezing with all of her strength, pushing her backwards to the murky sea below.

Melissa poised and ready for any opportunity knew what to do, remembering her vision, the way this *would* end now.

She screamed the words she used to describe her vision back in Simone's flat, but not the way Kirsten had understood them, not 'falling, falling, falling,' but how she knew the girl who came to her for a reading must die.

'Fall in! Fall in! Fall in!'

That was the only way to end this now, give it what it wanted, break the mental daisy chain she had become a part of by fulfilling the creature's prophecy, giving the creature what it wanted the most, to drag Kirsten to the bottom of the sea… dead or alive.

She aimed the rifle and pulled the trigger.

The rifles barrel exploded.

Kirsten's head shot back on its neck, the bullet making a hole the size of a twenty pence piece on her forehead, an instinctual shock tensed through her features.

Her head fell forward, eyes locked on Melissa.

Fall in… fall in… Falling backwards, she slipped from the pier, the siren grabbed her, they sprawled over the old iron railings, twin girls flying through the air.

'*Falll innnn*!' Melissa screamed, dropping to her knees, and they did, down with a loud splash into the cold, night waves.

They fell deeper beneath the surface, both holding onto one another as they sank down to the ocean floor, silhouettes to the world above. Then silence.

Mellissa's head eased; slowly it cleared of the sirens' wail, her own thoughts and feelings becoming clear at last. The tethered mindscape the three of them shared instantly broke, cut off forever. Shakily, she stood to her feet and limped over to the point where they had fallen in, looking down at the still rippling impact point. She exhaled, finally it was over.

Smiling the first smile in a very long time, she turned to walk away, but all of a sudden the sirens' wail returned in her ears. This time ten times more powerful than before, making her clutch desperately at her head as she fell to her knees again, nose and eyes bleeding.

'It's supposed to be over,' she pleaded 'Why isn't it over?'

She looked down in front of her, the rifle lying there. Grabbing it, the noise in her head destroying her mind, she understood what the final thing was she had to do to empty the sound from her brain, the one thing she didn't want to do. The other option to rid herself of it – the last resort.

Raising the barrel under her chin and gritting her teeth, she closed her eyes, ready to leave this plane of existence for good. Peace at last.

But as suddenly as it had begun, the sound in her mind stopped. The crystal clarity of normality coming back over her face as the thing in her head that haunted her, that drove her an inch from insanity and death, vanished.

She smiled like a crazy person, falling down on the pier's wooden boards and laughed into the night sky.

Whether it was the creature's way of saying thanks, that one final push in her headspace, or just a simple act of cruelty, a thing that she knew these sirens thrived on, she didn't know, nor did she care. She was free now, she had been unhinged from the situation, left to live her own life again.

Hearing the police sirens in the background, she wiped the gun with the sleeves of her black cashmere jumper, eradicating her prints from it permanently, then dropped it in the sea watching it sink as easily as the two girls had moments before.

The black insides of the two other sirens, the things that looked like Mickey and Geena, slithered from their remains to the sides of the pier and dropped down into the water.

Exhausted, tired and done with the whole thing, she slumped face down on the boards and closed her eyes, dreaming of her free stay in A&E, getting patched up and nursed back to health.

It was over, she had survived and now in the world on her own, she would find a new way to continue. She had resisted the loneliness after her husband's death, now she longed for it, longed to be alone in the quiet confines of her own mind once more.

CHAPTER 40

Epilogue

The newspapers had a field day the following week, sensationalising what was found on the end of the pier.

The daily rags had rung every last drop of fabrication from the story, one that was already ripe with enough of the juicy stuff to keep readers of such material salivating like rabid animals.

Some called it the 'Brighton Blood Bath,' focussing on the dead bodies of Simone and Mickey. More gaudy papers focussed on the naked, mutilated body of Geena, 'Sordid Seaside Sex Crimes' trumping up the fact that the police would not comment if the bodies on the pier were defiled in any way. Both stories corroborated on one fact, another girl was still missing, the cousin of the one on the pier, Kirsten Costello.

No one had heard from her, no one had seen her. They all thought that this story could be tied to the disappearance of the other young girls, attractive ones just like Kirsten, and the vanishing crew of the drilling rig out at sea.

A whole new hyperbolic dynamic was made up. This was part of something bigger, something more depraved that could be hauled into to sell more papers.

Only the remaining survivor, Melissa Clarke – the one the police had found battered and broken on the pier, but still with a pulse – had any of the answers.

Answers she wouldn't tell any form of tabloid without the right price included.

Melissa had known the fate of the girls. It was inevitable, she knew they had to die, there was no stopping the siren, and now she would use that situation, make the most of it for her own advantage.

It's been said destruction is a form of creation, and now with the loss of life around her, the physical and mental impact of the siren's wail shattering her psyche like a glass window, she would use this experience to move forward, to fix the other problems in her life.

After a few days, as with any tragedy, life simply went on, the pier reopened, kids rode the amusements, other exaggerated stories took their place in the newspapers and people's consciousness, and slowly – like they always did – the public would forget.

It simply became a thing of the past, something that became washed away, like debris in the sea. As the sun set on Brighton Pier, burning like a giant, glowing eyeball, shining down as the seawater cut in, the tide slowly rose up to the pebbled beach, and the distant wailing of a saxophone began to rise with it.

The girl playing, the girl who had been victim to Simone stuffing a chip wrapper into the end of her horn, now blew long, soulful notes into the evening air.

A couple sat looking out to sea on an iron bench, taking in the nuances of the moment as the sky overhead faded into pastel shades of pink and blue.

Then, unseen by anyone, two white hands reached up from beneath the pier, shrivelled fingers grabbing onto the iron railings, pulling itself up. Wet and dripping it staggered forward, leaving footsteps soaking into the wooden boards. It walked past the saxophonist, knocking into her, stopping her from playing as she puffed out another bum note, not the first or last that day, but the only one she could blame on something other than herself.

She looked up, recognition creeping over her face, daggers appearing in her eyes.

'You're as bad as your loudmouth friend!' she shouted, taking a moment to rebuke the pretty girl who looked like she'd fallen in the drink.

Brighton was a place where anybody could fit in, whatever

you were, whatever you wanted to be, everyone was different, everyone was homogeneous, and it was easy to be ignored because of it.

The figure from the pier, its hair dangling like seaweed, its skin pale, washed out, clothes wet and skin-tight to its body, a sight that anywhere else would draw attention, here was left alone, completely undisturbed as it went about its business.

Wandering to Simone's flat, it pulled apart the police tape that covered the door, kicking the makeshift lock the law had added to seal the crime scene away.

It walked to the bedroom, looking at the mattress, staring at the red stains that corrupted its whiteness. It felt nothing.

It walked to the bathroom, seeing the mirror above the wash basin, wiping a layer of water stained filth from it to stare at its visage, its *new* visage.

There in the mirror stood Kirsten, the thing beneath her skin getting its first decent look at the face it wore above water for the first time.

It prodded at it, feeling her soft skin, sensing how nicely it had formed beneath, not upsetting those cheekbones, moving in and feeling cosy like a new tenant in the new structure it dwelled in.

But somewhere, caged off in her membrane, Kirsten was there, too, the original one, now just a passenger in her own body as something else took the reins and steered. She had survived the bullet to the head, the siren made sure of that, it had work to do now, nothing would stop it.

It probed into her consciousness, saw into her past, watched her memories like old home videos on a screen, it was a skill it had drawn from Melissa – finding all the things it needed to know, the real Kirsten just becoming a spiritual memory bank it could tap into.

She screamed in her own mind, just like the thing itself once did in Melissa's, psychically it enveloped Kirsten like a black, plastic bag, suffocating her.

She thought of being trapped in the iron grid work of the pier, caught like a caged bird, just like the cocooned flies webbed in Simone's living room window – incapacitated, only able to watch as the spider literally pulled the silky strings to manipulate her like a marionette.

And as it did, it found something in her past, something it liked, something it could use for its survival in the present, a thing it was almost made to do.

It felt something like happiness.

It showered and made itself more presentable in that human way that would make it accepted.

Packing some bags, taking things it knew belonged to the girl it possessed, it went to leave, pausing for a second, touching a cracked iPad on the floor and stroked its way through Kirsten's photography portfolio. It understood that this was once something of importance, then discarded it, knowing what the girl was meant for now was better than this. It dropped the iPad, callously stepping on the photograph displayed on the screen, and, as simply as that, walked away from everything she was.

It walked from Brighton, wandered down the motorways, stopping once it had collected the information it needed from the screaming tortured girl in its head. It made a late night phone call in a motorway cafe to someone Kirsten promised herself she would never speak to again.

Apologising, promising things – sexual things, things she would never want to do with such a person.

She had once hit him, and now for her insubordination, she was willing to let him do what he wanted to her.

It was an offer he couldn't refuse, her feisty turn, the one that got away, it turned him on. Immediately, he agreed.

She walked to Hackney, back into the photo studio waiting room, where the same dull-eyed women, each one chewing gum, now just in different outfits, still in their own shallow world, all looked up at her for a moment.

The nature of the thing inside Kirsten was to be looked at, to draw people in, to make itself wanted, and when its victim was at its most vulnerable, it would completely consume them.

And now, using its instinct, its cunning, it could do that in a way no siren was able to before. After make-up and a wardrobe fitting, she was back in front of the studio lights, now more nimble and flexible than before. The voice of the tinpot Karl Lagerfeld jeered her on, the photographer, with the East London beard, the skinny jeans and the branded cup of corporate coffee.

His tone now enthusiastic, electrified, taking picture after picture with the snap and flash of his camera, his words almost sexualised, crude and derogatory, but for some reason, now, the girl who used to answer back, was anything but incompliant.

She had slipped a nipple, spread her legs, shown him her warmth between them, hadn't cared when he continued to flash away.

The siren was in control now, and this is what it wanted.

And as she sensually moved in front of the camera, enjoying being the centre of attention, with a fur around her neck, luring in the gaze of everyone, the flash popping faster and faster in her face, her eyes appeared empty for a second, glowing like an animal, like what she really was now, a siren from the sea.

In the back of her mind, caged away, only able to watch all this happening was Kirsten. Before she had the free will to escape all of this, but now she was just a prisoner, trapped forever, watching her life led by another through the filter of her own eyes, only able to do one thing now.

Internally, she screamed. On and on. Forever.

Cosmic Egg Books

FANTASY, SCI-FI, HORROR & PARANORMAL

If you prefer to spend your nights with Vampires and Werewolves rather than the mundane then we publish the books for you. If your preference is for Dragons and Faeries or Angels and Demons – we should be your first stop. Perhaps your perfect partner has artificial skin or comes from another planet – step right this way. If your passion is Fantasy (including magical realism and spiritual fantasy), Metaphysical Cosmology, Horror or Science Fiction (including Steampunk), Cosmic Egg books will feed your hunger. Our curiosity shop contains treasures you will enjoy unearthing. If you have enjoyed this book, why not tell other readers by posting a review on your preferred book site. Recent bestsellers from Cosmic Egg Books are:

The Zombie Rule Book

A Zombie Apocalypse Survival Guide

Tony Newton

The book the living-dead don't want you to have!

Paperback: 978-1-78279-334-2 ebook: 978-1-78279-333-5

Cryptogram

Because the Past is Never Past

Michael Tobert

Welcome to the dystopian world of 2050, where three lovers are haunted by echoes from eight-hundred years ago.

Paperback: 978-1-78279-681-7 ebook: 978-1-78279-680-0

Purefinder

Ben Gwalchmai

London, 1858. A child is dead; a man is blamed and dragged through hell in this Dantean tale of loss, mystery and fraternity.

Paperback: 978-1-78279-098-3 ebook: 978-1-78279-097-6

600ppm

A Novel of Climate Change

Clarke W. Owens

Nature is collapsing. The government doesn't want you to know why. Welcome to 2051 and 600ppm.

Paperback: 978-1-78279-992-4 ebook: 978-1-78279-993-1

Creations

William Mitchell

Earth 2040 is on the brink of disaster. Can Max Lowrie stop the self-replicating machines before it's too late?

Paperback: 978-1-78279-186-7 ebook: 978-1-78279-161-4

The Gawain Legacy

Jon Mackley

If you try to control every secret, secrets may end up controlling you.

Paperback: 978-1-78279-485-1 ebook: 978-1-78279-484-4

Mirror Image

Beth Murray

When Detective Jack Daniels discovers the journal of female serial killer Sarah he is dragged into a supernatural world, where people's dark sides are not always hidden.

Paperback: 978-1-78279-482-0 ebook: 978-1-78279-481-3

Moon Song

Elen Sentier

Tristan died too soon, Isoldé must bring him back to finish his job… to write the Moon Song.

Paperback: 978-1-78279-807-1 ebook: 978-1-78279-806-4

Perception

Alaric Albertsson

The first ship was sighted over St. Louis...and then St. Louis was gone.

Paperback: 978-1-78279-261-1 ebook: 978-1-78279-262-8